MOLLY CI
BECAUSI

Mary 'Molly' Clavering was born in Glasgow in 1900. Her father was a Glasgow businessman, and her mother's grandfather had been a doctor in Moffat, where the author would live for nearly 50 years after World War Two.

She had little interest in conventional schooling as a child, but enjoyed studying nature, and read and wrote compulsively, considering herself a 'poetess' by the age of seven.

She returned to Scotland after her school days, and published three novels in the late 1920s, as well as being active in her local girl guides and writing two scenarios for ambitious historical pageants.

In 1936, the first of four novels under the pseudonym 'B. Mollett' appeared. Molly Clavering's war service in the WRNS interrupted her writing career, and in 1947 she moved to Moffat, in the Scottish border country, where she lived alone, but was active in local community activities. She resumed writing fiction, producing seven post-war novels and numerous serialized novels and novellas in the *People's Friend* magazine.

Molly Clavering died in Moffat on February 12, 1995.

TITLES BY MOLLY CLAVERING

Fiction

Georgina and the Stairs (1927)
The Leech of Life (1928)
Wantonwalls (1929)
Susan Settles Down (1936, as 'B. Mollett')
Love Comes Home (1938, as 'B. Mollett')
Yoked with a Lamb (1938, as 'B. Mollett')
Touch Not the Nettle (1939, as 'B. Mollett')
Mrs. Lorimer's Quiet Summer (1953)
Because of Sam (1954)
Dear Hugo (1955)
Near Neighbours (1956)
Result of the Finals (1957)
Dr. Glasgow's Family (1960)
Spring Adventure (1962)

Non-Fiction

From the Border Hills (1953)

Between 1952 and 1976, Molly Clavering also serialized at least two dozen novels or novellas in the *People's Friend* under the names Marion Moffatt and Emma Munro. Some of these were reprinted as 'pocket novels' as late as 1994.

MOLLY CLAVERING

BECAUSE OF SAM

With an introduction by
Elizabeth Crawford

DEAN STREET PRESS

A Furrowed Middlebrow Book
FM70

Published by Dean Street Press 2021

Copyright © 1953 Molly Clavering

Introduction © 2021 Elizabeth Crawford

All Rights Reserved

First published in 1953 by Hodder & Stoughton

Cover by DSP

ISBN 978 1 914150 53 1

www.deanstreetpress.co.uk

INTRODUCTION

Because of Sam (1954), Molly Clavering's ninth novel, was welcomed by readers and reviewers, as had been its forerunners, for being, as the *Manchester Evening Chronicle* emphasised, 'As rural and refreshing as the Scottish scene in which it is set. There's the real stuff of country village life here.' For Molly's novels centre on life in the Scottish countryside, particularly in the Borders, the setting for the village of 'Mennan', home of 'Millie Maitland', the principal character in *Because of Sam*. In this novel, as in others, occasional forays are made into Edinburgh, but it is in Mennan that the story is played out, the characters drawn from all strata of society, their mores reflecting those of post-war Britain. As ever, Molly Clavering is excellent at evoking a sense of place, both of rooms, such as Millie's kitchen with 'the clean white-wash of walls and ceiling, the blue plates on the old-fashioned dresser, the big solid kitchen table in the background . . . all neat and clean and comfortable', and of the countryside where 'Larks rose from the red furrows of ploughed fields beside the roads, singing with all their might, and higher up the hillsides curlew were wheeling, in wide slow spirals, to the sound of their lovely lonely crying'.

Born in Glasgow on 23 October 1900, Molly Clavering was the eldest child of John Mollett Clavering (1858-1936) and his wife, Esther (1874-1943). She was named 'Mary' for her paternal grandmother, but was always known by the diminutive, 'Molly'. Her brother, Alan, was born in 1903 and her sister, Esther, in 1907. Although John Clavering, as his father before him, worked in central Glasgow, brokering both iron and grain, by 1911 the family had moved eleven miles north of the city, to Alreoch House outside the village of Blanefield. In an autobiographical article Molly Clavering later commented, 'I was brought up in the country, and until I went to school ran wild more or less'. She was taught by her father to be a close observer of nature and 'to know the birds and flowers, the weather and the hills round our house'. From this knowledge, learned so early, were to spring the descriptions of the countryside that give readers of her novels such pleasure.

By the age of seven Molly was sufficiently confident in her literary attainment to consider herself a 'poetess', a view with which her father enthusiastically concurred. In these early years she was probably educated at home, remembering that she read 'everything I could lay hands on (we were never restricted in our reading)' and having little 'time for orthodox lessons, though I liked history and Latin'. She was later sent away to boarding school, to Mortimer House in Clifton, Bristol, the choice perhaps dictated by the reputation of its founder and principal, Mrs Meyrick Heath, whom Molly later described as 'a woman of wide culture and great character [who] influenced all the girls who went there'. However, despite a congenial environment, life at Mortimer House was so different from the freedom she enjoyed at home that Molly 'found the society of girls and the regular hours very difficult at first'. Although later admitting that she preferred devoting time and effort to her own writing rather than schoolwork, she did sufficiently well academically to be offered a place at Oxford. Her parents, however, ruled against this, perhaps for reasons of finance. It is noticeable that in her novels Molly makes little mention of the education of her heroines, although they do demonstrate a close and loving knowledge of Shakespeare, Dickens, Thackeray, and Trollope.

After leaving school Molly returned home to Arleoch House and, with no need to take paid employment, was able to concentrate on her writing, publishing her first novel in 1927, the year following the tragically early death of her sister, Esther. Always sociable, Molly took a lively interest in local activities, particularly in the Girl Guides for whom she was able to put her literary talents to fund-raising effect by writing scenarios for two ambitious Scottish history pageants. The first, in which she took the pivotal part of 'Fate', was staged in 1929 in Stirlingshire, with a cast of 500. However, for the second, in 1930, she moved south and in aid of the Roxburgh Girl Guides wrote the 'Border Historical

Pageant'. Performed in the presence of royalty at Minto House, Roxburghshire, this pageant featured a large choir and a cast of 700, with Molly in the leading part as 'The Spirit of Borderland Legend'. For Molly was already devoted to the Border country, often visiting the area to stay with relations and, on occasion, attending a hunt ball.

In the late 1920s Molly published two further novels under her own name and then, in the 1930s, another four as 'B. Mollett'. The last of these, *Touch Not the Nettle*, was published in 1939 and then, on the outbreak of the Second World War, Molly joined the Women's Royal Naval Service, based for the duration at Greenock, then an important and frenetic naval station. Serving in the Signals Cypher Branch, she eventually achieved the rank of second officer. It would seem that, although there was no obvious family connection, the Navy had long had an appeal for Molly as many of her most attractive male characters are associated with the Senior Service.

After she was demobbed Molly moved to the Borders, to Moffat, the Dumfriesshire town where her great-grandfather had been a doctor, and in 1953 published a paean to the surrounding countryside. This, *From the Border Hills*, was her only work of non-fiction. Living in Moffat for the rest of her life, Molly shared 'Clover Cottage' with a series of black standard poodles, one of them a present from D.E. Stevenson, another of the town's novelists, whom she had known since the 1930s. D.E. Stevenson's granddaughter, Penny Kent, well remembers how 'Molly used to breeze and bluster into North Park (my Grandmother's house), a rush of fresh air, gaberdine flapping, grey hair flying with her large, bouncy black poodles, Ham and Pam (and later Bramble), shaking, dripping and muddy from some wild walk through Tank Wood or over Gallow Hill)'. Similarly, although perhaps rather more sedately, in *Because of Sam*, Millie Maitland walks her dogs in the hills around Mennan. An impoverished widow and, fortunately, like Molly, a dog lover, she has found that operating a boarding kennels is 'the only thing I can do at home that pays me'. It is because of Sam, a young, black Labrador, that her fortune changes.

During these post-war years Molly Clavering continued her work with the Girl Guides, serving for nine years as County Commissioner, was president of the local Scottish Country Dance Association, and active in the Women's Rural Institute. She was a member of Moffat town council, 1951-60, and for three years from 1957 was the town's first and only woman magistrate. She continued writing, publishing five further novels, as well as a steady stream of the stories that she referred to as her 'bread and butter', issued, under a variety of pseudonyms, by that very popular women's magazine, the *People's Friend*.

When Molly Clavering's long and fruitful life finally ended on 12 February 1995 her obituary was written by Wendy Simpson, another of D.E. Stevenson's granddaughters. Citing exactly the attributes that characterise Molly Clavering's novels, she remembered her as 'A convivial and warm human being who enjoyed the company of friends, especially young people, with her entertaining wit and a sense of fun allied to a robustness to stand up for what she believed in.'.

Elizabeth Crawford

Chapter 1

THE organ boomed softly, and the choir, followed in rather a ragged fashion by the kneeling congregation, broke into "O Perfect Love". Millie Maitland—she had been christened Camilla, but no one ever called her anything but Millie—noticed that the hymn was having its usual effect on the older feminine element present. All over the little church there was a fluttering of dainty handkerchiefs, which were being discreetly applied to eyes wet with pleasurable tears. Mrs. Maitland felt her own eyes prickle in sympathy, but decided against producing her handkerchief. It was simply pandering to a far too easy emotion, and she knew that her daughter Amabel, who knelt beside her, bored but decorous, would be annoyed.

Millie swallowed a sigh. Barely acknowledged even to herself was the wish that her dear Amabel had grown up a little more like her name, a little less sharp and critical, a little less clever, in fact. *Amabel*—lovable, thought Mrs. Maitland, even as she sang in a small tuneful undertone; and lovable was the last adjective one would think of using in connection with that clever, capable Miss Maitland. If she had been like her name, Amabel might have been the figure kneeling there in a white dress before the altar, with a veil shrouding her glossy dark hair and a very new wedding ring on her finger, instead of being single at twenty-nine.

Loyalty and pride made her acquiesce when friends told her how lucky she was to have a daughter so much at home to keep her company, but in her heart she knew that she would infinitely have preferred Amabel to be married. *Every* mother, thought Millie, except for the extraordinary ones she read about in novels but had never met, every mother wanted to see her daughter married. Nor was it likely that she herself was the only woman to treasure her wedding veil and wreath of artificial orange-blossom, carefully packed away among layers of yellowing tissue-paper in a box in a corner of her wardrobe, for a daughter to wear some day.

But of course it was ridiculous to think of Amabel wearing orange-blossom and a veil; if she did marry, she would be in a dark severely-cut suit and a felt hat; and probably not in church at all, but at a registry office, as Mrs. Maitland persisted in calling it.

A prod from Amabel roused her from these profitless thoughts to find that the hymn was over and the wedding guests resuming their seats.

Hastily scrambling up from her knees, Millie straightened her hat with a gloved hand as she sat down. The service had almost reached its conclusion, the curate was leading the bride and groom towards the vestry, while bridesmaids and best man followed in an untidy huddle with the bride's mother and uncle (her father had been dead for several years), and the bridegroom's parents.

Davina was looking her best, Millie thought approvingly—the bride's mother was a friend of long standing—the dark sables round her neck toned down her naturally high colour to a more becoming shade than usual, and her expensive wool frock was very kind to her rather solid figure, why was it that mothers of the bride always were so much better turned out than bridegrooms' mothers? It seemed to be an unbreakable law, somehow, Millie thought confusedly; at least, she had seen it at every wedding she had ever been at.

Except her own, she remembered suddenly, for then, though her mother had looked ravishing, Maurice had been represented only by a strong-minded aunt, an ex-Suffragette, because his mother had died while he was still a schoolboy. The aunt was dead now, too, and Millie hadn't thought of her for years, which was really very ungrateful of her. Poor old Aunt Euphorbia! Could it have been from her that Amabel had inherited her most striking characteristics? "For she certainly isn't in the least like either of *us*," thought Mrs. Maitland. "Maurice so easy-going and happy-go-lucky, and me so weak that I almost always give in to avoid unpleasantness!"

And she sighed, upon which Amabel hissed in her ear, "For goodness' sake, Mother, don't *sigh* so! What is there to sigh about?"

"I'm sorry, dear. I was only thinking," her mother whispered back apologetically. "They are taking a long time in the vestry, aren't they? And it's so small, too!"

"Indulging in an orgy of kissing," replied Amabel with ineffable scorn. Having once been an unwilling and ungracious bridesmaid to a school-friend, she had first-hand knowledge of what went on in the vestry after a marriage ceremony, and thought poorly of it.

Mrs. Maitland sighed again, but managed to repress the slight sound. After all, what was the good of worrying about Amabel's unmarried state, when Amabel herself seemed perfectly content to be single? To take her mind off it, Millie Maitland glanced cautiously round, noticing who were all there. She had not really had a chance to do this before, because they had arrived rather late, and of course once the bridal procession had gone up the aisle, one did not look at anyone else.... There was little Miss Kennedy, looking exactly like a field-mouse, with what appeared to be an entire rose-bed stuck on her last summer's hat, weeping openly and loving it all. In the pew in front of her was old Miss Emerson, wealthy and mean, whose only weakness was her overfed disagreeable pug. Numbers of rather smart strangers, of course, but they did not interest Millie. The two maids from Netherton were there, of course, and some of the local W.R.I. members, among them Mrs. Denholm, the shepherd's wife whom Millie sometimes walked up the burn to visit. It was nice of Davina to have asked them, but what did Susan think of these guests? There were very few of her own generation present, apart from the bridesmaids.... Then Mrs. Maitland smiled. This was really Davina Gray's show, and her daughter knew it. Probably Susan wasn't thinking of anything or anyone but her bridegroom.... There was young Jade Ross at least. He was Susan's friend. How spruce and correct he looked, wearing all the right clothes, with a handsome pink carnation in his buttonhole! How nice it was to see men in morning dress, even if some of them did diffuse a slight aroma of naphthalene! But it was a pity that Jack should be sitting beside that little yellow-haired Mrs. Noble, instead of his own wife, Pat of the sunny smile. Mrs. Noble was a newcomer about whom nobody in Mennan knew anything, and this, as well as her alien smartness of appearance, made her an object of suspicion in a place where everyone's background was familiar.

. . . Of course Pat's baby was almost due, which explained her absence to-day.

Mrs. Maitland wondered if Pat was remembering that just over a year ago she had been the bride in this same church, the object of everyone's congratulations and good wishes, the central figure of the day. Now her trousseau had all been worn, the wedding gown converted into an evening dress which for months she had not been able to get into. . . . Mrs. Maitland, with the sudden rather sick feeling of fright which assails older people at such moments, was conscious of the inexorable ticking away of Time's clock. Her own wedding, Pat's wedding, and now this one to-day, were all over, and nothing, no power on earth, could bring them back. Two were already part of the past, this third soon would be, and the years went round, faster and faster as fewer remained to one. Presently the hour would come when she, Millie Maitland, would shut her eyes in a sleep which would not end in this world; and though she believed, quietly and simply, that there was another life ahead, the trouble with her was that she did not want to leave *this* world. It was a distressed world, made miserable by its own inhabitants and their constant wars, a world where even everyday domestic life was subject to nagging little irritations, yet it held such moments of beauty and happiness, it was so dear, that Millie could not bear to think of it rolling on its round without her. *"Timor mortis conturbat me,"* she thought, and shivered involuntarily.

At this moment the organ, which had been softly playing to pass the time, burst with all its might into Mendelssohn's Wedding March, and the bridal procession, neatly paired off now, emerged from the vestry and came pacing down the aisle to the door. All Mrs. Maitland's dismal thoughts and fears were blown away like mist by a breeze in her eagerness to get a good view of the newly-married couple. They were hand-in-hand, she noticed, confidingly, like children, as if they had instinctively felt that the more conventional link of bride's hand through the crooked arm of her husband was too cold and formal.

"Sweet!" thought Mrs. Maitland.

And beside her Amabel muttered: "Did you ever see anything so childish? How silly they look!"

For once her mother answered back. "They look happy, and that is what matters most," she said, sharply for her, and though Amabel still looked scornful, she said no more.

Halted in the porch among the slowly-moving crowd, Mrs. Maitland found herself next to Jack Ross, and asked in an undertone how Pat was.

"She made me come," he muttered back. "You know Susan was one of her bridesmaids, and so—"

"Of course," said Mrs. Maitland understandingly. "As Pat can't be here herself she wanted you to come, and you can tell her all about it afterwards."

Jack's boyish face lost its look of anxiety and creased in an engaging grin. What a good sort she was, Mrs. M.! It was like her to realize that he wasn't just gallivanting while Pat stayed at home with the suitcase ready packed, waiting to go to the Cottage Hospital any minute now. . . . All the same, he wished he hadn't left her, and as soon as he had wished Susan and her new husband joy, he would slip away from the reception and go home to her. . . .

"Oh, Mr. *Woss*! I've dwopped my bag!"

The plaintive, fluting voice came from somewhere just below his left shoulder, and he glanced down to meet the limpid gaze of Mrs. Noble's large blue eyes.

"Confound the little woman!" he thought unchivalrously. "She has an idiotic way of talking, and I don't like hair the colour of a newly-hatched chicken! She's an attractive little piece; for all that, but how the devil does she think I'm going to get her bag for her in this jam?" Aloud he said politely, "Too bad, I'll see what I can do."

It was impossible, of course, he knew that, but he tried to bend down and get a glimpse of the tiled floor of the porch at least, shielding his top hat as best he could.

"Give me your hat," said Mrs. Maitland. "You don't want to dent it." And as, with a grateful look, he handed it to her, she exclaimed again, "Mrs. Noble, your bag is hanging on to one of the spokes of your umbrella!"

"Dear me. So it is. How awfly clever of you," murmured Mrs. Noble, though Millie Maitland had an idea that *she* was not grateful, if Jack Ross was.

"So stupid of me," went on the fluting voice. "But then, I feel quite lost without a man to look after me, and I do hate a cwowd! Don't you?"

"Yes," replied Millie simply, though what she was longing to do was to ask whether Mrs. Noble was without a man because she was a widow or for some other reason. "But one has grown so accustomed to crowds—queueing and all that, don't you find?" To herself she added, "But I bet she has never stood in a queue for fish in her life."

Opening her blue eyes even wider, Mrs. Noble said, "But there aren't any queues in the village, are there?"

"Not now. But there were during the war," Mrs. Maitland replied grimly. "You should have seen our fish queue! And haven't you ever gone shopping in Crossford on a Saturday? There are queues there all right."

"I don't shop in Cwossford," Mrs. Noble said. "What do you buy there?"

"Dog-meat," said Millie, whereupon her daughter poked her in the ribs and muttered crossly, "For heaven's sake, Mother, don't let us have dogs or their meat at a wedding!"

Obediently Mrs. Maitland became silent, and as the surge of people swept them all out of the porch into the chill April sunshine, she was separated from Mrs. Noble and there was no need for her to enlarge upon or explain her remark.

"Just as well," she thought. "It *was* silly of me to say it—dragging the dogs in like that! But she irritated me, talking as if she hadn't even heard of having to queue!"

All along the quiet road where the little Episcopal church stood behind a belt of laurels, car doors were slamming, engines were being started up, while voices called, "Can I give you a lift?" to those who had no cars of their own—of course it was understood that the one or two local taxis had been booked for the day by the bride's mother; they always were on the rare occasions of a wedding in Mennan village. But no one would have to walk to the Royal Hotel, where the reception was being held, for Mennan was a friendly place, and its inhabitants fully conscious of their duty towards their neighbour.

"I'll take you and Amabel, Mrs. Maitland," said Jack Ross, suddenly appearing beside them. "Unless you're going with anyone else?"

"Oh, thank you, Jack. How good of you," Millie said gratefully, smiling at him. Really, Jack was an exceptionally nice person. What a delightful son he would be, and an equally delightful husband. Now he was asking little Mrs. Noble, telling her there was plenty of room as he led them to where his car was standing on the far side of the road.

Mrs. Maitland was rather amused to find herself firmly directed to the front seat, and the two young women put in behind, an arrangement which suited her (and presumably Jack, since he had made it), but was not to the taste of either Amabel or Mrs. Noble. They sat, each in a corner, silent, as far withdrawn from one another as possible. Childish and a little ill-mannered, thought Mrs. Maitland, her amusement altering to slight momentary irritation. They ought, both of them, to be able to behave civilly for a few minutes, however antipathetic they were, and of the two Amabel, of course, was the more tiresome, for she did not even try to *look* agreeable, while Mrs. Noble, catching sight of herself in the driving mirror, composed her neat little features to a patient smile. Mrs. Maitland had just time to think, very inconsistently, that she would like to throw something hard at that smugly smiling face, when the car drew up at the doorway of the hotel.

As Jack Ross got out and went round to the near side to open the door for his passengers, a small boy thrust a note into his hand.

"Ma mother sent me," he said.

"It's from Pat," said Jack, tearing it open and reading it. "Look, Mrs. Maitland, will you make my excuses to Susan and Mrs. Gray? I must dash to the hospital at once—"

"Of course." Millie Maitland might not be intellectual, but she was quick-witted, especially where her sympathies were engaged. Refraining from adding that it was useless for him to go near the hospital for hours yet, she was out of the car in a flash and urging Mrs. Noble to hurry. Amabel, spurning assistance, had already descended on the other side, and was standing waiting in the entrance.

Before Mrs. Noble had ceased her plaint that it was "so howwid" to have to face the wedding reception without a male escort, Jack had swung the car round and vanished down the High Street with a roar in the direction of the Cottage Hospital.

"Why was he *wushed* away like that?" asked Mrs. Noble.

"Because his wife is having her first baby," Mrs. Maitland said baldly.

"Good gwacious!" exclaimed Mrs. Noble in tones of blank astonishment.

"People quite often have babies," said Amabel impatiently, and shooting a glance of extreme dislike at Mrs. Noble. "Do let's go in, Mother."

The glance was returned with interest, but little Mrs. Noble said no more, and the three ladies proceeded to join the long line which was filing slowly past the reception committee of the parents, and thence making its way round the big room towards the bride and bridegroom.

All about them the usual remarks were being made. "Such a pretty wedding!" . . . "Doesn't Susan look *radiant*?" . . . "The bridegroom is handsome, isn't he?" . . . "Oh, do you think so? It's not a type I admire, but, of course, tastes differ." . . . "How lovely the flowers were in church!" . . . "My dear, that dress must have cost the *earth*!"—"What I say is, there's nothing so pretty as a spring wedding, is there?"

Champagne was fizzling palely in shallow glasses, its bouquet mingling with the scent of flowers, but it was the party feeling and not the wine which went to Millie Maitland's head. Reckless of Amabel's lifted eyebrows, she raised her glass high and called, "All good luck and happiness, Susan dear!" as she took her first sip of it.

Already the smart little hat with its massed violets and tiny veil was crooked, her silvery curls sprayed out under it, her cheeks were flushed. After all, what was the use of going to a wedding if one didn't enjoy it? In two hours it would all be over, the newly-married pair gone, the drift of silver paper horse-shoes and rose-petals lying trodden in the street, and she herself, dressed in her old blue skirt and thick jumper, rubber boots weighing her down, would be trudging across the wet fields giving the dogs their afternoon walk. ... All the more reason, Millie thought, to appreciate the present to its fullest, not to brood over the horrifying price of the hat she had bought with such extravagance for the occasion, which she would probably never have another opportunity of wearing, but to remember instead how becoming it was. Mrs. Maitland gave the hat a little push which set it even more askew, though happily for her she did not realize it, and took another sip of champagne.

Just for the moment she had no one to talk to, for Amabel had moved away to speak to some acquaintances. This did not worry her at all, she was quite content to stand looking at people in their best clothes, all lifted out of their everyday round by the festive feeling, to hope that when the cake reached her she would get a piece with both kinds of icing attached, to admire the glimpses she caught of the bride among the throng.

It was the bride herself, Susan Penistone, really grown-up at last, though it was only an hour ago that she had still been Susan Gray, the youngest and most docile of Davina's four daughters, who noticed that Mrs. Maitland was alone. Dear Mrs. M. with her pretty hat crooked, bless her, and rather pushed into a corner while everyone was chattering round her. Susan had a warm heart and a share of her mother's decisiveness. She darted from her new husband's side, regardless of the fact that Mrs. Gray had just guided her there, ready to listen to speeches and congratulatory telegrams, and made her way swiftly towards Mrs. Maitland in her backwater.

"Hi, Susan, come back!" cried the bridegroom, in a panic at this desertion, but she only threw him a glance over her white satin-clad shoulder and sped on.

"Mrs. Maitland!" she said. "Oh, Mrs. Maitland, I did want to thank you so much for the little china jug! It was far too kind of you to give me another present as well as the electric kettle from you and Amabel. I'll always use it for the milk for our porridge."

Millie Maitland smiled. "I know you wanted a useful present, my dear," she said. "And of course it's much more sensible to be given things you need, like kettles and irons and Pyrex dishes, but—" she hesitated. "I daresay it is very silly of me, but I *did* want to give you something—something more pretty than useful, just as a little extra."

"Your little jug is both, and I love it," said Susan.

"It seems to me," went on Mrs. Maitland, as if talking to herself, "that everything must be for use nowadays, and I know all those home magazines always say that useful things can look nice, but it's no good telling me that an electric iron or a kettle can be *pretty*! And when you're getting married, it does seem so— so *drab* to be given only presents that are useful. Life is so very drab now—I thought perhaps you would use the little Spode jug to put flowers in—"

"Well, of course I will," Susan agreed. She was a little puzzled, because it had never occurred to her that life was drab, and her array of wedding presents, all of which had been chosen with a view to their utility, left nothing to be desired in her eyes. Across the room she caught her bridegroom's appealing eye.

"Oh, Tim wants me, I must fly!" she said, rather relieved, but not wanting to leave Mrs. Maitland by herself still.

She turned and seized the arm of a man near them. "You two must know each other quite well, I'm sure—Martin Heriot, Mrs. Maitland," she babbled hastily. "He was a great friend of Dad's. . . . Look, Uncle Martin, you'll take care of Mrs. Maitland, won't you, and see that she has tea and everything?"

She was gone, her long train over her arm, leaving her two elders to look at one another in silence.

Mrs. Maitland felt a little annoyed. She did not want to be left in anybody's care; she had been quietly enjoying herself, in her own way, and now, she supposed, she would have to make an effort to talk to this man Heriot, on whom she had been dumped, yes, dumped was the only word for it, by Susan!

To say that they knew one another was hardly true; each knew the other by sight, of course, and to exchange casual remarks about the weather when they met on the road. It was impossible in a little place like Mennan not to recognize everyone; but there were very few occasions on which Martin Heriot, a prosperous farmer, who hunted and shot and played bridge, would be likely to meet Mrs. Maitland. She had too little time, and too little money, to go about much. A few sedate tea-parties, strictly feminine, a whist drive or two, in aid of local affairs such as the Agricultural Show or the Unionists, were the sum of her social activities, whereas he went about and saw people all over the scattered neighbourhood.

Millie Maitland sighed a little, her face suddenly was wistful. It would be such fun to be able to live like that. . . . Then she roused herself and looked at him, to find him still staring at her.

"I suppose my hat's crooked?" she said ruefully. "It almost always is. I have the kind of head that no hat stays on properly—" and she put up a hand to push it straight.

Martin Heriot started. "I'm sorry. I didn't—why should your hat be crooked?"

"You were looking at it," said Millie. "Is it better now?"

"I'm sorry," he said again. "I didn't mean to stare—I—yes, it's all right. I thought it was supposed to be like that."

With every word he became more confused, because while he had been staring at her, he had been thinking vaguely that this was how she ought always to look, wearing a little flowery hat and soft frills at her neck. He had never seen her before when she had not either been shopping, with a big basket on her arm and an old felt hat crammed down over her soft hair, or out walking, surrounded by dogs, in rubber boots and a dirty waterproof. She looked quite different today, younger and gayer. It was a shame that a woman like Mrs. Maitland should have such a hard life. Naturally he could not say any of this, so he floundered, wishing heartily that he had been elsewhere when Susan had thrust him upon her.

It was distressing to Millie's kind heart to see a big man of Mr. Heriot's age and standing tongue-tied and embarrassed, and she forgot her momentary annoyance in pity.

"What a dear Susan is!" she began, hoping to set him at ease.

"S—sh!" several voices hissed. "The speeches are going to be made now!"

The owners of these voices, though they had been talking at full pitch only a few seconds earlier, managed to make their hushing sound so disapproving that Mrs. Maitland felt quite abashed. Instinctively she glanced at her companion for sympathy and received a fellow-criminal's look of dismay which was oddly comforting.

When the speeches were over in a burst of clapping and laughter, Mrs. Maitland's eyes met Martin Heriot's again.

"It's a funny thing," he observed reflectively. "But I can never listen to speeches without feeling as if my collar had got far too tight for me. If I were a dog I know I'd howl."

Mrs. Maitland smiled. "Yes, I kept on waiting for him to hope all their troubles would be little ones," she said. "He didn't *actually* say the words, but they were sort of hanging in the air, weren't they?"

At that he laughed outright, a cheerful carefree sound. "Well, they're over, anyhow," he said. "Come and sit down at one of these little tables and I'll bring you some tea—or would you rather have champagne?"

But Mrs. Maitland thought that a cup of tea would be very nice, and sank into the chair he pulled out for her, feeling that even nicer than the prospect of tea was the being waited on, because it was such an unaccustomed luxury.

"Hullo, Mother," said her daughter Amabel suddenly, breaking in on her thoughts, "Are you all right? I got separated from you." She flung herself into the chair opposite and added rather too loudly, "What a bore these functions are!"

"Oh, dear! Why must Amabel be so *farouche*?" wondered her mother, even in her own mind avoiding the adjective rude; but she knew that to expostulate would only irritate Amabel to say something more, so she looked a little unhappy and wished Mr. Heriot would come with the tea.

"What on earth are we sitting here for?" was Amabel's next remark.

"Well," said Mrs. Maitland mildly, "I am waiting for tea. I suppose you want some too, don't you?"

"It will be ages before we get any, sitting here. Everyone else is standing up."

"You can stand up if you want to, dear," said Mrs. Maitland. "I'm thankful to sit for a little. And—" she was going to add that she didn't think they would have to wait very long, when Mr. Heriot appeared, followed by a waiter who carried a tray laden with steaming cups. "And here is our tea," she ended.

If Martin Heriot felt that two women on his hands was more than he had bargained for he showed no sign of it. Introduced to Amabel he greeted her pleasantly, sat down between her and Mrs. Maitland and proceeded to talk easily on a variety of uncontroversial subjects. Even when Mrs. Noble came fluttering towards them, crying affectedly, "Oh, *do* let me sit beside you, Mrs. Maitland! I'm *dropping* with exhaustion!"—even then Martin Heriot took it calmly.

He rose, found a chair and a cup of tea for the addition to their party and included her in the conversation with complete composure. Mrs. Noble basked like a sleeping cat in the sun on finding herself with a man to look after her. Her remarks were uttered in a voice as nearly a purr as human speech could attain, Mrs. Maitland thought, listening as she drank her tea. But far more surprising, because so unexpected, was the way Amabel melted and became pleasant. Not even Mrs. Noble's presence seemed able to excite her normal sharpness of tongue.

"How very kind Mr. Heriot has been!" said Millie, after they had been left at the end of their drive by the obliging gentleman in question. "Hasn't he, Amabel?"

"Oh, very kind," Amabel said gloomily.

Her mother looked at her. Sharpness in her daughter she was quite used to, but this depressed tone was new.

"I shouldn't have enjoyed Susan's wedding nearly so much if he hadn't looked after me," she said. "And to have had *three* of us on his hands! Not many men would have—"

"Oh, Mother!" cried Amabel. "Three of us! You don't suppose he *minded* looking after that horrid Mrs. Noble, do you? She's the sort that any man likes to dance attendance on! Look at the way she made him drop us first, though her house is far nearer!"

"Well, I wanted to get home quickly, and she said she wasn't in any hurry," said Mrs. Maitland reasonably.

"Of course she wasn't in a hurry! She'll probably get him to take her out to dinner at the hotel, the nasty little creature! With her nasty yellow hair like raw egg yolks!" Amabel answered with extreme bitterness.

Mrs. Maitland opened her mouth to speak, thought better of it, and closed her lips without saying anything. It sounded as if Amabel would have liked to go out to dinner with Mr. Heriot; Amabel, who had no use for men! Mrs. Maitland felt puzzled, and would have thought more about it, but the dogs, who had heard their return, were yelping and barking from their kennels, and must be attended to at once. In the bustle of changing her dress, slipping on a large blue overall, mixing four bowls of rather horrible dog-meat and brown bread and gravy, feeding her charges and later taking them out for then evening walk across the fields, Mrs. Maitland had no more time for thinking of Amabel and her unusual mood.

Chapter 2

Sometimes, in a rare moment of leisure, when Mrs. Maitland looked back across the thirty years of her short married life and long widowhood, the nineteen-year-old girl on the other side of that gap seemed a total stranger, incredibly young and untried, incredibly ignorant. Of course nineteen is young for marrying, and Millie, though she knew what are called the Facts of Life in theory, was quite ignorant of life itself. She still had the comfortable childish belief that "grown-ups" could do anything they wanted without restraint; also that once married, she and Maurice would live happily ever after, as in the novels she read.

The shock of discovering that married life was not in the least what her novel-reading or her mother's halting attempt at explanation on the eve of her wedding had led her to expect, was a severe one, but Millie was fortunate in that her husband showed her more consideration than a worthier man might have done.

She neither realized nor appreciated his gentleness then, but she did now, and it made her think very kindly of her young husband, who had died after they had been married for three years, and before she had begun to recognize the faults in his character.

He left her only a daughter two years old, and Fernieknowe, the house on the outskirts of Mennan village where she still lived; but he had always been easy-going and kind, never out of temper in spite or all Millie's inability to run their establishment, which would have exasperated most men.

Maurice had bought the house in one of his impulsive moments. It had taken almost the whole of his small capital, but he was perfectly certain that he would make plenty of money quite quickly, and told his wife in a very business-like way which she greatly admired, that it was a sound investment. Not that Millie knew anything about investments, sound or otherwise, or about money matters at all. When she needed money she used the allowance made over to her by her father, and when that was done she asked Maurice for more and he gave it freely. She was ready and willing to believe him when he said there was plenty of money to be made, shared his optimism, and thought Fernieknowe a dear little house. Neither of them could foresee that, long before he had even begun to replace the capital spent so confidently, Maurice would be dead of pneumonia following a neglected cold.

His widow, dazed and bewildered, listened with stunned incomprehension to the lawyer explaining the state of her affairs, while Amabel's roars of baffled fury at having been banished from the drawing-room during this interview rang through the house. What he had to tell her did not make sense; this talk of liabilities and assets, words which she never used, simply defeated her.

At last she said meekly, "If you could tell me how much money there is, perhaps it would be easier—"

"It would," the lawyer said grimly. "To put it quite shortly, Mrs. Maitland, you have this house, and the money your father left you, and that's all."

Mrs. Maitland never forgot her sensations on hearing this; even now when she remembered Mr. Ramsay's words, she could feel again the dreadful sinking inside her. It is probable that she grew up suddenly in the moment that passed after he had spoken them.

The lawyer was afraid she might burst into tears or faint; but she did neither, though she was very pale. And at last he cleared his throat and asked if there were no relations who would help her.

She shook her head. Her parents were both dead now, as were Maurice's. There was no one to whom she could turn.

Mr. Ramsay thought with the irritability of distress that she reminded him of Amelia Sedley, except that Amelia would undoubtedly have wept, and that she had had parents almost as silly as herself, who gave her a home of sorts. "What about Miss Maitland?" he said suddenly. "Your husband's aunt."

Again Millie Maitland shook her head. "Aunt Euphorbia? Oh, no, it would be quite useless to ask *her*, Mr. Ramsay. She made it very plain that she doesn't—didn't—approve of us. She said Maurice was shiftless and I was a fool, and though we called Amabel after her—Amabel Euphorbia, you know, such a mouthful!—she only softened enough to send her a christening mug. Plate, not solid silver." A most un-Amelia-like twinkle appeared for an instant in her pathetic eyes. "Anyhow, I don't really know where she is, and I don't suppose you do. She's probably off on one of those strange expeditions to unknown China or Persia, and may not be heard of for years. No, I shall have to try to manage on what I've got."

She rose, a small, black-clad figure suddenly adorned with a new dignity, and held out her hand. "You have been very kind and patient," said Mrs. Maitland. "Thank you."

With a touch of grim amusement the lawyer realized that he was being kindly, gently and unmistakably dismissed. He held her hand while he said, "I am truly sorry that you should have been left like this, Mrs. Maitland. Anything I can do, of course—"

"Thank you, but that would cost money, wouldn't it?" she said. "I mean, one can't expect lawyers to give their help free, or they wouldn't be able to live, would they?"

Under her candid gaze he reddened slightly. "Oh—well—your affairs were left in our hands by your husband, naturally we should expect to look after them," he muttered. "And being Miss Euphorbia Maitland's man of business as well—"

Inwardly he was telling himself that he would let the old eagle know exactly how badly her nephew's widow had been left. "So you see it would be quite in order for you to consult me if you found it necessary," he ended, and to his relief Mrs. Maitland said no more until they stood on the step outside the front door. Then, just as he was turning to walk back to the village to catch his slow train north to Edinburgh, she said, "Mr. Ramsay—there are a lot of—bills, aren't there?"

"I'm afraid there are," he assented.

"If there is any money at all of Maurice's, could you use it to pay them for me?" she asked. "It would be—easier—if I could start without debts."

"There will be enough for that, and I will see to it," he promised.

Not like Amelia Sedley at all, really, he thought, tramping down the stony drive to the gate. Much more like one of Trollope's heroines, who were all young women of sense.

Millie Maitland watched him out of sight, unaware that she was being compared to Mary Thorne and Lucy Robarts and Grace Crawley. She did not feel like a heroine at all. She wanted to go upstairs to her room, lock the door, and fling herself on her bed to cry until she could not cry any more. In the past, indeed, until this final blow of Maurice's death, she had wept like a child over all her sorrows, from a broken teacup to the loss of her mother, and like a child her tears had washed away her grief. But now, she suddenly realized with a feeling of utter desolation, there was no one to comfort her, and tears were a luxury she could not permit herself. The wailing of baby Amabel, which had died down, now rose again to an even more piercing note.

Mrs. Maitland sighed, rubbed her eyes with her handkerchief, and prepared to start her new life by quietening her child.

Even in retrospect the next four years seemed a nightmare of continuous struggle. The money left to Millie Maitland by her father, invested in War Loan, brought her an income of just over £100 a year. A hundred pounds went a great deal farther then than it does now, but it did not go far enough even while Amabel was a baby, and the problem of how to educate her child caused Millie many sleepless nights. She wondered if she ought not to sell the house in order to get a lump sum, though it would leave them without a home, but Mr. Ramsay advised against this, pointing out that the sum realized would be quite inadequate. Nor did he approve of raising a bond on Fernieknowe because of the difficulty Mrs. Maitland would have in paying the interest. He counselled patience, and just going on carefully from day to day, which drove Millie almost frantic, it was so useless. What she did not know was that Mr. Ramsay, who had written in very plain terms to his client, Miss Euphorbia Maitland, was always hoping for a favourable reply from that wandering eccentric. But time went on, and any brief communications which Mr. Ramsay had from Miss Maitland mentioned neither his letter nor her nephew's widow.

Somehow Millie battled with circumstances. She did sewing and knitting and mending in order to pay rates and taxes—fortunately very low by present-day standards—keep the house more or less in repair, and feed herself and Amabel. As she had started her married life with a very large and handsome outfit, she was able to alter and turn these garments for herself, or cut them down for the child. But all the time, the day when Amabel must begin lessons loomed nearer. She was three, she was four. . . . Millie Maitland's forehead showed a perpetual wrinkle of worry, there was grey in the pretty brown hair round her temples, young though she was.

There was the village school, of course, the board-school, as it was then called, but it happened to be going through a bad period under an elderly master due to retire in five years. Discipline was maintained by the lash of Mr. Grigor's savagely sarcastic tongue, which his pupils feared and hated almost more than the "tawse", that strap used in Scottish schools, though he used it as freely. The teaching was uninspired, to say the least of it, and Millie Maitland felt that for Amabel, clever and quick as she was, to start her education under Mr. Grigor's sway would be disastrous.

Yet there appeared to be no alternative. Attempts to teach the child herself failed miserably, the lessons usually ending by reducing Millie to exasperated tears, while Amabel remained mulishly intractable.

"I want a governess like the Grays," she said in answer to her mothers piteous cry of "*Why* won't you learn your ABC, Amabel darling?"

"Nobody does lessons with their mothers."

"I can't afford a governess for you," said Millie with a sigh. "If you won't do lessons with me you will have to go to Mr. Grigor's school, I'm afraid."

Amabel stuck her chin out. "I won't," she said, and that was all.

Matters were at this very unsatisfactory stage when Mr. Ramsay paid one of his rare visits. Arriving unannounced in order to spare Mrs. Maitland a flurry of unnecessary preparation, he could hear the dreary argument going on in the dining-room. The voices carried to him through the open windows, Millie's vainly imploring her daughter to "say A B ab like a good girl", Amabel's flatly reiterating "I won't do lessons 'cept with a guv'ness."

A vague idea which had been growing in his mind for months, and had indeed brought him down to Mennan this morning, suddenly hardened to resolution. Without waiting to ring the bell he marched straight into the shabby, friendly little house, opened the dining-room door, and confronted the stubborn daughter and tear-stained mother before they—or rather, Mrs. Maitland—could muster a conventional smile of greeting. Amabel merely scowled and muttered "Beastly Ramsay."

Mr. Ramsay paid no attention to this. "Go into the garden, Amabel," he said abruptly. "I want to talk to your mother."

And as soon as Amabel, sulky but cowed by his manner, was out of the room, he asked Mrs. Maitland to marry him.

The offer was made in much the same tone as he had used to Amabel, so that it was a moment or two before Millie took in the meaning of his astonishing words. When she did understand, she was torn between laughter and tears. It was so absurd, it was so touchingly kind. The thought of an old bachelor like him—he was about eight years Millie Maitland's senior, but his gravity and precise manner made him seem elderly to her—saddling himself with a wife and a stepdaughter made her tremble with suppressed half-hysterical laughter. But she could have wept just as easily, and for an instant the temptation to burst into tears, accept his offer and push all her heavy burden of care and anxiety on to him was almost irresistible. The Millie of three years earlier would have done just that without a second thought, unhesitatingly. This Millie was different, and had learned by hard experience that the easy way out of difficulties was no good.

She blew her nose hard, drew a deep breath, and in a steady voice thanked Mr. Ramsay very much for the honour he had done her, but refused him. It struck her even while she was speaking that she sounded like an early Victorian young woman, or a character out of Jane Austen. Imagine calling a man who had just asked one to marry him "Mr. Ramsay"! There was nothing else she could call him, for she did not know his Christian name, his legal communications were always signed P. Ramsay, but it brought home the absurdity of the whole situation again to her, and she had to bite her lip to restrain a smile which might hurt his feelings.

He was asking her to reconsider her decision, in those very words, in his dry legal voice, which gave no hint of his feelings.

Mrs. Maitland shook her head. "It's very, very kind of you," she said earnestly. "Don't think that I don't appreciate it, Mr. Ramsay, but I really mean that I can't marry you."

"Have you any reason for refusing?" he asked.

"Yes, I have. Two reasons," said Mrs. Maitland. "One is that you don't care for me in that way, and the other is that I don't care for you."

He murmured something about admiration and esteem, and this time she did smile. She could not help it.

"Oh, my dear, good man!" she thought hopelessly, but she remained silent.

"Ah, well!" said Mr. Ramsay, and she fancied there was a certain relief in the exclamation, and that he squared his shoulders with a gesture wonderfully like that of a man ridding himself of a load. "What are you going to do about the child's education? Send her to the village school?"

"She won't go."

"Won't go?" he was genuinely shocked. "Do you mean to tell me that she refuses to do what you say like that?"

"Yes, that's just what I mean. And please, Mr. Ramsay, don't start telling me that I must use my authority, because it just isn't any good."

"Surely if you took her there and left her she would stay?"

"How am I to take her?" demanded Millie. "She's much too heavy for me to carry even when she wants to be carried."

"Good heavens!" exclaimed Mr. Ramsay. "Then you will have to go on teaching her yourself, is that it?"

"So far she refuses to learn even to say the alphabet," Millie said wearily. "You see, she wants a governess—"

"Haven't you explained to her that she can't have a governess?"

"I've tried to explain it every day for three months, or four, I forget how many."

"Good heavens!" said Mr. Ramsay again. Then he added: "Shall I explain it to her?"

"You can try, if you like, certainly," Mrs. Maitland agreed, and called Amabel in from the garden.

"Now, Amabel," said Mr. Ramsay, looking down at the small sulky figure before him . . .

He put the matter very fairly and sensibly, Mrs. Maitland thought. The only trouble was that Amabel was not in the least convinced by his arguments. She continued to say "Why?" and "But I want a governess", until Mr. Ramsay, conscious that he was not doing very well, lost his temper.

"Now listen to me," he said. "Either you will learn what your mother teaches you, or you will go to school in the village, and if you won't walk there I shall come and carry you myself."

Amabel glared at him, but she realized that he would get the better of her in this argument, since his physical strength was so much greater. "I hate you," she said passionately.

"I don't care in the least," said Mr. Ramsay coldly. "What is important is that you should understand I mean exactly what I say. You will promise to be good and do lessons with your mother, or I shall come and take you to school."

Mrs. Maitland made an impulsive movement to stop him, for she felt he was being much too severe; but neither Mr. Ramsay nor Amabel paid any attention to her. They frowned silently at one another, until finally the child said sulkily, "All right. But I do hate you. Beastly pig Ramsay."

"Amabel!" cried her mother in horror.

"Never mind," said Mr. Ramsay impatiently. "What does it matter what she calls me? We dislike each other heartily, and we know it. As long as she keeps her word, Amabel can hate me for all she's worth."

And he had proposed to become Amabel's stepfather, thought Millie dazedly. Perhaps something of this showed in her face, for he smiled rather sourly.

"I know, I know," he said. "But I would have done my duty by both of you. And now I must be off to my train." He shook Millie's hand in his usual formal way, looked at Amabel and said, "Don't forget!" and was gone.

Harsh though he had been, his treatment of Amabel was apparently successful, for she now began to show a slightly less hostile attitude towards lessons. She certainly did not try very hard and her imperceptible progress was maddening to her mother, who had a shrewd suspicion that this stupidity was assumed; but at least she no longer demanded a governess, and Millie was humbly aware that she herself was no born teacher.

So the two plodded through the reading-book, its pages blistered with tears and grimed from the clutch of Amabel's unwilling fingers, until the day, several months later, when a telegram from Mr. Ramsay regretted to inform Mrs. Maitland of the death of her late husband's aunt, Miss Euphorbia Maitland, in Brazil.

"Oh, dear!" exclaimed Mrs. Maitland, standing with the message in her hand. "Poor old lady!"

Amabel, delighted with the unexpected break in lesson-time, had picked up the flimsy orange envelope from the gravel where it had fallen, and was quietly opening it out. At the note of mild regret in her mother's voice she looked up.

"What is it?" she asked. "Who's the funny little letter from, Mummy? Who's the poor old lady? Why didn't Postie bring it with the other letters?"

"It's from Mr. Ramsay, to say that your great-aunt is dead," replied Millie, and then wondered if a good mother would trouble her child's young consciousness with the thought of death, even the death of an unknown great-aunt.

Amabel, ignoring a fact which meant nothing at all to her, said apprehensively, "Is Mr. Ramsay coming here?"

"So he says—though why he should think it necessary," said Mrs. Maitland, forgetting that she was talking to a five-year-old, "I *cannot* imagine—unless it's because she had no other relatives."

"He—you won't let him take me to school?" cried Amabel. "You won't, will you, Mummy? You won't let him, will you?"

Mrs. Maitland calmed her daughter, but continued to wonder why Mr. Ramsay had added in his telegram that he would call on her the following forenoon. She hoped he did not mean to renew his offer of marriage, for this would only embarrass them both.

Mr. Ramsay, sober in his stiff dark suit, wore a curious air of triumph which roused Mrs. Maitland's fears, for he really did look not only as if he meant to ask her to marry him but sure of being accepted. His first words, however, set her mind at rest on that score.

"I have brought with me Miss Maitland's Will," he announced as he took her hand in greeting.

"Oh, yes? How kind of you. Do come in and let me make you a cup of tea. It is such a tiresome walk from the station," Millie said vaguely, full of relief because his errand was not what she had dreaded.

Mr. Ramsay looked coldly at her. What infuriating creatures women were! Did she not understand the significance of his having brought Miss Maitland's Will to read to her? He had arrived hugging to himself a feeling of personal achievement, which he fondly supposed was completely hidden behind his decently grave demeanour. Without conceit, he was sure that this Will was the direct result of his strongly-worded letters to his difficult and eccentric old client, and though he had no wish to wave his victory like a banner, he *had* rather expected the beleaguered garrison, in the person of Mrs. Maitland, to receive him with suitable gratitude and relief.

And she offered him cups of tea! And prattled about the walk from the station. *Women*, thought Mr. Ramsay disgustedly. Even Amabel, spoilt, selfish little brat though she was, had a better brain than her mother.

But he had his revenge when, after refusing the tea, he read the terms of Miss Euphorbia Maitland's Will, for Mrs. Maitland listened with almost strained attention, uttering no sound at all. When he had finished, he laid the paper down, took off his reading glasses, and looked across at her with a small tight smile, the only sign of gratification he permitted himself.

He was disconcerted to see that her eyes were full of tears, which brimmed over and ran down her cheeks.

"It's—it's all right!" she said shakily, fumbling for her handkerchief. "Very silly of me, but somehow good news is harder to bear than bad! I'm so sorry!"

With real tact and kindness, he went over to the window and stood looking out, leaving her to struggle with the tears which, once started, were so hard to check. He was more moved himself than he liked. Knowing how difficult Mrs. Maitland had found life since her husband's death, admiring her for her unexpected courage, it was only now that he realized, from this breakdown, a little of her mental distress during those years.

At last he heard her say, "There! I've pulled myself together, Mr. Ramsay. Do you think you could tell me about the Will again? Somehow it doesn't seem quite true yet."

He turned at once. "Don't go running away with the idea that this is a very satisfactory Will, Mrs. Maitland," he said. "We could have drawn up one that would have been much fairer to you. I wish we had been allowed to do so. But Miss Maitland had peculiar ideas, and liked to go her own way—"

"Oh!" Millie stared at him in sudden dismay. "You—you don't mean that we can't use the money now, when we need it so badly, surely?"

"No, no, no!" he hastened to reassure her. "The income can be put at your disposal immediately, but only for Amabel's use, do you understand? Miss Maitland has left her entire estate to Amabel, who is life-rented in it. That is to say, she cannot touch the capital, which is to go to her children, failing whom, or should such children predecease her, the money is then to be divided in equal parts among several charities named by Miss Maitland."

Millie Maitland's sigh was one of pure relief. "You gave me such a fright!" she said. "But of course all we need the money for *really* is Amabel, her education, her clothes and dentist's bills and doctor's. What a load off my mind it is! How very, very good of the poor, queer old lady to leave it to her!"

Mr. Ramsay felt that he would never understand women—or at least this particular woman. "It is very much to your credit that you should take it like this," he said patiently. "I don't think, however, that you quite realize what an invidious position it places you in. This money is Amabel's, the income will be paid direct to her as soon as she is twenty-one. It can never benefit you except as she chooses. I do not approve of it at all."

"Don't you? I do," said Mrs. Maitland. "If I don't have to worry about Amabel I won't have any real worries at all. I certainly never expected Maurice's Aunt Euphorbia to leave *me* anything. I told you she considered me a fool!"

Mr. Ramsay made a small deprecatory gesture, but privately he was rather inclined, if only for the moment, to endorse Miss Maitland's opinion of her niece by marriage.

Yet when he was sitting quietly in the corner of a first-class non-smoker on his way back to Edinburgh, he suddenly said to himself, "All the same, fool or no, I wish the money had been left to *her*. It would make no difference to her character and outlook, for she is one of those whom money can't spoil. But I doubt very much if it will do Amabel's character any good. I doubt it. Amabel will have more intelligence than heart."

Chapter 3

THOSE of her acquaintances who congratulated Millie Maitland on having a daughter at home were apt to qualify this—though not in her hearing, of course—by the remark that it was a pity Amabel Maitland was so sharp and impatient with her mother.

"A pity, do you call it?" said big, bouncing Mrs. Gray of Netherton, whose own pretty daughters had always had a wholesome respect for her which continued even now that they were all married. "*I* call it an outrage! When I think how Millie has slaved for Amabel, and never so much as hinted that that queer old aunt of her husband's might have left the money to her and not to the child, my blood boils, absolutely *boils*! I should like to give that young woman a piece of my mind, and I would, if I weren't sure that she would tell Millie, and Millie would be hurt."

When she held forth like this her audience always agreed heartily, especially with the last part of her statement. None of them was anxious to hurt Millie Maitland's feelings, however much they disapproved of her daughter's attitude to her, and so nothing was ever said, directly or indirectly, to Amabel. Which no doubt was a good thing, words uttered in heat being extremely apt to do more harm than good.

Since there was nothing wrong with Amabel's intelligence, she quite soon realized that a great many of her friends and neighbours did not approve of her, and shrugged it aside as being of no importance. What did it matter to an independent young woman with a good job if a lot of old tabbies had a low opinion of her? In her own estimation she did a lot for her mother, and would have done more financially if Millie would have let her. If her conscience ever murmured that she might show a little of the affection which she knew Millie would infinitely prefer to a new electric iron, Amabel told it firmly that she considered deeds more valuable than mushy sentiment, and conscience retired vanquished.

Amabel's job was that of organizing secretary to a combine of youth organizations, and she carried it out extremely efficiently. So long as she got through her work, she was able to use her own discretion as to hours, and found that her presence in the office in Edinburgh was only necessary for three or four days each week. This meant that she could frequently have a day at home as well as week-ends, and made it quite possible for her to live with her mother and go by train or her little car to her job, returning at night.

Millie Maitland liked this arrangement, but for almost a year now Amabel had been urging her to sell Fernieknowe and buy a small flat in Edinburgh where they could live together and not be "completely cut off from everything like the theatre or concerts", as Amabel insisted they were in Mennan. Because her mother was unexpectedly firm in refusing to sell her house or even to begin to consider doing so, Amabel's behaviour to her during the past few months had become almost bullying and certainly most, if not all, of what Mrs. Gray and others said of it.

Mr. Ramsay had never met Mrs. Gray, nor would he have expressed his opinions in her violent robust way, but he felt that he had been right all those years ago, when he had first doubted the wisdom of old Miss Maitland's leaving her money to Amabel and not to her mother.

This feeling was particularly strong as he faced Amabel across his big desk in his dusty, paper-laden office, a few days after Susan Gray's wedding.

"Perhaps you will tell me why you wish me to speak to Mrs. Maitland about selling Fernieknowe?" he asked, and his tone was not promising.

Amabel glanced at him warily. In her memory there still lurked the picture of the look on his grave face, the sound of his voice when, years and years ago, he had told her that if need be he would carry her to school, unless she promised to be good and learn her lessons from her mother. Mr. Ramsay himself had forgotten the occasion, but Amabel had not. Because of it she had never treated him to the good-naturedly contemptuous, slightly patronizing manner she was a little too apt to use with her mother and others of Millie's generation.

She did not call him a beast now, of course, even in her thoughts, nor say that she hated him; but there was always a feeling that they were antagonists. Now, even while she stiffened at his tone, she smiled composedly, glad that she had taken the trouble to wear her new suit and the becoming hat in which she looked her best The outfit might have been too severely business-like for a wedding, but the well-tailored dark grey set off her tall figure, and she knew it.

"You sound terribly disapproving," she said lightly, but with the wary look in her eyes.

"If you will give me your reasons for wanting this, I shall be in a better position to approve or disapprove," said Mr. Ramsay stolidly.

Amabel realized that he had no intention of making this easy for her. "Well," she began, "Mennan is a dreary little hole, and I dislike it, and its inhabitants. The house isn't easy to run, it's old-fashioned and inconvenient. Mother would be much more comfortable in a flat in Edinburgh, and it would be less bother for me if I didn't have to travel to and fro every day."

"I didn't know that you did travel every day," observed Mr. Ramsay.

"Oh, well, almost every day, then," said Amabel impatiently. "It's a nuisance and an expense, even if I only have to go up three days in the week."

"Then why not take a room in Edinburgh and go back to Mennan at the week-ends?" suggested Mr. Ramsay, and now his voice was bland. "With your salary and the income from your great-aunt's money, diminished though that is now, you could surely afford it."

If Amabel had been fifteen years younger, her movement at these words could best have been described as a squirming wriggle. Mr. Ramsay could always attack one's weakest point! Her voice as she muttered, "I hate digs," might have been a sulky schoolgirl's.

Mr. Ramsay raised his eyebrows. "I'm afraid I could not possibly advise Mrs. Maitland to sell her home simply because you dislike the thought of digs," he said. "The only solution that

I can see is for you to give up living with your mother at Mennan altogether, and rent a small flat in Edinburgh for yourself."

"You know I can't do that!" Amabel burst out. "Mother would have to work even harder than she does now with those wretched dogs to manage, and even then it would mean pinching—"

"Quite so," said Mr. Ramsay, who knew this perfectly well, but had wondered how Amabel would react to his suggestion. His voice remained dry, but his eyes had a kindlier glance, though his client did not notice it. There was, it appeared, a limit to her selfishness, and Mr. Ramsay was mildly pleased to discover this. Before she could say anything he went on: "Bear in mind that your mother has been for years, and still is, in the rather ignominious position of having very much smaller means than her daughter. If she had not been a woman incapable of envy, and without a single mercenary instinct, you might have felt it very awkward indeed."

"Oh, I know that, of course!" Amabel exclaimed ungraciously. "But I get pretty sick of being reminded of other's sacrifices, so you needn't start telling me about them again. It isn't my fault that Great-Aunt Euphorbia left her money to me, is it?"

"Certainly not," said Mr. Ramsay emphatically.

"Well, then—" Amabel found that she did not know what to say. His prompt agreement had taken the wind out of her sails. She darted an angry glance at him, feeling baffled.

Quite unperturbed, Mr. Ramsay said, "I had no intention of reminding you of sacrifices made for you by your mother. What I want to suggest is a small sacrifice on your part—"

He broke off suddenly to remark with unexpected force: "How ridiculous all this exaggerated talk of 'sacrifice' is, Amabel! I am sure your mother never speaks or even thinks of anything she has done for you in these terms! Surely any normal person is willing to give up a little for the sake of others? Surely it isn't asking too much of you to let your mother keep her house? It means that she can feel independent, or at least not entirely dependent on you, if the house belongs to her."

Amabel was amazed at the feeling the dry reserved man showed in these words. He must think a great deal of Mother, she thought confusedly, and her manner when she answered was much less confident than usual. Her hesitation made her seem younger, softer; for the first time in her life, Mr. Ramsay saw in her a slight resemblance to Millie.

"I—I never thought of it that way," she murmured. "I hate to see her slaving with those dogs and the housework. But if you really think it means so much to her I won't say anything more about selling Fernieknowe."

Already Mr. Ramsay had resumed the grave look of composure normal to him. His voice when he spoke next, about her investments, was level and business-like. If he approved of Amabel's capitulation he showed no sign. And Amabel herself, although she had given up her longing for an Edinburgh flat because at the moment she was thinking of her mother's feelings, soon had another thought, less disinterested. It looked as if Mr. Ramsay had a soft spot in his heart for her mother; perhaps he would ask her to marry him, and then Amabel could go off and live her own life with a clear conscience—if her mother accepted him. There was a vague recollection in Amabel's mind, a memory of which she had always been ashamed, of a child sent out of the room to play, but lingering at the door and listening, and hearing Mr. Ramsay ask Mother to marry him. . . . It would solve all their problems if Mrs. Maitland would marry Mr. Ramsay, thought Mrs. Maitland's daughter, and wondered why the idea, with its promise of freedom for her, did not altogether please her.

Millie Maitland did not bother very much about the salve to her pride which owning the roof above her and Amabel's heads was supposed to give. She had her own reasons for wanting to keep Fernieknowe. She was fond of the house because she had always liked it, and now was accustomed to it; and it reminded her of Maurice, when she remembered to think of him, which was not very often now. The first reason was the stronger, of course, for Fernieknowe and she had grown together during thirty years, and she knew all its faults, and all the shabby corners were dear to her now. Besides, Fernieknowe was completely satisfactory as a place to board dogs; there were plenty of outhouses, a large untidy garden at the back, and best of all, there was no other house near enough for its inhabitants to be disturbed when the dogs barked or howled, which they sometimes did.

Millie could not understand why Amabel objected to the dogs. They were infinitely less troublesome than human lodgers, they made no complaints about their beds or food, they did not have to be spoken of as "paying guests", they could be scolded or even beaten if they were troublesome. Millie found them an excellent source of income and didn't mind the work they caused her. It was quite hard work, especially in bad weather, when she had to plod out through the rain or snow to feed them, and take them out for exercise, but they were so grateful and affectionate, they repaid her care and trouble.

If she sold Fernieknowe and bought a flat in town, Millie would be deprived at one blow of her little extra money and her chief interest, for the fact was that Mrs. Maitland really liked the dogs, and in the mass, preferred them to human beings, while the dogs liked her. She was quite sure that it had been a fortunate day for her when, by mere chance, five years before, Mrs. Gray had lamented the difficulty of knowing what to do with her old spaniel while the family was away on holiday at a seaside hotel. The house was to be shut up, the hotel was being very sticky about taking a dog—and Millie had said suddenly, "I'll have him, Davina. I'd like to."

And so it had begun, as easily as that. Mrs. Gray had been delighted, had insisted on paying Millie for looking after Sambo—and Millie, who had no false pride about money, had gladly accepted it—and had told everyone she knew who kept dogs to send them to Fernieknowe if they required a temporary home.

The thing had grown like a snowball rolled downhill, as more and more satisfied dog owners passed on the information about "that little woman at Mennan who boards dogs" to their friends in turn. It was very rare indeed now for Millie to be without at least one dog, either in the house if it happened to be what she called a "parlour boarder", or in the old stable which she had converted into dogs' quarters; more often there were three or four.

Mrs. Maitland sometimes said that the name of her house should be changed from Fernieknowe to Dog Hall, for, though there were large clumps of fern growing on the high bank behind the house, and clustered thickly on either side of the steep, winding drive, the dogs were much more noticeable.

Fernieknowe was quite near the village, but Mennan lay in a hollow with many trees about it, so that it was only by looking down from her bedroom window that Mrs. Maitland could catch a glimpse of slated roofs and the rosy spire of the parish church, peering among the green, with its gilt weathercock glinting as it turned to the wind and the sun caught it. Though she was always too busy to feel lonely, and in any case she had the dogs to keep her company while Amabel was at her job in Edinburgh, Millie liked to be able to see even this little peep of the village. It gave her a comforting, companionable feeling, perched as she was halfway up a hillside, with the great wide sweep of the open moor on the other three sides of the house, to be reminded that she had neighbours almost within a stone's throw.

This steep approach to Fernieknowe was one of Amabel's many objections to it, and as the shed which had been made into a garage for her little car was down by the gate, she always had to do the last fifty yards on foot. Millie rather liked that walk up from the gate. The front garden on its steep slope seemed to be tumbling downhill to meet one, and behind it the house looked out with a welcoming twinkle from its windows, rather as if it stood on tiptoe to see over the flowers and shrubs. It was a low house, built before the craze for ornate architecture had set in during the nineteenth century, and its proportions and style owed a great deal to the inspiration of the brothers Adam. The door had a shell-shaped fanlight above it, and a large window on either side, matched by the three windows of the upper storey. Tall chimneys rising at each end added to its appearance of eager watchfulness. Inside, a hall ran back to unexpectedly large kitchen premises behind the dining-room and drawing-room which looked to the garden, and upstairs there were three bedrooms, a bathroom, and a box-room where Millie kept her ironing-board and sewing-machine, and a dressmaker's dummy with a knob on a stalk instead of a head, lurked in a corner, its anatomy bristling with pins. Amabel, whose taste in clothes was always for impeccably cut tailor-mades, and whose pocket allowed her to indulge it to a modest extent, despised poor Berengaria, but Millie found her invaluable and pinned garments on to her with tremendous enthusiasm, for she always hoped, with each dress she made, that *this* one would turn out perfect.

The whole house was shabby, the chintz loose covers so many times washed and mended that their original patterns had vanished, the carpets faded and worn, the curtains in no better case; but everything was brilliantly clean, and the furniture and floors shone with faithful polishing. Not even the dogs' muddy footprints could take away me effect of exquisite cleanliness which Fernieknowe presented. Mrs. Maitland's greatest joy was the electricity which now replaced the paraffin lamps and bedroom candles of her earlier days there. Amabel on her eighteenth birthday had persuaded Mr. Ramsay without difficulty that to use her money to install electric light and power was quite legal; and her mother felt an innocent delight when she pressed down a switch and flooded a room with light.

To her friends' lamentations over the change—"oil lamps look so much more attractive and give such a lovely soft mellow light!"—she replied simply that having to fill and clean the lamps every day robbed them of their attraction, and she preferred to be able to see to sew and not to have to blind herself by a softer light, no matter how mellow.

Millie enjoyed sewing, though her hands were really too rough from gardening and housework and dogs for handling fine materials, and she was making a tiny dress for Pat Ross's baby while she waited for Amabel to come home from Edinburgh. Because the April evening was cold, she was sitting by the window in the big kitchen, where the corners were already shadowy, and all the light seemed concentrated on the space immediately inside the window. A slow combustion stove, which heated the water as well as cooking, filled the room with pleasant warmth. This was the quiet hour of the day that Millie Maitland liked, when she had time to sit down for a little. The dogs—there were three of them at present—had all been fed and walked and were bedded in clean dry straw in the old stable. Millie had put on a woollen dress of a soft dark blue which suited her, and exchanged her shoes for slippers, and was enjoying the feel of silk stockings instead of thick lisle thread.

A round table nearer the stove was all set for supper, a handful of daffodils in a pewter mug reflected the last of the sunset. In the oven was one of Amabel's favourite dishes, a fish-pie made with cheese sauce and covered with fluffy creamed potato now slowly turning brown, and Millie had been given a piece of real farm butter that morning, a great treat in these days of severe butter rationing.

She was feeling contented and at ease, tired with her day of household duties and dog-walking, but not over-tired. If only Amabel came home in a pleasant temper, everything would be perfect, she thought, as she put quick neat stitches into the little blue dress. Pat had had a hard time with this first baby, but she was doing well now, and delighted with her son, Jack reported. Jack himself had suddenly acquired a responsible air which changed him from the pleasant-mannered boy of his first year of marriage, to a man. He even seemed to have grown an inch taller when he had looked in an hour earlier to give Mrs. Maitland the latest news of Pat and the baby, and to say how much Pat had liked the flowers Mrs. Maitland had taken round to the Cottage Hospital for her.

"But of course that isn't *possible*!" Mrs. Maitland said aloud, sewing away. "Unless reaching man's stature really means something like that."

She could not remember that Maurice had shown any such signs of maturity when Amabel was born; perhaps all men didn't react in the same way as Jack Ross, or perhaps she herself had been too young to notice. But Maurice had remained boyish until his death, and Millie wondered now if he would ever have grown up at all. From her rather hazy memories of her husband she was inclined to think that he would have continued incurably optimistic about money, incurably careless, happy-go-lucky and Micawberish. . . . Quite suddenly and for the first time, it struck her that life might have been even more of a struggle if Maurice had not died. She had never thought that before, but now she knew that he would never have been able to suffer the indignity of his young daughter being his aunt's heir instead of himself. He would have brooded over it, allowed it to embitter him, and they would all have been miserable. "Oh, poor Maurice! I am glad he didn't have to know about that!" said Millie, again aloud, for she quite often spoke to herself, as people who are much alone tend to do.

Thinking of Maurice induced a gentle melancholy, which the fading afterglow in the sunset sky and the gradually darkening room increased. She could no longer see to sew, and, too comfortable in the old wicker chair to get up and put on the light, she folded her work and leaned back against the cushions. There was a pricking under her closed eyelids, and with considerable surprise Mrs. Maitland realized that there were tears gathering, slow, pleasant, almost luxurious tears which she would rather enjoy to feel rolling down her cheeks. "Good gracious!" she thought. "What on earth can be the matter with me? It must be the spring!"

For a moment she made no attempt to blink back the tears, and two had already escaped when the thought of Amabel's annoyance if she came home and found her mother weeping dried the flow as if by magic. Only just in time, too, for as she found her handkerchief and mopped her eyes, she heard the front door open, and Amabel's voice called, "Mother! Where are you?"

"I'm here, dear. In the kitchen," Millie called back, and began to make her way towards the light.

Before she had reached it Amabel had opened the kitchen door and pressed the switch briskly. The big room sprang into light which dazzled Millie after the twilight gloom to which her eyes had grown accustomed.

"I—dear me, I must have been nearly asleep," she said in the deprecating manner which Amabel's sharply matter-of-fact tones so often produced in her. "But supper's almost ready. I'll have it on the table as soon as you have taken off your coat and hat."

"Oh, that's all right. There isn't any great hurry for supper," Amabel replied with unusual mildness. "But Mr. Heriot's here. He wants to ask you something about boarding a dog."

Millie, blinking a little, saw that a tall broad figure was standing behind Amabel in the kitchen doorway, as if uncertain whether to come in or not.

"I hope I haven't come at an awkward time," he said now. "We—your daughter and I—travelled down together and it seemed a good chance to see you about this dog, but—"

"Of course I'm very pleased to see you, Mr. Heriot," said Millie promptly. She had had time to recover her scattered wits, and he sounded so shy that she felt more composed herself, and sorry for him at the same time. "I hope you don't mind sitting in the kitchen. It's much the warmest place in the house."

Amabel dragged forward another old basket chair with cushions and frills of faded chintz. "Come and sit near the fire," she said brusquely, and Millie sighed inwardly, for she knew Amabel meant to be kind and hospitable, and yet she sounded like a female sergeant-major addressing a new recruit.

"Oh—er, thanks." Martin Heriot came right into the room and looked about him appreciatively, noticing the clean whitewash of walls and ceiling, the blue plates on the old-fashioned dresser, the big solid kitchen table in the background, and the little round one so neatly set for two people in front of the stove. It was just as he imagined Mrs. Maitland would have things: all neat and clean and comfortable. "I like your kitchen," he said suddenly, smiling at her.

"It's terribly big and out-of-date," Amabel objected.

"I expect that's why I like it," he answered. "Those modern kitchens that look like operating theatres are so comfortless. I never feel that a real satisfying meal can be cooked in one of them, just something that is well balanced and has all the necessary vitamins. This is the sort of kitchen where the cook would always have a little batter over for children to make drop scones when she had finished and the girdle was still hot."

"Terribly big and out-of-date" seemed rather a good description of the man himself, Mrs. Maitland thought. On an impulse she said: "I don't know if our supper is well balanced and full of vitamins, but I know it will taste good. It's a fish-pie, and I make it rather well. Won't you stay and have some?"

Immediately the words were spoken her heart sank. Amabel would be certain to disapprove of this carelessly-issued invitation to share their supper, and in the kitchen too! But she had asked him now, and must put a bold face on it, since she could not withdraw.

"Yes, do stay," Amabel said quite eagerly. "Mother's fish-pie is something rather special."

"Are you sure it wouldn't be a bother?" he asked.

"Of course it isn't a bother!" cried Mrs. Maitland. "I'll lay another place in a minute. The only thing is," she added doubtfully. "There isn't anything to *drink*."

At her tone, which seemed to imply that he could not exist without quantities of alcoholic refreshment, Martin Heriot laughed. The deep sound rang through the kitchen pleasantly. "What's wrong with water?" he said. "I drink the stuff quite often, Mrs. Maitland."

"Oh—well—" Millie said with relief. "If that will be all right—Amabel drinks a glass of milk, and I have tea—"

"Better still."

"Well, I'll go and wash and tidy my hair," Amabel said. "I won't be a minute."

Martin Heriot noticed that she made no offer to help, and that her mother did not seem to expect it. She opened a drawer of the dresser and put out extra knives and forks and a table-napkin, and took another plate and cup and saucer from a cupboard, moving quickly and quietly about the room, while he stood by the stove looking very tall, and watched her neat movements of hand and arm, the turn of her head with its clustering silvery curls, and wondered at the difference between her and her daughter.

Then Amabel came in again, her hair shiningly neat, her silk shirt daisy-fresh under a dark cardigan, and they gathered round the supper-table.

The meal was a great success. The fish-pie, piping hot, with its deliciously brown top and succulent cheese-flavoured contents, was eaten to the last scraping. Mrs. Maitland was very glad she had made such a big one. It was a pleasure to satisfy a hungry man's appetite, and she encouraged Martin Heriot to enjoy his supper, pressing the home-baked wholemeal scones and gingerbread on him, pouring out cup after cup of tea, quite forgetting that Amabel disapproved of what she called "forcing food down people's throats".

Amabel seemed to be in an unwontedly gentle mood this evening. When Martin said to her apologetically, "I don't believe I've eaten such a lot since I was a schoolboy!" she looked pleased and replied, "Mother is a very good cook, isn't she? And it's a compliment to her when you appreciate her cooking."

"I don't think I have ever paid a compliment so wholeheartedly," he said. "Mrs. Maitland, your cooking is marvellous!"

Millie smiled and coloured with pleasure, but it was not because of what he had said, but because her dear Amabel was being so sweet and kind that her heart felt light and she forgot her tired feet and aching back.

Even the inevitable washing-up was fun, for Martin insisted that they should all do it together, assuring Mrs. Maitland quite seriously that he was a very good hand at drying dishes. Rather to her surprise this proved to be no empty boast, and he laughed at the astonishment which she could not hide.

"I used to do a lot of this when I was a boy," he said. "My mother was a great one for making her children take a share in household chores, and we didn't get off dish-washing just because we were boys, my brother and I!"

Mrs. Maitland would have liked to ask him about his boyhood, and how many brothers and sisters he had, and where they were now; but Amabel was anxious to talk, she could tell, and stories of his childhood would not interest her.

So Millie took out her knitting and sat quietly in her corner by the warm stove, listening to her daughter's clever, sensible questions about farming and the difficulty of getting labour so far from picture-houses and shops, and was aware that Martin Heriot found her intelligent and spoke to her as to an equal.

Yes, she decided to herself, it was a very pleasant evening, and she was quite sorry when he looked at the clock and exclaimed, "Good Lord! Is it that time? Quarter to eleven? I must go!"

Standing in the kitchen where he had left her, feeling the strong clasp of his hand as he had said good-bye, remembering the genuine sound of his voice thanking her for her kindness, Millie

Maitland yawned with sheer sleepiness and hoped that Amabel would not be too long over her farewells at the door. She thought of her bed with pleased anticipation, and pulled the kettle further on to the stove to fill the hot-water bottle which even with daffodils and scillas flowering outside was more of a necessity than a luxurious pampering of the flesh.

Amabel came in again, bringing a rush of chill night air with her, just as the kettle began to sing.

"Oh, it's *cold*!" she exclaimed. "Would there be enough hot water for me to have a bottle too, Mother?"

"Of course there's enough," said Millie. "I'll fill this one for you first."

"I don't really need it, but it would be nice, to-night," Amabel said, watching her mother carefully pouring the steaming water into the red rubber bottle. "Oh, Mother! Do you realize that Martin Heriot came here to ask you about keeping a dog for him, and he forgot to say anything about it?"

"He can either ring up or come again and tell me," Millie replied calmly. "Here's your bottle, dear. Take it up and put it in your bed before it gets cold."

Chapter 4

THE great drawback to even a slight escape from the daily rut is the disagreeable bump with which one falls back into it afterwards. Having Martin Heriot to share their evening meal could not have been described as madly exciting, yet the days that followed seemed unusually humdrum and dreary to Mrs. Maitland, and she imagined, from Amabel's irritability, that she felt the same, although she scoffed at such an idea.

"Good heavens, Mother!" she exclaimed, Millie having been unwise enough to suggest it. "Surely we aren't so hard put to it for entertainment that having a man unexpectedly to supper should rouse us to such a pitch that we can't take it! This is what comes of living in a Backwater like Mennan. The whole thing's ridiculous!"

"It does sound ridiculous when you put it like that," Millie agreed, passing over the reference to Mennan. "But—it was a *break*, you see, and much more fun than inviting someone and having to fuss over preparations beforehand."

"Then why fuss? No one expects more than a simple meal nowadays," said Amabel.

Millie opened her mouth to explain, but thought better of it and said nothing. She was always starting to say things to Amabel and having to think better of it. If Amabel did not realize that there must always be a certain amount of preparation to be made for guests it was because she did not want to. Millie thought of it all: the fresh flowers for the table, the looking through dinner-napkins to make certain there was one without too obvious dams, the choice of pudding, the filling of salt-cellars and pepper-pots, all the thousand and one little extras which make such a difference. Nor did she really think this a bother, for while it had been fun, as she had said, to have an unexpected guest, she also found it fun to arrange things for one who had been invited.

"What were you going to say?" Amabel asked now.

"Perhaps I do fuss too much," was all that Millie replied.

"Of course you do! The next time we have anyone, just leave it to me. I'm sure I could do it without making myself a nervous wreck."

"I didn't know I did make myself a nervous wreck," Millie said meekly. "But I'll certainly leave it to you if you like, dear. And will you do the cooking too?"

"Oh—well—I know I can't cook like you do," began her daughter, who might more truthfully have said that she couldn't really cook at all. "I thought if you would do the actual *cooking* and I did the rest, it would be a fair division."

A peculiar expression crossed Millie Maitland's gentle face as she remembered the numberless times when she had managed everything, with housework thrown in, and no question of a division of labour, fair or otherwise. But she said nothing, and Amabel fortunately was not looking and did not notice.

"We could try it, certainly," Mrs. Maitland said after a short pause. "Are you going to the village this morning, dear?"

"I might be. D'you want anything?"

"If I gave you a list—" Millie began hopefully. Amabel moaned.

"Oh, Lord, Mother! That means a whole basketful of stuff, and you'll want it in time for lunch, or something!" she said. "Honestly it isn't worth being able to manage my job three days in the week if I have to do all sorts of things when I stay at home! How on earth do you get on when I'm in Edinburgh?"

"I have to do it myself, of course, and it means a bit of a rush," said Mrs. Maitland.

She spoke quietly, but there was a flash in her mild eyes. Amabel was being so—so infernally disagreeable, she thought, that it would be infinitely preferable never to have anyone to the house again, if this was to be the result!

Amabel knew a suddenly extraordinary longing to rush at her mother, fling herself into her arms and say that she knew she was being a beast, but she had promised not to bother her again about selling Fernieknowe and taking a flat in Edinburgh, and she liked Martin Heriot much better than any man she had ever met, and he seemed to like her too, and she did not know how or when she would have a chance to talk to him again. . . .

Being Amabel, she curbed this impulse at once, and the moment for a better understanding between mother and daughter was gone without either realizing that they were missing an opportunity.

"Sorry," she said gruffly. "I must have a touch of liver this morning. If you'll give me your list I'll get the things."

Millie accepted this *amende*, and presently paused in her dusting to watch her daughter's tall form stalking down through the garden towards the green gate, swinging a basket.

"Poor lamb!" she murmured. "I do wish she would get married. She would be so much happier and so much less thorny. Poor lamb!"

And she sighed. Then the absurdity of calling Amabel a lamb struck her, and she laughed. But it did not occur to her that, in view of her own brief married life and struggling widowhood, it was hardly a kindness to wish the same fate for her daughter. She was quite firmly convinced that marriage would be the best possible thing for Amabel.

When she had finished the housework and prepared vegetables for lunch, Mrs. Maitland took the two dogs which required exercise out for a walk. The third, an elderly bulldog for whom a dignified waddle about the garden was enough, lay snoring in his bed of straw, but the two rather foolish fox terriers leapt about her with shrill hysterical yelps, eager to go out. Millie had no intention of taking such excitable creatures into the fields or across the hills, where young lambs might be disturbed by them. Calling her charges to heel in a very firm manner, she set off along the road in the opposite direction to the village. It was a quiet road with little or no traffic, and the terriers could run and sniff about the hedges as their own erratic fancy dictated.

Mrs. Maitland walked briskly, reminding the dogs now and then that they were not entirely free from authority, enjoying all the signs that spring was at hand. Hawthorn hedges were misted over with gay fresh green, the distant woods showed a bloom like that on a ripe damson which told of swelling buds. Larks rose from the red furrows of ploughed fields beside the road, singing with all their might, and higher up the hillsides curlew were wheeling, in wide slow spirals, to the sound of their lovely lonely crying.

As with so many people, the spring was Mrs. Maitland's favourite season, not so much because of its beauty, for Millie thought autumn the most beautiful time of the year, but for the promise of new life breathed by every hint of mildness in the air, shown by every springing blade of grass. Autumn in its very fulfilment had a wistfulness, only felt, perhaps, by those no longer young. But spring, coming after the long dreary winter which was so hard on older people, spring seemed to say, "Well, you see, you've weathered it all right, and here I am, with summer not far behind me, long warm days and sunshine on the way!"

Millie forgot Amabel's peevishness and her own flat spirits in the sheer pleasure of being out, able to walk lightly and quickly, with the short grass of the road's verge under her feet and the sun shining with tempered warmth from a pale blue sky. She whistled to the dogs, more to hear the mellow note than to summon them—Millie's only musical accomplishment was a singularly clear sweet whistle, almost like a blackbird's—and since it hardly came under the heading of parlour tricks, especially in a woman of her age, she had few opportunities of practising it. But the road was empty ahead of her, there was not even a shepherd striding far away across the hill, and the spring had gone to her head. Suddenly she was whistling a tune quite loudly, and it sounded so pleasant to her ear that she went on, passing from one tune to another as the fancy took her.

Engrossed in this unladylike performance so unsuited to her years, it was with a horrid shock that Mrs. Maitland heard someone hailing her from the rear. She stopped whistling at once, of course, and took another step or two, hoping against hope that the voice had not really been calling to her; but a louder shout of "Mrs. Maitland!" brought her, most unwillingly, to a halt, and she looked round.

Martin Heriot was hurrying towards her with long strides.

"Oh dear, oh *dear*!" thought Millie. "Of course it *would* have to be him instead of the butcher's boy or postie, or the Wardlaw shepherd!"

As she stood waiting for him to come up, she wished she could sink into the ground and vanish. For she had seen that her difficult, finicky Amabel was attracted to him, and she wanted him to have a good impression of Amabel's mother. Up to date she had not done badly. She had been absolutely ordinary at Susan Gray's wedding, and had provided a good supper for him when he had appeared at Fernieknowe, though, to be sure, it would have been more to the point if Amabel had cooked the supper—but *this*! To be caught tramping along the road whistling like a schoolboy. ... Annoyance and embarrassment heightened the colour which brisk walking had brought to her cheeks, and made her look ten years younger than her age, though of this she was not aware. The flush, indeed, was merely an additional irritation. "Turning pink like a schoolgirl to match the whistling boy!" she said to herself. And then, in her mind's eye, she suddenly saw the pink-faced girl and the schoolboy with lips pursed to whistle, for Millie's thoughts very frequently took the form of tiny pictures, flashing on her brain as on a miniature cinema screen, and sometimes at very awkward moments. On this particular occasion it was rather a help, for it made her smile, and she was still smiling when Mr. Heriot, raising his tweed cap, said cheerfully:

"Good morning, Mrs. Maitland. What a pace you walk! I thought I should never catch you up."

"I didn't know I walked fast," Millie replied. "I suppose it's because I never have a great deal of time and I like to give the dogs as much exercise as possible."

"You're very conscientious about those dogs, aren't you?"

"Well, I'm paid for it, you see," Millie said simply.

"I feel sure you would take just as much trouble even if you weren't," he suggested.

"Oh, I expect I should. But then, of course, I'd never have a whole drove of the creatures," Millie explained. "I should just have one. It would be nice to have a dog who belonged to the house, instead of all the boarders. They are constantly changing, and if you get fond of them it is horrid when they go home."

"D'you mean to say you *haven't* got a dog of your own?" he exclaimed. He sounded amazed.

She shook her head. "No. It wouldn't be fair always filling his house up with other dogs. You see, a dog does expect all your affection and attention, he doesn't like it if you spread it out on others, especially when they aren't really part of the household."

"Do you believe that dogs have so much intelligence?" he asked rather doubtfully.

"Not *all* dogs, of course, but a great many are intelligent, and very sensible as well," Mrs. Maitland said with calm authority, as one knowing her subject. "There are thick-heads among them just as there are among humans—and that reminds me, I must call Snip and Snap in before they go off rabbiting." She whistled, and two reluctant fox terriers hesitated for a moment, thought better of their impulse to pretend they had not heard, and came tearing back, their little straight legs going like clockwork.

"You certainly have them in excellent control," said Martin Heriot. "They came at once when you whistled."

Millie's flush, which had subsided, rose again. "I—did you—did you happen to hear me whistling just now, when you first called to me, I mean?" she asked.

"Yes, I did," he told her, smiling. "I thought you whistled very prettily, it was so sweet and true, and not a bit shrill."

Millie was in no mood to be complimented on her doubtful accomplishment. "I hope you don't think I am in the habit of whistling when I'm out, except to the dogs," she said. "I really hardly ever do it, and I don't know what started me to-day, unless it's the spring."

"Why on earth shouldn't you whistle if you feel like it?" he said.

"It's very unladylike," said Millie primly; and spoilt the effect by adding anxiously, "Please don't tell anyone you heard me, Mr. Heriot!"

"Of course I won't," he promised. "If you'll ask me to supper again one night soon."

"Bribery?" murmured Millie.

"Or blackmail," he said cheerfully. "But I hope you will ask me. I enjoyed the other evening."

"So did we," Millie said. "And we'd love to have you again. We could play Canasta, or something," she finished vaguely.

"Would we have to? Are you very keen on Canasta?"

"Oh, no. It was just—I thought it would amuse you."

"I'd much rather sit and talk," he said.

"So would I, but I thought it might be dull for you," said Millie thankfully. "I really ought to go home now and see about lunch. Come along, dogs!"

"Half a minute," said Martin Heriot. "I didn't call at Fernieknowe and gallop after you along the road just to cadge an invitation to supper. It's about that dog."

"What dog?"

"A young black Labrador, name of Sam, that a cousin of mine wants to park somewhere for a bit," he explained. "I can't have him at Wardlaw during the lambing—no time to walk him—and I promised to ask you if you could board him. Could you?"

Millie became very business-like, or what she imagined to be business-like. "I'll have to look in my book," she began. "Would he be an ordinary boarder, or parlour?" Then, as she saw his bewildered look, she laughed. "I'm sorry. I mean, is it kennel or house?"

"Do you keep them in the house? A Labrador is pretty large for indoors," said Martin Heriot.

But Mrs. Maitland said she preferred a big dog because it was never so likely to get under her feet and trip her up, and if Sam was a house-dog he had better come as a parlour-boarder. "I could take him ten days from now, I'm almost sure, but I'll look in my book and ring you up," she concluded.

So it was arranged, after she had named terms which seemed to Martin extremely moderate, and they parted, he to climb the road to his hill farm, Mrs. Maitland to conduct her two charges home to Fernieknowe.

It was only when she had actually reached the house that she realized he had never so much as mentioned Amabel's name during quite a long conversation.

"Oh well, I daresay he is a little shy, these big men often are," she consoled herself. But as she set about giving the dogs their dinners it did strike her that he had not seemed in the least bit shy this morning. It is always easy to convince oneself of what one wishes to believe, so Mrs. Maitland determined that his ease of manner with her was because he looked on her as a friendly old thing.

Yet when Amabel returned from the village, announcing that she had managed to get a nice young rabbit but there was no off-the-ration cheese to be had this week, Mrs. Maitland found it curiously difficult to say with the right degree of casualness, "Oh, I saw Mr. Heriot while I was out with the dogs."

She could not imagine why she should feel so self-conscious about it, except for Amabel's sake, and hoped the words sounded more natural to her daughter than in her own ears. Presumably they did, for Amabel answered with a rueful laugh:

"You were luckier than I was, for I only met old Pearson, and he *would* tell me about his inside, or what is left of it. You know how deaf he is. I bawled myself hoarse at him, and then I don't believe he heard a word I'd been saying. Oh, and Mrs. Gray, of course. It's impossible to go to the village without seeing *her*. She was asking for you, by the way, in her usual reproving way.

I nearly told her I had left you chained up in the coal-cellar. It's what she always appears to expect!"

"Amabel *dear*!" murmured Mrs. Maitland from the stove—for they were in the kitchen, that being, as in so many other establishments of to-day, the most lived-in room of the house. "I'm sure you are exaggerating. It's just Davina's manner—"

"It's a manner I don't like, and belongs to a woman I can't stand," Amabel said cheerfully. "But then she can't stand *me*, so it's fair enough. Never mind, Mother, I know you and she like one another, so I won't say any more about her. What did you and Mr. Heriot talk about?"

"Oh, dogs, mostly, and whistling," Mrs. Maitland answered without thinking, and then, wishing she hadn't mentioned whistling, added hastily: "He wants to come to supper again soon."

Evidently the walk to Mennan and back had rid Amabel of her bad temper, for though she remarked that she wondered what in the world had made them talk about whistling, she did not probe into it in her usual rather inquisitorial fashion, but went on: "It's quite clear that he appreciates your cooking, Mother, and I don't blame him. When shall we ask him to come?"

"I should be sorry to think he only came because of my cooking," said Mrs. Maitland. "You had better suggest an evening, dear. It doesn't matter to me, but you may prefer a day when you haven't been at the office. You won't be so tired."

"I will be if I keep my word and do all the getting ready except the cooking."

"But you were going to do it to show me how little fuss there need be, so it shouldn't be tiring," exclaimed her mother, thinking: "Mercy me, are we back again to the same old argument?"

"I think Martin Heriot is the type who would appreciate having a fuss made of him—oh, in the nicest way, I mean," said Amabel. "He'd like to think people took the trouble to make a fuss just for him. I think he's a very modest sort of man and wouldn't just take it for granted."

"How clever of you, dear!" said her mother with genuine admiration. "I've never heard you sum up a person so well. You're perfectly right about Martin Heriot, I'm sure—and you want to leave all the preparations for having him to supper for me to do as usual?"

Mildly though she spoke and without a hint of an underlying meaning, Amabel flushed a little.

"I'll do it if you like. I didn't really mean to go back on my word," she began hastily. But Millie only laughed.

"No, of course not, dear. I'll do it. I—I rather like the fussing, as you call it. Will you ring him up and suggest an evening?"

"I think it would be better if you did it," said Amabel, and Millie, though once again surprised by her daughter's co-operative and gentle mood, agreed, because she wanted to tell Mr. Heriot when she would be able to take his cousin's dog Sam. And once more Amabel proved unexpectedly amiable, though as a rule she disliked any reference to her mother's unorthodox method of earning a living.

"Yes, that's a good idea," she said. "We don't want him to think we're running after him."

"As it was he who asked to be invited I hardly imagine there is any danger of his thinking that," Mrs. Maitland pointed out with the tiny hint of astringency in her tone which saved her from often being branded as "sweet". "And in any case, if he really *is* modest as you say he is, dear, it would be out of character, wouldn't it?"

Amabel only laughed and said she wished that some of the silly old hens who were always telling her what a sweet woman her mother was could hear her now, and the rest of the day passed in placid happiness.

Chapter 5

Mrs. Maitland went to bed that evening convinced that the prevailing amiability must be too good to last, and quite resigned to finding her daughter a thundercloud next day.

But Amabel continued to be more like her name than ever before, so Millie decided that it must be due to the prospect of seeing Martin Heriot in three days' time, took the goods the gods had provided, and rejoiced in the sunshine both outdoors where daffodils were gilding the grass, and the more heartening warmth of the atmosphere caused by good humour in the house.

It would have astonished Millie Maitland very much had she known the real reason of her daughter's lack of acerbity, which had little to do with Martin Heriot. The truth was that now she had given herself time to grow accustomed to it, Amabel found that she was almost enjoying having given up her cherished plan of trying to persuade her mother to sell Fernieknowe and join her in Edinburgh. No matter what Mr. Ramsay had said—and Amabel remembered his sudden unexpected outburst with quite disconcerting sharpness—it *was* a sacrifice to her, for she did not like living in the country, and found Mennan as dull as ditchwater. If Martin Heriot came to see them every day of the week she would still find Mennan dull; though not so deadly dull, she acknowledged, for he was interesting and intelligent on his own subjects. To do a kindness, or even, as in the present case, to refrain from an unkindness and keep it secret, was a source of queer pleasure to Amabel, and resulted in her feeling an extra benevolent fondness for her mother, who was never to know what was being given up for her.

Possibly Mr. Ramsay might have snorted derisively if he could have read Amabel's mind. Possibly he might have taken this as the first shoot grown from the seed of unselfishness, beginning to grow in rather unfavourable soil. Mr. Ramsay devoted more thought to the character of his client Miss Amabel Maitland than anyone was ever likely to guess. Under his rather disapproving manner there lay a constant hope that she might turn out in time to be a really fine person. He had never had the slightest doubt as to her brilliant intelligence; what he privately longed to see was a bigness of heart to match it. At times he felt that Millie, much as he liked and admired her, did not fully appreciate her daughter's possibilities. Certainly Millie was by far the more agreeable of the two, but she lacked the greatness which he felt sure was latent in Amabel, and however uncomfortable greatness may be to live with, it deserves recognition. Since he was positive it would be bad for Amabel to know what he thought of her, he preserved his slightly antagonistic attitude, though whether he was right or wrong is open to question. On the whole, then, he might have considered Amabel's feeling of sacrifice exaggerated, but he would have applauded her resolution not to worry her mother.

None of these cross-currents of thought stirred the quiet surface of life in Mennan. Millie Maitland looked after the dogs and the house, did Amabel's washing and ironing and mending, and made a dark moist gingerbread, heavy with treacle, to add a party look to the meagre ration of mousetrap cheese when Martin Heriot came to supper.

Amabel travelled up to Edinburgh twice and spent long busy days in her office, clearing work with swift efficiency.

Martin Heriot was in the thick of lambing, up at four or five each morning and out all day on the hill with his shepherd until he returned at nightfall almost too tired to keep awake until he had swallowed a meal.

And Mr. Ramsay wrote a letter from his office.

"Good gracious!" exclaimed Mrs. Maitland blankly, staring at the sheet of paper covered in fine crabbed writing which she held. "What on earth is the meaning of this?"

She was standing on the wide shallow step at the front door where postie, a few minutes earlier, had given her a handful of letters: two seedsmen's catalogues, a cheque from the elderly bulldog's owner (he had been restored to his family two days before), a charity appeal and the electricity bill, and this which she had opened first on recognizing the handwriting.

"Have you tried reading it?" Amabel asked, putting her head and shoulders out of the open window overhead. "It always helps."

"Naturally I've read it," said her mother with dignity.

Amabel laughed. "Sorry. I thought you were having the usual guessing competition with the unopened envelope," she said.

"I have opened my letter and I have read it, but I don't understand it," Mrs. Maitland said, raising her voice slightly, as if speaking to someone deaf.

"Why not? Is it in a foreign language?"

"Don't be silly, Amabel. Of course it isn't."

"It might have been, if you can't understand it. Who's it from?"

"Mr. Ramsay."

"Business? He usually makes himself only too clear," said Amabel. "Is it unpleasant?"

"No, no, it's not business. It's—he says may he come here to-morrow for the week-end," Mrs. Maitland explained. "I suppose he wants to, but it is all most confusing."

"He-wants-to-come-and-stay?" repeated her daughter in accents of stupefaction. "But he's never stayed for so much as a cup of tea before, has he?"

"Never," said Mrs. Maitland. "He always comes by one train and rushes away by the next. Do you think he's made some mistake?"

"If your name and address are on the envelope and he begins 'Dear Mrs. Maitland' I don't see how there can be a mistake."

"He begins '*My* dear Mrs. Maitland'," said Millie dubiously.

"That makes it all the more certain. May I read the letter?"

"Yes, of course."

Amabel's head disappeared and in a minute she came out to stand beside her mother, who was sniffing the mild air, sweet with the scents of earth and growing grass and a faint hint of blackthorn blossom.

"How heavenly everything smells on a morning like this!" said Mrs. Maitland, waving the letter dreamily to and fro.

Amabel had no time to spare for the beauty of the morning. She took the letter from her mother's hand and read it through quickly.

"Not a shadow of doubt, I should say," she announced cheerfully. "He is certainly inviting himself here for the week-end. Well, that's all right, I can bring him down with me to-morrow in good time for supper. I didn't mean to take the car, petrol costing what it does, but this being something of an occasion, I will. Are you going to ring Mr. Ramsay and tell him, or shall I? There isn't time to write."

"Oh, dear," Mrs. Maitland sighed. "Do wait just a moment, Amabel, and don't rush me so. I wish he'd written a day earlier. How can you go up to Edinburgh to-morrow?"

"What's to prevent me?" demanded Amabel in what her mother always thought of as her bristly voice, used when she imagined her own affairs or arrangements were being interfered with.

Hastily Mrs. Maitland said, "It's to-morrow that Martin Heriot is coming to supper. I thought you'd decided to stay at home because of that."

"Oh! Oh, yes." Amabel frowned, but in concentration rather than displeasure. "Well, I don't see that it matters," she added. "I did mean not to go to Edinburgh the day he was coming, but I really think I'll have to go to-morrow, after all. And if I take the car for once I can come home early in the afternoon. It would save Mr. Ramsay a tiresome train journey."

Millie wondered just how, if Amabel intended to leave Edinburgh early, she would prise Mr. Ramsay away from his office before his usual hour, but prudently resolved to say nothing about this, and leave Amabel to work it out.

"You'll be able to manage by yourself, Mother, won't you?"

"Oh, dear me, yes. I've always been able to manage," murmured Mrs. Maitland. "I hope I can find a decent pair of sheets to put on Mr. Ramsay's bed."

She spoke rather absent-mindedly, as if it were not of very great importance, but Amabel sounded quite horrified as she cried:

"Surely we *must* have enough respectable sheets for one extra bed, Mother!"

"I don't know really why you should suppose so," Millie said tranquilly. "I've never been able to keep up a good supply of linen, and during the war they required so many coupons, and now the prices are so fantastic that it's impossible to buy sheets and things. I won't put *holey* sheets on Mr. Ramsay's bed if that's what you're afraid of, though I doubt if he would notice."

"Of course he would notice!" Amabel cried in such a passionate voice that her mother stared at her in amazement.

"I thought you said that *I* made far too much fuss about guests," she observed after a short but awkward silence, during which Amabel fidgeted about, pulling the tiny leaves from a long woody stem which grew up the house beside the front door. "Do leave that honeysuckle alone, Amabel! You'll kill the poor thing."

"It will grow again," said Amabel, throwing away the unfortunate leaflets. "But about the sheets, Mother—"

"Oh, *blow* the sheets!" cried Millie. "I can't think what has happened to you! You've never paid the slightest attention to them before, so why are you bothering now? All I meant was that I must find a pair that hasn't been turned sides to middle, and without too obvious darns or patches, that's all!"

"Sorry, Mother," said Amabel more mildly, astonished in her turn by Millie's unwonted flare of temper. "It's only—you always talk about Mr. Ramsay as if he was a doddering old idiot, and he isn't!"

"Well, my dear child, if you feel like taking the sheets off your own bed and washing and ironing them," said Millie, "you are welcome. But if not—and it's a big job, let me tell you—I think you had better just leave things to me as usual."

The thought of Amabel struggling to wash anything larger or heavier than a pair of nylons restored her sense of humour, and she laughed. "I certainly didn't mean that I consider Mr. Ramsay a dotard. Why should I? He's only about ten years older than I am, after all."

"Eight," muttered Amabel, and then, mumbling something about having a lot to do, hastily retreated into the house.

"Upon my word," said Millie, addressing a cock blackbird which had stopped digging for worms among the grass to look at her with a beady inquisitive eye. "I really don't know what in the world possesses Amabel these days! My grandmother would have recommended a good dose of treacle and sulphur! She might be a changeling, she's so odd."

Odd or not, standing there wondering about Amabel was no help with a room to be prepared for Mr. Ramsay, the bed to be aired, sheets to be looked out and perhaps darned, and to-morrow's rather special supper to be planned.

"Bother Amabel and Mr. Ramsay too!" thought Millie crossly, and where Mr. Ramsay was concerned, ungratefully.

She was a quick worker, and it did not take her long to get the bedroom ready. Everything was shabby, but Mr. Ramsay would not expect anything else, and it was clean and fresh. Short white curtains blew in the soft breeze which entered at the open window, a white counterpane was covering the bed, and though the sheets were undeniably old and thin in places, they were linen, smelling faintly of lavender, and the only darn was in the under one, and came well up to the top where the pillows hid it.

"I hope he isn't a restless sleeper, or he will probably poke a hole in that top sheet," thought Mrs. Maitland. "Now for some flowers and it's ready."

Coming back into the room a little later with a handful of polyanthus in an old lustre mug, she was surprised to find that there was already a green earthenware jug full of daffodils on the chest of drawers. Water had been spilled from it on to the shining mahogany surface. This time Millie said "Bother Amabel!" aloud, as she fetched a duster and dried it. "Of course it has left a mark! Why is she interfering like this? I always thought she rather disliked Mr. Ramsay!"

Very much did she wish she had the courage to ask her daughter what she was playing at, but Millie hated a scene, and Amabel's forbidding expression warned her to keep quiet on the subject of daffodils. So she carried her little gay mug, smelling faintly of honey and sunshine, to her own bedroom, where she did not always have time to put flowers, and set it down beside the silver-framed photograph of her husband on the dressing-table.

After more than twenty years the gesture had lost its original significance; the empty space next to Maurice's photograph was the place where she was in the habit of putting flowers, just that and nothing more. This morning, however, perhaps because of Amabel's odd behaviour, Millie Maitland was thinking more than usual, so that as she set the little dish of polyanthus down carefully to avoid spilling—Millie always filled her flower vases to the very brim—she glanced at the photograph almost hidden behind the brilliant velvety colours.

It was the first time she had really looked at it with a seeing eye for years, and she realized with shocked surprise that she was looking at the face of a stranger. The features were familiar, of course, and the little close-clipped moustache, and the ready smile; but she no longer knew the man they represented, if indeed she had ever known him. Why did one keep the photograph of an unknown man on one's dressing-table and put flowers in front of it? Suddenly Millie found it slightly embarrassing that this face had smiled at her unnoticed while she brushed her hair, hastily creamed her face at bed-time (when she remembered to do it, which was not nearly often enough), or dabbed powder on her nose. . . .

"Ridiculous!" she said sternly. "Don't start being fanciful, my good woman. You've no time for that sort of nonsense!"

But she pushed the little dish of flowers so that it hid the photograph altogether before she left the room, and felt that after this display of idiocy she could not in fairness blame her daughter for acting so strangely out of character. There was something queer about the day, no doubt about it: it *must* be the spring!

Her mind continued to turn over this question of her husband's picture, and "Amabel," she said, while they were putting away the dishes after lunch, "you haven't got a good photograph of your father, have you?"

Amabel turned from the kitchen cupboard in astonishment, with the plates still in her hand. "No," she said. "The glass of mine got broken that time years ago when there was a bad storm and the wind blew everything off my table near the window. Remember? We never discovered it until the rain had soaked the photograph and ruined it. Why, Mother?"

"I thought perhaps you might like to have mine," Mrs. Maitland said. "You really ought to have one."

"What, the one on your dressing-table?"

Mrs. Maitland nodded.

"But—wouldn't you miss it, Mother?" asked Amabel, bewildered and rather hurt for the sake of the father whom she did not remember.

"Not desperately, now," said Mrs. Maitland honestly. "And I'd still see it every day when I dust your room."

"If you *want* me to have it, of course—"

"Yes, I do. I think it would be nice for you to have it," said her mother.

"Silver frame and all?" Amabel sounded incredulous, and Mrs. Maitland flushed a little, but stuck to her point.

"Silver frame and all. But you'll have to keep it properly polished," she said.

"Well—it's very sweet of you, Mother," said Amabel slowly.

"It isn't, my dear. I want you to have it," Mrs. Maitland repeated with perfect candour. "I won't miss it. I can't exactly explain why, but there does come a time when one stops missing things like that. It is different for you, because you have never really missed your father. I *can't* explain," she ended rather hopelessly.

When Amabel, still somewhat puzzled, had taken the photograph away to her room, Mrs. Maitland looked at the denuded dressing-table and decided that she liked it better. "If Maurice were alive he might be fat and bald by this time and he would hate to be constantly reminded of what a handsome young man he used to be—and he'd hate it even more for me to be reminded of it," she thought, for Maurice had always been a trifle vain of his good looks. "I should certainly have had to put it away in a drawer. Far better for Amabel to have it."

She made these explanations—or excuses—to quell the one or two very slight pangs of conscience which she felt. Possibly she would not have felt them at all if Amabel had not eyed her uneasily from time to time during the rest of what Millie called to herself "the strange day". It was no use blinking the fact that Maurice was no longer a part of her life, had not been part of it for many years.

The strangeness of the day, however, did not make any difference to the usual household tasks which had to be done, and by the time Mrs. Maitland crept to bed she was too tired even to look at the flowers standing on her dressing-table where the photograph of her husband had stood that morning.

Chapter 6

The next day began badly.

Mrs. Maitland, dashing about doing half a dozen things at once, forgot the milk which was heating for the breakfast coffee, so it promptly boiled over, making a mess of the stove and filling the kitchen with the horrible smell of burning.

Amabel, who had overslept and was in a bad temper and a tearing hurry in consequence, wrinkled her nose in disgust when she came in.

"Poof! What a frightful smell!" she said crossly.

"If you had been down in time to keep an eye on the milk for me while I set the table there wouldn't have been any smell," said Millie, almost equally crossly.

Then they both looked blankly at each other and finally laughed unwillingly.

"You never used to snap like this, Mother. It must be the effect of keeping all those dogs over a long period," said Amabel.

To which Millie responded with spirit that she didn't see why Amabel should enjoy a monopoly of snapping in their household, and they had better have breakfast at once as it was late and she had a great deal to do.

Breakfast was eaten in a Passover-like fashion, neither lady sitting down for more than a minute at a time. Mrs. Maitland had constantly to rush across to her shopping list which was on the kitchen dresser to add items to it which otherwise she was sure to forget. Amabel, between gulps of coffee and bolted mouthfuls of toast and marmalade, was putting on her shoes and hat and looking for her gloves, and presently, with a great whirring of the car's self-starter and slamming of its doors, removed herself to Edinburgh and her job.

Mrs. Maitland was left to get on with her own affairs. The dogs had already been fed and let out, but it was the day when their kennel was thoroughly cleaned and fresh straw put in their beds. That would have to wait until the beds in the house had been made and the rooms swept and dusted, and the breakfast dishes washed up.

"Lucky I did the flowers yesterday," thought Mrs. Maitland, busy with mop and a basin of very hot soapy water at the sink. "Oh, *damn!*"

A cup slipped out of her wet hands, poised itself for an instant on the edge of the draining-board, as if in doubt, and then, while

Mrs. Maitland made a wild clutch at it, slid with diabolical malicious slowness over the side to break into a score of pieces on the floor.

"And *that* means only two breakfast cups left! We'll have to use an odd one to-morrow," said Mrs. Maitland with the calm of despair. She swept up the bits, flung them into the dustbin outside the back door and prepared to tackle the housework.

This did not go very smoothly either, for the carpet-sweeper, an old and valued friend, which had always conducted itself in a most exemplary manner, suddenly jibbed and spat out a quantity of dust and fluff in the middle of the drawing-room. Mrs. Maitland, feeling that a mere "damn" was quite inadequate, compressed her lips tightly, fetched the dustpan and brush, and swept up the mess. As she rose to her feet, she caught sight of a singularly ugly little green and brown pottery jug on which was written in squiggly lettering: "NEVER SAY DIE. UP, MAN, AND TRY!"

It occupied a place on the drawing-room mantelpiece from purely sentimental reasons, having been given to Millie by a school-friend whom she had much admired in her early teens; but now its inspiring message seemed an insult to its enraged owner. She advanced upon it with a purposeful step and a menacing gleam in her eye.

"You horrid little object!" she said. "I'm going to put you in the darkest corner of the china cupboard where I won't be able to read your loathsome motto every time I come into this room!"

She never knew how it happened, for she had not meant to damage the thing, but the next moment there was another crash, and she was looking at fragments of green and brown earthenware, rather badly glazed, scattered about the fireplace.

"'Never say die!'" quoted Mrs. Maitland grimly, and added the remains of the jug to the contents of the dustpan. Then, because she firmly believed that things went in threes, particularly breakages, she took a jam-jar out with her to the dustbin and bashed it with a stone.

This seemed to break the spell, for the rest of the household chores were unaccompanied by any further incident, and she had time to make a chocolate *mousse* for supper before taking the fox terriers out.

"You'll have to come to the village for your walks to-day," she told them. "On *leads*."

Snip and Snap flattened their ears and looked dejected, but submitted to having leads attached to their collars, and holding both in one hand and her capacious shopping-basket in the other, Mrs. Maitland set off down the hill to Mennan.

On the open road they trotted demurely beside her, as good as gold, two well-bred, well-trained little dogs.

"*Sweet* little pets!" observed little Miss Kennedy sentimentally as they passed her.

But the very first cat they saw, sitting washing its face with insolent disregard on the sunny doorstep of a cottage on the outskirts of the village, transformed them into raging demons.

"I wonder if Miss Kennedy would think you so sweet now, you hell-hounds!" muttered Millie when she had succeeded in yanking her charges past their enemy, and stopped at a safe distance to disentangle their leads.

Snip and Snap, panting a little, looked up at her with bright defiant eyes. "More cats! Show us more cats and we'll show *you* something!" they seemed to be saying.

"Behave or I'll beat you both!" Mrs. Maitland said fiercely, shoving her felt hat straight with the hand that held the basket.

By some unlucky chance it appeared to be a cats' day in Mennan. Millie was sure that she had never met so many cats along the one and only street before, and at each one they sighted, no matter whether it was close at hand or sloping away round a house in the distance, the terriers' fury and excitement increased. Their passage was as noisy as a fire engine and attracted more attention. People turned to stare, people even hurried out of shops to see what the noise could be, and were a little disappointed to find it was only Mrs. Maitland.

"Good heavens, Millie, what possessed you to bring two such badly-behaved brutes to the village with you?" was Mrs. Gray's greeting, when she came face to face with her dishevelled and breathless friend outside Thomson & Liddle, Licensed Grocers by Royal Appointment to H.M. Queen Victoria.

Mrs. Maitland was fond of Davina Gray, but there were occasions when she longed to bite her and this was one of them.

"I brought them because I've shopping to do and I hadn't time to take them for a walk as well," she answered curtly. "It's the first time, and it will be the last."

"I should hope so," said Mrs. Gray. "Dreadful little beasts. I can't stand fox terriers!"

Millie Maitland felt that she couldn't stand them either, at the moment, but Mrs. Gray's sweeping statement roused her to defend the culprits.

"They can't help it," she said. "All terriers chase cats, especially fox terriers—"

"Don't know why on earth they're called *fox* terriers! Cat terriers would be nearer the mark, ha-ha!" laughed Mrs. Gray, delighted with her own wit. "Well, I must be getting on. Come and see me soon, Millie—and don't bring your cat terriers!"

She strode off along the High Street, leaving Millie looking resentfully at her broad, tweed-covered back. "As if I ever took any of the dogs with me when I go to see people!" she thought, and turned towards the grocer's.

A car, proceeding slowly, passed, stopped, and a voice shouted cheerfully. "Hi, Mrs. M.! Don't take 'em in there! Thomson & Liddle's old tabby has kittens, and she'll go for them as sure as fate!"

Mrs. Maitland turned, saw Jack Ross beaming at her, and smiled ruefully.

"Well, what am I to do, Jack? I *must* go in and I can't leave them outside. I need coffee and biscuits and soap powder—"

"Shove the little brutes into the car. I'll keep them for you and run you all home," he offered. "I'm going out that way—"

Never before had Mrs. Maitland so highly approved of Jack Ross's job with the Forestry Commission. She had always thought it a wholesome outdoor occupation, but now when it offered her this solution of her difficulties, it appeared to her to be the only job for an active young man worth consideration.

"Oh, Jack, you angel!" she exclaimed gratefully. "Are you sure?"

"Of course I'm sure! Here, come in, you terrors. Nice-looking little beasts, aren't they?"

"Handsome is as handsome does," said Mrs. Maitland darkly, thrusting them without ceremony into the back of Jack's shabby but serviceable Austin. "I won't be a minute, Jack—"

She was a little longer than that, but she was out of Thomson & Liddle's again within five minutes, breathless and triumphant.

"You've been very quick," said Jack, cuffing the fox terriers, who were trying madly to break the windows in their efforts to reach their keeper. "It must be a record for T. & L.'s!"

"I was terribly lucky," Millie explained, as she got in beside him and balanced the shopping-basket on her knee. "There was nobody in the shop that I knew."

"You have the queerest notions of luck, Mrs. M.," said Jack, driving off down the road in the direction of Fernieknowe. "Most people think they're lucky if they do see their friends—"

"You know quite well what I mean," said Mrs. Maitland with dignity. "If the shop had been full of people I know—as it usually is—I would have wasted a great deal of time asking how they were and how their children were, and—"

"Well, I think you might ask me how *my* child is," said Jack with a grin. "Never to mention my wife."

"How are they both?" asked Mrs. Maitland eagerly. "I really did mean to ask you the minute I saw you, but the dogs made me forget everything except wanting to kill them. Is Pat getting on all right? Who is the baby like?"

"Both doing well, thank you. The baby is the most hideous object I have ever seen in my life. Dark red all over, and squirming," said the proud father. "They're coming home this afternoon."

"Oh, Jack, how lovely! How pleased you must be—"

"H'm. It will be heaven having Pat home again, of course. I've missed her no end, though people have been very decent about asking me out to dinner and bridge and so on. Mrs. Noble has turned out to be much better value than she looks," said Jack. "But it's not the same as going out with Pat."

"Naturally it isn't," said Mrs. Maitland a little tartly, for she did not care to hear him utter even this temperate praise of Mrs. Noble. "Why did you say ' h'm' like that?"

"Well, I'm not so sure that it will be all joy having the son and heir in the house," Jack said doubtfully. "I hope he won't yell all night."

"He won't," Mrs. Maitland assured him. "Babies don't nowadays. They are very well regulated. Besides, you've got a nurse, haven't you?"

"Lord, yes, an absolute Gorgon of a woman," said Jack. "Only till the first month's up, thank goodness! I doubt if we could stand her for longer. I hope she won't frighten off Mrs. Miller, that's all. She likes everything just so—that's what she told me—and nothing must interfere with the baby's routine. Well, you know Mrs. Miller. She's a very good hand, works away in the house, and cooks quite decently. She has looked after me jolly well while Pat's been in the hospital, but she doesn't begin to know the meaning of routine."

"I'm sure it will be all right, Jack. Don't worry. Just think about having Pat home and leave the rest to sort itself out. Things do, you know," said Mrs. Maitland, vaguely but consolingly. "Oh, we're at the gate already. How short it seems in a car! Thank you so much for the lift. It's been the most enormous help."

She got out, let the dogs loose, and stood for a moment to wave as he drove away.

Then she trudged up the steep slope from her gate to the house, pausing to look at the first tightly-curled fronds that were rising from the brown tangle of last year's growth in the clumps of fern bordering the path, and wondering, not for the first time, if they had anything to do with the name of her house.

When she had shut the terriers into their loose-box and eaten a rather sketchy lunch of bread and cheese and coffee, Mrs. Maitland spent a busy hour or two preparing supper. As the meat ration this week happened to be steak, there was a reasonable quantity of it, and the butcher had added a small piece of kidney. A beefsteak and kidney pie, therefore, was to be the mainstay of the meal. Mrs. Maitland made very good pastry, and she was glad that she would be able to provide such a satisfying dish when there were two men to eat it. She had cooked the meat, made her pastry and set it away until the time to cover the pie, when she suddenly realized that it would be exceedingly agreeable to sit down for a short time and drink a cup of tea while she looked at the morning paper.

So she set a tray with her favourite cup, a little Crown Derby one standing in a very large saucer, the blue and gold beginning to vanish from its surface with age, brewed a pot of China tea, forgot her spectacles but found them almost at once on the kitchen mantelpiece, and sat down at the table in the window with the *Scotsman* propped up against the teapot.

Millie had taken the first luxurious sip or two of scalding tea, and had discovered no names she knew under "Deaths", when the telephone rang.

"Oh, bother the thing!" she said, rising in a hurry and rushing to the hall to answer it.

An agitated elderly female voice wailed at her as soon as she had said "Hullo".

"Oh, Mrs. Maitland, I'm in *such* a quandary! It's poor Pug. Could you take poor Pug just for a night or two? He really needs *very* little attention and hardly eats *anything*. Just a little rabbit—or some very fresh fish, steamed—in the middle of the day, and some nice milky pudding at night, and a weeny drinkie of milk at breakfast, and—"

"Just a minute, Miss Emerson, please. It is Miss Emerson speaking, isn't it?" said Millie firmly. "You want to leave your Pug with me for a few days, is that it? I can't have him in the house, I'm afraid."

"Oh, but the poor darling *always* sleeps with me, Mrs. Maitland, on my *bed*, you know. Of course he has his own blanket—"

"I'm sorry. If you like to leave him I promise he'll be looked after properly and fed right, but he will have to be in the kennels. He will be quite comfortable," said Millie, more firmly than ever. She had had some experience of Miss Emerson, and of poor Pug. Indeed, this was an annual performance. . . . "The usual terms. When do you want to leave him?"

"I thought perhaps you could *fetch* him this evening. He *does* so hate it when his mother has to go and leave him, the darling, and he eats so *little*, perhaps a tiny reduction in your fees?" Miss Emerson's wailing voice rose hopefully. "*Just* for five days, you know, or perhaps a little longer, while I go to see my sister at Hawick—"

"I'm sorry, Miss Emerson, but I can't reduce my fees, and I can't fetch Pug. I think you should leave him when you go to the station to-morrow!"

"Oh, dear, well—if you *can't*, of course! Let me see, it was five shillings a day, wasn't it?"

"Two guineas a week, or seven-and-six a day for shorter periods," Millie said. "Very well, I'll expect him to-morrow morning. You're going by the ten-twenty-two, I suppose?"

Knowing her client, she then added, "Pug will be quite all right. Good afternoon," and rang off.

"What a really very stupid old lady she is," she added aloud to the telephone. "Mean, too, but I'm certainly not letting her off with less than the usual fee. She can well afford to pay it, and considering what a pest poor Pug is, and that not a soul will have him but me, I really ought to charge her double for boarding him."

It was annoying to find, on returning to the kitchen, that her tea was quite cold.

Mrs. Maitland poured the now revolting brew into the sink-basket and washed up her cup and saucer and the teapot, realizing that her brief time of leisure was over without her having had it at all, and she might as well start on the cheese and onion soup which was to be the first course at supper.

It is well known that one interruption inevitably leads to another, so Mrs. Maitland was not surprised, though rather irritated, when she heard a ring at the front door, followed by the sound of footsteps in the hall.

"I'm in the kitchen!" she called, and in a moment Jack Ross burst upon her, looking distraught.

"Thank the Lord you're in, Mrs. M.!" he exclaimed. "I was afraid you might be out with the dogs—look here, could you possibly come along with me to Hillend? I'm in the most awful hole!"

Mrs. Maitland dropped the knife she was holding and seized his arm with an onion-scented hand. "Jack! Nothing has happened to Pat and the baby?" she cried, picturing every imaginable calamity from a hospital in flames to an accident with the car.

"No, no. It's not so bad as *that*," he said. "But Mrs. Miller has had to go off to the other side of the country to her old father, who's had a stroke or something—I say, I'm sorry if I gave you a fright—"

"And well you may be," Mrs. Maitland answered indignantly.

"But don't you understand?" Jack said. "Pat and the baby and that awful nurse are arriving at six, and there's nothing ready for them, and it's five now!"

Mrs. Maitland, having recovered from her fright, was quick to appreciate the difficulties of the situation.

"Oh, dear! It *is* awkward," she said. "Well, I suppose you want me to come with you now, Jack, do you?"

"If you could, Mrs. M.—"

"Well, I couldn't really," said Mrs. Maitland candidly. "But I will. Just let me wash my hands and put on a coat—and you can be writing a note for Amabel to tell her what's happened."

"God bless you, Mrs. M.!" said Jack rapturously, and imprinted a kiss on her cheek. "What an angel you are!"

"Nothing of the kind. I'm a fool who can't say no, that's all. Here I am with two men coming to supper and one of them staying the week-end, and I go rushing off leaving everything half done," Mrs. Maitland said crossly. "For goodness' sake write that note to Amabel, Jack, and let me go and get ready."

"Can't Amabel manage?" asked Jack hopefully, looking up from the message he was scribbling on a leaf torn out of his pocket diary.

"She'll have to, that's all, but she won't like it. Oh, Jack, if we could just spare a minute I'll cover the pie and then she'll only have to put it in the oven," exclaimed Mrs. Maitland.

With incredible speed she rolled out the pastry, clapped it on top of the pie and added a pastry rose and four triangular leaves. "There! I feel better now that's done," she said. "I'll get my coat—"

The crowded hours that followed left her no time to wonder how things were going at Fernieknowe. Mrs. Miller had swept and dusted Hillend Cottage, the Rosses' little house, and fires were burning in sitting-room and bedroom; but she was quite obviously one of those who leave all their cooking to the last possible moment, and there were no signs of preparation for a meal. Mrs. Maitland's first act was to put two kettles on the gas cooker, and to order Jack to fill hot-water bottles for Pat's bed.

"And the nurse's too," she added breathlessly, as she whirled between larder and kitchen opening tins, beating up eggs for a *soufflé*, searching for cheese to grate.

She was very tired indeed when, assured that Mrs. Miller had promised to send her neighbour in the next morning to give them a hand, she finally left, driven by the grateful Jack, for her own house. But Pat was tucked up warmly in her own bed, the baby asleep in his cot beside it, and the nurse, well-fed and pleased with the electric fire which had been turned on in her room, was disposed to be gracious and turn off the unfortunate absence of Mrs. Miller with a laugh.

Mrs. Maitland, as she crept in at her own front door, felt that it had been worth the effort, if only Amabel was not annoyed at having been left to cope with everything.

The house was very quiet: everyone seemed to have gone to bed, and Mrs. Maitland suddenly realized that it was long past her own bedtime, half-past eleven by the brass-faced grandfather clock ticking loudly and slowly beside the sitting-room door. To stave off the evil moment when she must go upstairs and begin the exhausting process of getting ready for bed, she went to see if the kitchen boiler had been stoked properly for the night, and to her great astonishment found her daughter quietly washing up.

"It was going to spoil the evening if I did it when we finished supper, so I left it until now," Amabel explained, in answer to Mrs. Maitland's exclamation. "No, Mother, you are not to dry a single dish. You've done plenty this evening, and you look like a ghost. Sit down for a bit until I've finished, and then we can fill the bottles and go to bed."

"Did everything go off all right?" asked Millie, sitting down as she had been told. "I was truly sorry to leave you in the lurch, but what else could I do?"

Amabel nodded. "I quite understood, and so did Martin Heriot and Mr. Ramsay. I think things were as they should be. I brought some *foie-gras* from Edinburgh, so we started with that and hot toast and butter—it was margarine really, but they didn't seem to notice—and I cheated rather with the potatoes, because I didn't leave myself enough time to do them, so we had crisps instead."

"That was very sensible," murmured Millie drowsily. "I hope the pie was good."

"We—ell—the pastry wasn't up to your usual standard," said Amabel.

"Wasn't it? I'm sorry. It should have been just the same as it always is," said her mother. "Perhaps you didn't have the oven hot enough—" She broke off, because Amabel was staring at her, dish-cloth in hand.

"Oven?" she said faintly. "*Oven?* But I didn't put it in the oven—"

For a moment the two gazed at one another in wild surmise. Then Millie broke into the half-hysterical laughter of extreme fatigue.

"You gave them raw pastry? Oh, Amabel, *dear!*" she cried. "Didn't you see it wasn't cooked? I hope they won't be ill! Oh, dear, how—how awfully funny!"

Amabel's face assumed its least pleasant expression. "Well, how was I to know?" she began, but as Mrs. Maitland continued to shriek with helpless laughter, she became alarmed.

"Stop, Mother, do stop!" she said. "You'll wake Mr. Ramsay—or if he isn't asleep you'll frighten him. Wait, I'll get you a drop of brandy from the medicine chest! You're tired out, that's what's wrong with you. Slaving for those miserable Rosses—"

The mere mention of the precious brandy, hoarded against a much greater emergency than this, brought Millie to her senses. She blew her nose hard, dried the tears that had escaped from her eyes, and announced that she had better go to bed.

"I'll fill your bottle," said the greatly relieved Amabel. "If you go on up. And—and—Mother—you won't *tell* them about the pastry, will you?"

"No, I won't, of course not," her mother promised.

But once in bed, cuddling her comfortable hot-water bottle to her, she laughed again.

"Raw pastry!" she thought. "I do wonder what on earth those wretched men thought they were eating. Poor dear Amabel!"

Chapter 7

As if to make amends for all the trials of the day before, Saturday morning began smoothly. Mr. Ramsay appeared punctually at breakfast brisk and refreshed; obviously he had taken no harm from his odd meal, for he commented on his night of unusually sound sleep. The discovery of a large basket in the larder, left by Martin Heriot and containing a handsome chicken, a dozen eggs and a piece of real farm butter, rejoiced Mrs. Maitland's heart, for it solved the meals problem. Amabel was in a very good temper, and even the prospect of Miss Emerson's revolting Pug's arrival seemed amusing rather than annoying.

Sunlight streamed into the shabby, friendly rooms, showing up all their deficiencies, it is true, but also showing how faithfully the old furniture had been polished, so that it reflected the sun in its faint mellow sheen. With the warmth of a bright fire bringing out the scent of the bowl of violets from Mrs. Maitland's carefully cherished bed below the south wall of the house, the drawing-room was a very pleasant place, and Mr. Ramsay, to his hostess's unexpressed but great relief, seemed willing to sit there with the *Scotsman* after breakfast.

Mr. Ramsay, who had finer perceptions than most of his acquaintances gave him credit for, felt the gracious welcome which the room offered; but all he said, in a tone of approval, was:

"A good fire, Mrs. Maitland, is very cheerful, and your *Scotsman* arrives wonderfully early for a country place."

"It's an extravagance really," she confessed. "I have it sent by post, and it comes with the morning delivery."

He smiled. "Well, it's the first extravagance I've ever known you to indulge in, and a very mild one," he said. "I'll just look through it now, if you're sure you don't want it yourself."

Mrs. Maitland shook her head, wondering how he imagined she had time to sit down in the morning and read the paper.

"Amabel, then? Would she not like it?"

But Amabel had gone out, saying that she would do any shopping that was needed and bring it back with her shortly before lunch. She was going to walk up to Wardlaw, it appeared, meet Martin Heriot, and see his lambs. That she had made this arrangement mainly to give her mother and Mr. Ramsay a chance of talking to each other uninterrupted was quite unsuspected by either of them.

"Dear me," said Mr. Ramsay in some surprise when Millie told him where Amabel had gone. "I didn't know that Amabel took any interest in that kind of thing."

Millie hesitated for an instant, then she answered, "She doesn't as a rule, but she is interested in Martin Heriot himself, I think. It is the first time in her life that she has ever bothered about any man to my knowledge—"

"Dear me!" murmured Mr. Ramsay again.

"I think it's splendid!" cried Millie rather defiantly for some reason, perhaps his tone. "I'm delighted, and I shall encourage it as much as I can!"

"Of course, of course," said Mr. Ramsay, suddenly sounding as if his thoughts were far away. "I suppose Mr. Heriot is fairly well-off. It sounds very suitable. But—I didn't think he was exactly Amabel's type, if you will forgive my saying so."

"I doubt if that enters into it, Mr. Ramsay," said Millie. "I mean, when one begins to think about a particular person it really doesn't make any difference whether he happens to be one's type or not."

"I daresay you are right. Indeed, judging from the number of unsuitable marriages that take place every year, I am sure you are," Mr. Ramsay said in his driest voice.

He opened the *Scotsman* and rattled its pages so sharply that Mrs. Maitland, as she left him to peruse it in peace, began to wonder whether the raw pastry had had an ill effect on him, after all. . . .

Amabel had made the beds and tidied the rooms upstairs before going out, so there was not too much to do, which was just as well, because Miss Emerson, in her anxiety over Pug's welfare, arrived much earlier than she needed to. Millie's only consolation, after an exceedingly tiresome interview, in the course of which Pug's delicate digestion, sweet, sensitive nature and need of every possible care, were dwelt on at length, was that Miss Emerson would still have to wait at least twenty-five minutes at the station before her train was due.

Pug showed no signs of mourning the departure of his foolish mistress, to whom he bore a resemblance so striking as to be almost uncanny.

"Or else it's the other way about. I'm never quite sure," Millie Maitland said thoughtfully, looking down at the squat obese figure of her newest boarder.

Mr. Ramsay, who had peered cautiously round the edge of the drawing-room door on hearing Miss Emerson's taxi trundle away, shuddered as his eyes fell on Pug.

"Good heavens!" he exclaimed. "Do you have to look after this brute?"

"Oh, he's not too bad," Millie said tolerantly. "In fact, he would be quite a decent little dog if he hadn't been ruined; that is, if you care for pugs."

"But do you?"

"Care for pugs? Not awfully," Mrs. Maitland admitted. "I get so tired of hearing them snore."

"No, no, I don't mean that!" said Mr. Ramsay testily. "I mean, must you take any dog, whether you like it or not?"

"As long as they aren't vicious and haven't got eczema or anything, I can't very well refuse," said Mrs. Maitland. "It wouldn't be good for business if I did."

She spoke quite seriously, and Mr. Ramsay stared at her, his reading glasses pushed up among his thick grey hair.

"Do you know, this is the very first time I have ever really considered your looking after other people's dogs as a business venture?" he remarked. "And that is very short-sighted of me, because of course it *is* a business, and quite a prosperous one."

"It's a very tiresome business sometimes, like when you have to walk them in bad weather," said Millie practically. "But it's quite natural that you shouldn't think of it as a real job, because I'm not the kind of person you could imagine making a success of any kind of business. It astonishes me when I stop to think about it—and I'm quite sure Amabel believes it is just a rather irritating hobby. But it does pay, Mr. Ramsay. It's about the only thing I can do at home that pays me."

"Sup'pose Amabel were to marry, not necessarily this farmer, but anyone, would you be able to manage without her help?"

"Without her help?" echoed Millie in surprise. "Oh, I see what you mean! Her share of the household expenses. Well, of course, I should have to live even more quietly, but I think I could still manage. I've always used the income from my own money for the big things like taxes and rates and absolutely essential repairs to the house, and the dogs do the rest."

Mr. Ramsay put out a foot and stirred Pug, now snoring on the rug between them, with a dissatisfied air. "You have never made enough use of Amabel's money," he said. "As you know, I have always considered that morally you have a right to it."

"I know," said Millie. "And I've never agreed with you. Maurice's aunt was perfectly entitled to leave her money as she liked, and I was only too thankful that she did leave it to Amabel. Do you make these rather unprofessional remarks about moral rights to many of your clients?"

He smiled rather sourly. "No," he admitted. "But very few of my clients care so little about money as you do."

"There is no point in caring for what you can't have," Mrs. Maitland said lightly. "I cared enough when I thought there wasn't going to be any to bring Amabel up on. Now that she's all right, and I can make a little to keep me from worrying I don't bother about it. Would you like to come out with the dogs and me?" she ended, smiling to soften the abruptness with which she had changed the subject.

Mr. Ramsay looked at Pug. "It won't be much of a walk—" he began.

"Oh, we're not taking *him*. Good heavens, it would kill him! No, I'll put him in his bed and let the fox terriers out. You'll find walking with them quite strenuous," Millie said.

Though hastening along the narrow road which followed the lower slopes of a long hillside in the wake of the terriers did not allow much time for admiring the lovely view of blue distances down the valley, Mr. Ramsay enjoyed his brisk exercise. On their return to Fernieknowe he told his hostess that he felt all the better for it. He repeated this remark to Amabel, who had just come in, with the addition that he really would have to try to walk to his office every day, as he had felt quite livery on getting up, and now was like a different man.

"I thought that walking with those fiends of terriers would help him to shake off any possible effects of the pastry," said Mrs. Maitland solemnly, but with twinkling eyes, when she and her daughter met in the kitchen a few minutes later. "How did Mr. Heriot seem, by the way?"

For a moment Amabel looked as if she might be going to sulk, then she suddenly burst out laughing.

"He hadn't turned a hair. I should think he's pretty tough," she said. "But I told him, Mother."

"You told him? About the pastry not being cooked? Oh, Amabel! What did he say?"

"It seemed so unfair that he should think your pastry could be so horrible," Amabel explained. "I had to tell him. He laughed—" she broke off.

Mrs. Maitland said, "Well, I can't say that I blame him—"

"Oh, no, of course not. It was idiotic of me, and he was really very nice about it."

But Amabel seemed disinclined to say more. "I'll set the table," she offered.

Like all well-trained mothers, Millie knew when to stop trying to talk to her daughter. "Do, dear, it will be such a help," she murmured.

As she set about preparing the light lunch which she thought suitable for an elderly man who had eaten raw pastry the night before, Mrs. Maitland indulged in the rather sentimental hope that Amabel was thinking about Martin Heriot.

"Bless her, she's at the stage when she doesn't want to talk about him in case she gives herself away," she thought.

Amabel was thinking about Martin Heriot, it is true, but her thoughts were resentful rather than tender. It was not that she minded his laughing about her mistake over the pastry; that was fair enough; it had been imbecile of her, and she had had to laugh herself. No, what had annoyed her had been his careless remark: "Poor old Ramsay! I don't suppose *he's* been feeling any too comfortable. I mean, raw pastry at his age—"

Always this assumption that Mr. Ramsay was practically on the brink of his grave, Amabel thought angrily, and the remembrance of Martin's innocent astonishment when she had retorted, "He's only a few years older than you, after all!" made her set a plate down so sharply that her mother murmured, "For heaven's sake don't *break* one of those plates, we've only got five left!"

"Mother!" she exclaimed. "Do *you* really think Mr. Ramsay is so terribly old?"

Amabel had often been impatient with her mother's habit of giving any question careful consideration before answering it, but now it seemed somehow right and oddly comforting, when Mrs. Maitland turned from the stove where she was stirring soup and stood for a moment with knitted brows, a large wooden spoon in her hand.

"No," she said at last. "It's queer that you should ask me that, Amabel, because I've suddenly realized that Mr. Ramsay isn't old at all. When I was a young woman he seemed like Methuselah to me, and then for years he was just Mr. Ramsay, but now, seeing him here off the lead, as it were, I suppose I've looked at him differently. As a matter of fact," she continued, absently stirring the soup again, "it was you who reminded me that he isn't so much older than I am. You flew out about him the other day, for some reason, and it made me think. It must be his dry legal manner that makes him seem older than he is."

Amabel nodded. "That's what it is," she said.

"Poor man, his ears should be burning!" Millie said. "If you've finished with the table, dear, I wish you would go and talk to him—and put a log on the drawing-room fire!" she added, as her daughter disappeared.

The week-end went quietly on. Mrs. Maitland was pleased to find how ready Amabel was to take the entertaining of Mr. Ramsay into her own hands. It saved her mother a great deal of time, and meant that she could concentrate on producing appetizing meals without having to neglect the dogs.

Mr. Ramsay was an unexpectedly easy guest. Wearing old-fashioned but incredibly neat and well-cut knickerbockers, he pottered about the garden casting ignorant and benevolent glances on saxifrages, primulas and grape hyacinths, or went for walks with Amabel. He commented on his good food with a discrimination delightful to his hostess's pride as a cook, he left his bedroom tidy, and did not create the usual male havoc in the bathroom; best of all, he was enjoying himself and said so.

Only one thing vexed Mrs. Maitland, and for it she could not blame Mr. Ramsay. It was hardly his fault that Martin Heriot should have chosen to call at Fernieknowe while Amabel was out walking, even though she was walking with Mr. Ramsay.

Millie felt more irritated than ever at the calmness with which Martin received the news that he had missed Amabel.

"Too bad," he said; that and no more. "But I really came to see you, Mrs. Maitland, you know. For one thing I never thanked you—"

"Thanked me for what?"

"My supper on Friday," he said, and his eyes met hers with just a suspicion of a twinkle.

"I think the less said about that the better," Mrs. Maitland answered repressively.

"All right. But I was sorry you weren't there," he said. "And I want to know when you can take Sam."

"Sam?"

"The black Labrador. I spoke to you about him."

"Oh, yes. He belongs to a cousin, didn't you say?" asked Mrs. Maitland.

For some reason he appeared a trifle disconcerted. "Oh—er—yes. Yes. He does. Could you manage him fairly soon, do you think?" he asked.

"Well—" began Mrs. Maitland doubtfully. "I could have, but I have the terriers until Wednesday, and now I'm saddled at short notice with old Miss Emerson's horrible pug for as long as she and her sister stay at their pet hydropathic without quarrelling with the management—"

"I shouldn't think that will be much more than a few days," he suggested, grinning broadly.

"Ten days is the record so far," Mrs. Maitland said. "Well, suppose you tell your cousin to send Sam on Thursday. How will he be coming? By train?"

"Oh, I'll bring him over myself," said Martin Heriot.

Mrs. Maitland looked at him in surprise. "Have you got him at Wardlaw, then? I thought you said—"

"Oh, yes. He's there all right," said Martin Heriot vaguely. "Tell Amabel I'm sorry I didn't see her, will you, Mrs. Maitland?"

"Why don't you come in and wait? She won't be long," said Millie, instantly diverted.

But Mr. Heriot was very sorry, he would have to be going on. "I'm dining with Mrs. Noble," he explained. "To play bridge. She's very keen, you know. I just hope they won't make too late a night of it, because I have to be up early just now with the lambing."

As he walked quickly away down the hill, Mrs. Maitland looked after him, and wished it had been anyone but Mrs. Noble he had been going to see.

Chapter 8

Spring comes slowly in Scotland, even in the south, suffering many set-backs of untimely frosts or snowfall, but when at last it has really arrived each lengthening day brings its own fresh delight of greening trees and newly-blooming flowers, and summer seems almost hand in hand with it. The daffodils wither, the pheasant's eye narcissi take their place, and, before they are over, the first lupins are in bud.

Mrs. Maitland, who was blessed with a peculiarly perceptive appreciation of places and seasons, rather forgot to think of her daughter's problematical interest in Martin Heriot as she walked out with the dogs or worked in her garden. When she did remember, with a slight feeling of guilt, she excused her forgetfulness on the grounds that it was useless to bother, since Amabel was hardly ever at home just now.

The organization for which she worked had arranged a drive to raise funds on an extensive scale, and Miss Maitland, their efficient secretary, divided her time between the office in Edinburgh and dashing about the country stimulating various branches to greater efforts.

This furious activity suited Amabel and brought all her organizing ability and her talent for administration into full play. Her short scribbled notes to her mother—not infrequently accompanied by parcels of washing or stockings to be darned—said that she was frantically busy and enjoying every minute of it all.

For her part, Millie was finding life alone extremely peaceful and pleasant. She did not mind solitude, indeed, she required a certain measure of it, and much as she loved Amabel, she did not miss her at all badly. This was what life would be like if Amabel were married: dull, perhaps, but arranged to suit her own wishes; and after all, one could never really be dull in the country, with a garden and dogs to attend to. Even the weather was of prime importance, not simply because, as in towns, it was a question of umbrella or no umbrella when one went out, but as it related to spring sowing, to turnip thinning, to the hens' laying and the young lambs: to the very groundwork of existence, in fact.

Where Mrs. Maitland herself was concerned, the garden and the dogs—or at least, one dog—were closely intertwined. Sam was in residence as a parlour-boarder and had proved himself to be an enthusiastic amateur gardener, constantly digging where she least wanted him to dig, pruning with a set of powerful teeth all the tender young twigs of low-growing shrubs, trampling rock plants underfoot on his tours of inspection. Nothing could convince him that his help was not wanted. Persuasion, admonishment, had no effect.

"He'll grow out of it," Pat Ross said consolingly on a fine June afternoon when she had wheeled her baby in its smart new perambulator over to Fernieknowe to have tea with Mrs. Maitland, and that lady was telling her woes. "Bless him, he's just like a child!"

"Nonsense, Pat!" said Mrs. Maitland. "He isn't in the least like a child, if you mean a human child. Mercifully for their parents the human young can't run fast. If they had anything like a puppy's turn of speed very few people would be parents. As for growing out of it, by the time he has there will be nothing growing *in* the garden!"

Pat looked at her with a twinkle. She knew Mrs. Maitland well. "Shut him up in the kennel, then," she suggested, and, as she expected, Mrs. Maitland flushed faintly and looked uneasy.

"Oh—well—it seems a shame to do that in this lovely weather," she said weakly, and Pat laughed outright, and even the baby produced a toothless grin.

"Oh, look, the *pet*. He's smiling!" cried Mrs. Maitland, and Sam's misdemeanours were forgotten while they hung entranced over the occupant of the pram.

"By the way, who landed you with the demon-dog?" asked Pat, when, after a pleasant tea and a chat about babies in general and one baby—her son—in particular, she prepared to go home.

"A cousin of Mr. Heriot's," Millie told her. It was quite true and she had no intention of concealing the part played by Martin Heriot in the transaction, but young Mrs. Ross went away with the idea that the unknown cousin had applied direct to Mrs. Maitland about Sam.

Mrs. Maitland, watching her slight figure as she went away down the hill, conversing in tones of besotted adoration with the comatose infant whom she was pushing, suddenly wondered how long Martin Heriot's cousin meant to leave Sam at Fernieknowe. The dog had been there now for almost two months, and that was a long time. Nor did his owner show any signs of wanting him back, or even write to ask for news of him.

It was true that Mr. Heriot showed a great deal of interest in his cousin's dog, paying frequent visits to see him, but Mrs. Maitland, who had been told so many times by Amabel that most of her impulses were foolish, had learned through this to look with kindly tolerance on other people's impulses. If Mr. Heriot liked to look in at Fernieknowe two or even three times a week to pat Sam rather absent-mindedly and then talk to her, there seemed to Mrs. Maitland no reason why he should not. Supposing Amabel to be the rose, then she herself was not only near the rose herself, but the rose's mother. It was natural that he should want to see her and he never failed to ask how Amabel was and to show an interest in the accounts of her activities which Mrs. Maitland gave him.

He dropped in an hour or so after Pat had gone, patted Sam as usual, and admired the garden. Apparently he had either not noticed the large excavations in various flowerbeds, or thought them intentional, for he did not mention them.

What he did say, quite unexpectedly, was: "Mrs. Noble seems very keen on her garden."

"Does she? I shouldn't have thought she knew anything about gardening," said Millie with genuine astonishment.

"Well, no, she doesn't, but I'm sure she would like to. I wish—" he said rather awkwardly, and paused.

Something inside Mrs. Maitland's brain uttered a small note of warning; but she only looked at him enquiringly and said nothing.

"You know, Mrs. Maitland, I believe she's lonely," he burst out.

"But everybody called on her when she came here, and I'm sure she must have been asked to people's houses," said Millie. "You can't say that Mennan isn't a kindly, friendly place, Mr. Heriot."

"She doesn't seem to get on with the people she has met. They—they aren't congenial, she says. Now, if *you* would ask her, Mrs. Maitland, and show her your garden, I'm sure she'd get on with you. And you would like her when you knew her," he said with true masculine stupidity.

If there is one thing calculated to set a woman against another, it is that remark, thought Mrs. Maitland, especially when made by a man!

But she kept it to herself. Aloud she said: "My dear good man, I am the last person to amuse or interest Mrs. Noble. I hardly ever go out, or ask people here. I haven't either the time or the means for purely social activities, as everyone knows. The dogs are a full-time job, and as for *my* gardening, it would kill a decorative little creature like Mrs. Noble if she tried to do it! I'm not one of those gentle potterers picking dead heads off pansies, you know. I dig and grub like—like fury, because I have to, or it wouldn't be done at all. Vegetables are what I work at most, anyhow—"

He looked obstinate and unconvinced. "It seems a shame," he muttered. "She's a sociable sort of person—"

"And I'm not, quite definitely," said Millie. "Doesn't she know Davina Gray? Of course she must. Davina is fond of bridge and plays well, as I am sure you know yourself."

"Davina didn't take to her somehow. Of course she's not a bit Davina's style, is she?"

"And do you seriously think she is *mine*?" Mrs. Maitland could not help laughing. "Why, there's nothing about my style or my lack of style, rather, that could suit Mrs.—"

"You're different," he said, and now he spoke with assured conviction. "Nobody could help getting on with you."

"That makes me sound a complete nonentity."

"I didn't mean it that way. You know I didn't," he said.

"Well, it's very nice of you. I'll ask Mrs. Noble to tea one day," said Mrs. Maitland, seeing that she would have to do something or speak her mind plainly and unkindly. "I'll have one or two other women, and I'll try to get Amabel to spare a day and be at home. She's nearer Mrs. Noble's age than I am."

"Oh, she doesn't I—I mean, I don't think she and Amabel would care for one another," he said very hastily, and Millie wanted to slap him, so fatuous did he seem, so obviously did he consider Mrs. Noble's likes and dislikes of paramount importance. And she had been thinking with pleased satisfaction that he was interested in Amabel!

Something of what was in her mind must have shown in her face, for he added, "Now I've annoyed you—"

"You must admit that Mrs. Noble seems to be a little difficult," Millie said rather tartly. "Well, to please you, I won't make a point of asking her especially when Amabel's at home, but if she does happen to be here the day Mrs. Noble is coming, they will have to take their chance of getting on with each other. I really can't promise more than that."

Then, because she was afraid he was about to burst into renewed thanks and asseverations that she would like Mrs. Noble (who at the moment she felt she disliked more heartily than ever before), Millie cut him short by announcing that it was time she made the dogs' supper, and he went away.

"Really, what awful fools men are!" observed Mrs. Maitland aloud as she mixed dog-food and divided it among the various bowls. "I suppose Martin Heriot has really fallen for that dreadful little Noble woman—my poor Amabel! She hasn't a chance against her, but there's nothing at all I can do about it!" And a tear or two of annoyance because of her helplessness fell among the brown bread and gravy, giving an unusual salty flavour to the kennel supper that evening.

Having given her word, Millie knew that she must try to live up to Martin Heriot's estimation of her. In fact, little as she wanted to, she would have to invite Mrs. Noble to tea.

"He seems to take me for a sort of middle-aged Kim!" she thought bitterly to herself as she wrote a short note to "the Noble woman". "Friend of all the world—ugh!"

After some consideration Millie decided to ask Mrs. Gray at the same time. She played bridge, and if Mrs. Noble had any sense she would try to make friends with Davina, who knew everyone and went everywhere within twenty miles of Mennan. To leaven the lump she rang up Pat Ross and implored her to come as well, and bring the baby, who would provide a topic of conversation if needed. Babies always do, thought Millie hopefully.

All three ladies accepted; Millie baked scones and a fruitcake and cut small neat sandwiches with savoury fillings, put on her only good dress, the black one she had worn at Susan Gray's wedding, and sat down in her drawing-room to wait for the party to arrive.

She had no hope that it would be a pleasant party, but it far surpassed any misgivings she had felt. To begin with, Mrs. Noble was late: not with the five-minute lateness which is permissible for a tea invitation, but really, unforgivably late. Davina, of course, had appeared just as the grandfather clock had struck its fourth rather hoarse note, and Pat with her son in a new blue coat had arrived almost immediately after.

For quarter of an hour the time passed easily in admiration of the baby, enquiries made and answered about Amabel, Susan and Mrs. Gray's other daughters, all well and happily married, some expecting an addition to their families. But then Davina Gray began to fidget and look at her watch. Soon she would ask her hostess point-blank, "Are you waiting for anyone?" and Millie, who had intended to spring Mrs. Noble upon them without warning, would be forced to say that she *was* expecting another guest, and would have to reveal the guest's identity.

Rather than do this, she said, "I think we'll just have tea now," and by hurrying away to the kitchen to make it, was able to avoid the question hovering on the tip of Davina Gray's tongue.

They were at their second cups, the fruit-cake had been cut, tasted, and warmly approved, and Millie was beginning to hope in a very cowardly way that Mrs. Noble was not coming at all, when the station taxi (Jno. Corsar, Funerals a Specialty) drove up to the door—Corsar, who always stopped at the gate of Fernieknowe and refused to face the hill with his elderly Daimler!

With a sinking heart Mrs. Maitland went to greet her guest, and brought her into the drawing-room, wishing that she had never invited her. She knew only too well that Mrs. Noble's appearance would be enough to antagonize Davina, that woman of strong and often unreasonable likes and dislikes.

Certainly the new arrival was a rather incongruous figure in that shabby country house. She wore a suit of fine white tweed and a small white hat set at a dashing angle on her butter-yellow head, which was exactly matched by a yellow high-necked jersey. Pearls, a diamond clip in her lapel, the sheerest of nylons on her elegant legs, white doeskin gloves and a waft of expensive Parisian scent completed a picture which might have stepped straight from the pages of *Vogue* or *Harper's*.

It was quite extraordinary, thought Millie as she poured out a cup of tea, now rather strong, for Mrs. Noble, how the two words "tweed" and "suit" could be used to describe garments so different in every respect as Mrs. Noble's creation and Davina Gray's solid serviceable brown Harris! As for Pat, who had removed her camel-hair overcoat and was sitting quietly at ease in a tartan skirt and white shirt, she just wasn't in the picture at all. Not that Pat would worry, thought Mrs. Maitland, giving her an affectionate glance.

"Do you like milk and sugar? And do have one of these scones. I'm afraid they aren't very hot any more," said Millie distractedly.

"I never eat anything in the afternoons, thank you," was Mrs. Noble's discouraging reply. "No milk or sugar—just a slice of lemon, please."

There was not a lemon in the house, and Millie said so apologetically.

"If I may just have it *vewy* weak, then," said Mrs. Noble, and Millie hastily added water to her cup, hoping that it was not cold like the scones.

"Mrs. Ross and I," said Davina suddenly in her impressive contralto, "were asked for *four o'clock*."

Mrs. Noble gave her a glance which said quite plainly, "What is that to me?"

"And," continued Davina, "we were *here* at four o'clock."

"You play bridge, don't you, Mrs. Noble?" cried Millie. "Mrs. Gray is very good and plays a lot. There's a bridge club in Mennan—isn't there, Davina?"

"I doubt if our little club would amuse Mrs. Noble," said Davina, and from Mrs. Noble's expression she fully agreed.

"Mrs. Ross has brought her baby," said Millie wildly. "He's such a darling, and so good—"

"Weally?" was Mrs. Noble's comment, and she did not even look towards the clothes-basket of Millie's providing in which Master Ross lay lost in contemplation of his own toes.

It was quite hopeless. Even Pat saw that, and very shortly announced that she must go, because she wanted to be home before Jack came in.

"He hates coming in and finding the house empty," she explained. "Thank you for the lovely tea, Mrs. M."

"Well, I think I should be going too. I've got my hens to feed," said Davina briskly. "Besides, I know you'll want to see to the dogs, Millie."

This remark was made so pointedly at Mrs. Noble that Millie quite expected her to get up and leave the house forthwith, because it really did sound rather rude; but Mrs. Noble, seated in a low chair with her legs crossed, smoking quietly, paid no attention at all. She bowed in answer to Pat's "good-bye", and to Mrs. Gray's even more pointed "How are you getting home, Mrs. Noble? Walking?" merely said with a lazy smile, "Oh, I am being fetched quite soon."

"Well, that's a mercy, anyhow!" said Mrs. Gray, barely waiting until she was in the hall. "My dear Millie, what possessed you to ask *her* to tea. Dreadful little person!"

"Oh, hush, Davina, she'll hear you!" murmured Millie unhappily. "I really only asked her to oblige Martin Heriot. He said she was lonely—"

Mrs. Gray snorted. "Lonely! Yes, about as lonely as a man-eating tigress on the prowl and for the same reason! As for Martin, it's all very well for him to make a fool of himself, but when it comes to victimizing other people, it is rather too much! What on earth does he see in her?" And, briefly thanking Millie for her tea, with the rider that it was good food wasted to have to eat it in that company, she took her leave.

"You won't mind my waiting until Martin comes?" said Mrs. Noble, when Millie went back to the drawing-room. "He's picking me up here and we are going to dine in Edinburgh."

"Of course I don't mind," Millie said untruthfully, for she was longing to get rid of her and wished she could say so. The tea-party had been the most dreadful fiasco. It just went to show what a mistake it was to try to please people.

Nor did she feel in the least rewarded by Martin Heriot's beaming smile when he appeared to remove the enchantress from Fernieknowe.

"Never again!" she vowed. "It's the last time I shall do anything for anyone! Davina was perfectly right, it *was* a waste of food and of a whole afternoon that I might have spent weeding the rose bed!"

She could not, however much she would have liked to, share Davina's wonder as to what Martin "saw" in Mrs. Noble. True, she was far from being the lonely little figure he imagined. She was nothing of the kind; she was a far more predatory type, with a flair for dressing well and for making the most of her appearance with all the beauty specialist's aids. She was supremely sure of herself, poised and confident: the sort of woman whom any man might like to be seen with. . . .

Millie went out into her garden after washing up the tea things and letting the dogs loose, feeling most depressed not only for Amabel but for big stupid Martin Heriot as well.

Chapter 9

"Millie, I've come to ask a favour," said Mrs. Gray, walking into the kitchen at Fernieknowe on a September morning when the whole countryside was washed in pale gold light.

"I don't care for the sound of it, or the look on your face," said Mrs. Maitland. "Both are much too business-like. What is this favour?"

"I want you to join the W.R.I. this winter. You are certain to be elected to the committee, and you would be the greatest help to me," Mrs. Gray said. "Now, don't refuse at once, without thinking about it, Millie! There really isn't any reason why you shouldn't do it. Yes, I know there are the dogs, but by the time the W.R.I. meets in the evenings the dogs are in their kennels, or ought to be. And with Amabel almost permanently in Edinburgh you *can't* have so much to do in the way of housework and cooking. Now, *do* join, to oblige me! I'll take you and bring you back in the car—"

"Well, don't try to rush me, Davina, or I *will* refuse," Mrs. Maitland answered firmly. "Sit down in the basket-chair, it's the only comfortable one, and have a cup of coffee, and give me time to think."

"I ought to be going to the village for the rations," began Mrs. Gray, but she sat down. "I must say a cup of coffee would be very nice, and you make the best coffee of anyone I know, Millie."

"No flattery," said Mrs. Maitland, pushing the kettle on to the middle of the stove and taking the coffee jar from its shelf. "Why do you walk into Mennan so often, Davina? It would save you a lot of time if you took the car—"

"George is using it this morning," said Mrs. Gray. "Besides, I need the exercise to keep my weight down—though what good walking is going to do if I drink coffee on the way, I do not know."

Millie laughed, and presently, when she had given her friend a cup of fragrant coffee and a biscuit, she said, "Very well, Davina, I'll join your W.R.I., though I hope I won't be put on the committee."

"Oh, you will!" Mrs. Gray assured her. "I'm very glad you have agreed to join, Millie. I'm sure you will enjoy the meetings. Some of them are *most* interesting!"

"I wonder!" thought Millie rather sceptically when she was alone again. "I know that sort of committee voice of Davina's when she is telling people that something is *most* interesting! It usually means she is trying to convince them for their own good!"

Apart from a natural dislike for being done good to, Millie had to admit that she might be better to have some outside interest when the long winter nights began to draw on. All that Davina had said had been true and sensible. Amabel had now a great deal more work to do, her job could not be kept going by attending at her office three or four days a week. The organization had moved into large new offices in a house which had been left to it, in one of the dignified grey Edinburgh crescents, and there was a small flat on the top floor for the secretary's use.

Amabel was delighted. She had kept her resolution not to try to over-persuade her mother to moving into an Edinburgh flat; now she was offered a flat for herself, and if she meant to do her job properly, she had to accept the offer. Mr. Ramsay approved—though he did not fail to point out to her how unnecessary her talk of "sacrifice" had been. With furnished accommodation provided for which she did not have to pay, she could quite easily continue to let her mother have something towards the upkeep of Fernieknowe. Again Mr. Ramsay approved, and had made Millie see that she ought to sink her independent feelings sufficiently to take this allowance.

"It will make Amabel feel that she really has a share in what, after all, has been her home for her whole life," Mr. Ramsay had told Millie during the course of another week-end visit to Fernieknowe.

Mrs. Maitland had agreed, and Amabel came down for short spells whenever she had time. Her interest in Martin Heriot appeared to have dwindled to nothing during the summer of hard work and new responsibility, and Millie thought this was just as well, since Martin was still dancing attendance on Mrs. Noble to a degree that roused considerable comment in the neighbourhood. What really astonished Millie was that he continued to drop in and see her—or Sam. She supposed it must be Sam, and yet he displayed remarkably little interest in the dog once he had sat down in her drawing-room. Millie thought he seemed rather out of spirits these days, rather tired and more silent than usual.

Perhaps the little Noblewoman—for so Mrs. Maitland always thought of her ironically—was a trifle exigent in her demands on a man who had not much spare time. Local rumour had it that Mrs. Noble, having gained her footing on the social ladder of the county through his introducing her to various members of the smart racing and bridge-playing set, now felt that a mere farmer, busy with harvest and other dull affairs, was rather beneath her notice.

Mrs. Maitland felt that this probably served Mr. Heriot right for being so foolish about so obvious a climber as the yellow-haired siren, but she could not help feeling sorry for him. Perhaps she also felt—though she did not say so even to herself—that he would turn to Amabel when he recovered from his brief infatuation. Of course she exaggerated the importance of it, as a woman always will where affairs of the heart are concerned, since no woman ever really believes or understands that to a man they are often no more than a secondary interest.

Since the day of her disastrous tea-party Millie had seen nothing of Mrs. Noble except for glimpses of a smartly-attired vision seated in a passing car, and as the latter had not troubled to return her invitation, Millie was only too thankful to let the matter drop.

She was thinking of all these things, sometimes aloud, a habit which was growing upon her, after Mrs. Gray had gone off purposefully towards the village, remembering how unhappy she had been during the summer for Amabel's sake, and for Martin Heriot's too; the silly blundering creature not able to see how worthless the object of his admiration was.

"Well, it doesn't seem to have upset Amabel," said Amabel's mother with unreasonable annoyance. "She *is* a phlegmatic creature! And I daresay that idiot of a man will soon get over it, so I've wasted all this lovely summer worrying for nothing! Come along, Sam. Walks!"

Sam, who was now almost a year old and extremely handsome, was quite ready to walk, and they set out up the winding path between the spruce-firs and silver birches which sheltered Fernieknowe at the back, towards the moor road.

There was a shepherd's cottage four or five miles away, hidden in a fold of the rolling hills, reached only by this rough unfenced little road, and the shepherd's wife kept hens, and sometimes had a few eggs to spare for Millie. Whether there were eggs or not, Millie always carried a basket when she went this walk, with a bundle of those glossy periodicals which follow the movements of the court and society, sticking out of it. She did not buy these papers for herself, but had them passed on to her by Davina Gray, and in her turn handed them to the shepherd's wife.

Millie liked taking them where they were so much appreciated. She had seen Davina idly ruffling over the pages in search of a familiar name or face, and she herself often had no time to look at them, but in the lonely cottage among the hills Mrs. Denholm pored over them, reading each publication, studying the photographs, from cover to cover, advertisements and all, of well-known people, as if she knew them personally. What she liked best were pictures of the Royal Family, in whom she took a passionate interest. She cut out the best of these, mounted them on cardboard, framed them with narrow strips of coloured paper, and pinned them up. The walls of her shadowy little kitchen, where home-cured bacon and ham in butter muslin bags hung from hooks in the ceiling, were almost covered by now. Millie sometimes wondered what would happen when there was no room for more. The shepherd's red first prize tickets won at many shows, the enlarged photographs of champion Cheviot tups, were being gradually crowded out by royalty.

On this particular morning Millie had a very special offering, a coloured photograph of the Queen in evening dress, wearing a tiara of diamonds and the ribbon of the Garter. It was a charming picture, the grave young face looking at the world which expected so much of her, with serious dark blue eyes, and Millie would have liked to keep it herself. But knowing how greatly Mrs. Denholm would prize it, she had resisted the temptation to cut it out, rolled the magazine up with the rest and now carried them up the path in her basket. Sam was her only boarder at the moment, so, as she had nothing to hurry home for, Millie had cut herself some sandwiches for a picnic lunch. She had a lovely free feeling of no domestic responsibilities which, added to the beauty of the September day, made her want to whistle.

The opening bars of a tune had escaped before she remembered how Martin Heriot had caught her exercising her unsuitable talent and she hurriedly changed it into a whistle to summon Sam. Then she laughed. Once she had got up among the hills she could whistle as much as she liked with nothing to hear her except a stray grouse or hare, and the round-eyed sheep.

After the first steep half-mile, the moor-road curled round a shoulder of hill and dropped into a long shallow valley, up the side of which it could be seen, a narrow band of red-brown, with a little stream running below it. Fernieknowe, the village, the scattered farms and cottages of the open country to the south-west, were all out of sight as soon as the first ridge had been passed. Instead, Millie had the bare hillsides, where outcrops of grey rock showed among the expanse of fading heather, and the "bent sae brown" of the old ballads. Far ahead, the tops of higher hills peered above the long humpback which shut in the valley at its upper end. The stream gurgled and chattered close by, running clear over stony stretches, foaming in miniature cascades down great rocks to pools where trout lurked, sometimes shaded by a hardy rowan covered with brilliant orange-red bunches of fruit, or slender delicate birches. There were no other trees at all, nothing but the rise and fall of rounded hills under a pale blue sky.

Millie walked easily and lightly in the sparkling clear air, enjoying the sensations of having the whole world to herself and of being ridiculously young. Both were illusions, both were wholly delightful, a part of the fine day and the lonely upland place. Cares and troubles fell away from her like Christian's burden. It would be lovely to stay up here and never come down again, she thought.

Then honesty made her admit that she had no desire to housekeep so far from even a small place like Mennan; *that* would only mean exchanging one set of domestic problems for another. And she was far too fond of her comforts, hot baths, electric light, a soft bed, to live in a cave like a hermit.

The shepherd's cottage was near now; she came over the last rise and saw it, nestled down on a narrow level shelf of ground beside the burn, and in a few minutes she was exchanging greetings with Mrs. Denholm.

When the coloured photograph of Her Majesty had been duly admired and promised a place of honour on the wall—"My, she's bonnie, the lassie! But there's an awful load she has to carry! I'll pit this up in the place o' yon one taken at the wee Prince's christening, for it doesna dae her justice." Mrs. Denholm laid it aside with tender care and offered Millie a glass of milk or a cup of tea. Millie chose milk, and took it outside to a wooden seat to drink while she ate her sandwiches and admired the colouring of the hillsides before her—tarnished bronze of withering bracken, deep purple brown of heather, green patches of grass, all turned to brilliance by the sun.

The shepherd's wife, too polite to voice her wonder at anyone's choosing to eat on a hard seat out-of-doors when she might be sitting cosily by the kitchen fire, came to stand beside her visitor in order not to miss a moment of her conversation.

"Mrs. Gray has persuaded me to join the W.R.I.," Millie said. "I don't suppose you can ever manage to go to anything like that, Mrs. Denholm?"

"Oh, whiles I get. I like the Rural," said the shepherd's wife. "And it's the day the grocer's van comes, so if my man's not ower busy, like at the lambing time, I get a lift into Mennan an' walk home. Only if it's a fine night, ye ken. There's no sense getting drooked."

Millie laughed. "And I was thinking as I came up the hill that living here one would never be bothered with things like the W.R.I. I wanted to stay here in the hills for ever, because it's so quiet."

"It's quiet, a' right," Mrs. Denholm said. "Ower quiet, whiles, an' we're snowed up often enough."

"The only thing is," said Millie, "I wouldn't really like a hermit's life. It would be too uncomfortable."

She was talking more to herself than Mrs. Denholm, hardly expecting an answer, but the shepherd's wife startled her by replying: "You'd be thinking of old Charlie, maybe?"

"Old Charlie? Who is he?"

"Oh, I thocht ye'd heard tell o' him. He was a great character, when I was a wee lassie and my father was shepherd seven miles farther on from here—there wasna ony road then, though, just a track through the heather." Mrs. Denholm was speaking in a slow reminiscent tone, her arms rolled in her blue apron, her eyes looking at the enclosing hills. Millie, who had never heard her talk of old times before, sat listening quietly. "Old Charlie lived in a wee bit hut, far up the hillside, he'd bided there for mony a year, until one day ma faither found him dead and cauld—it was a bitter February day, and the snow had drifted in through the cracks an' lay on him in his bed o' dried bracken. Like a fox in his den, ma faither said. He had a bit the look o' a fox, a queer slinkin' way o' walkin', an' red hair gone grey. Puir auld Charlie! It was a lonesome way to dee."

Millie shivered a little as the slow voice stopped, picturing the chill winter morning, with a bitter wind blowing the powdery snow into the frail dwelling where the old man lay dead. Yet, after all, was it a bad thing to die as he had lived, alone in the hills, undisturbed by all the panoply of mortal illness?

"Don't you think," she suggested, "that he'd rather have died like that? I mean, if he had been ill and taken to hospital it would have been far worse for him."

"Oh, it suited him best, nae doot," agreed Mrs. Denholm. "But it gave me awful bad dreams when I thocht o' him lying there wi' the hill foxes prowlin' in an' sniffin' at him—" She broke off abruptly.

"I dinna like to think o' it even yet," she confessed. "Maybe it's with bein' on my own that much. Would ye be wantin' some eggs?"

Millie said she would like some eggs, and while Mrs. Denholm went to fetch them, sat thinking in the sun. Probably an interest in the Royal Family was better and healthier, for people who lived in the solitary places, than thinking of old men dying alone.... People like Mrs. Denholm were too near the elemental forces of nature to enjoy their manifestations. One might as reasonably expect a fisherman's wife to admire a storm at sea.... "'I'd *orter* be thankful,'" thought Millie suddenly, remembering a story in an old book she loved, *Cinnamon Roses*. "I live in a country place without any of its drawbacks, and I can come here when I like in fine weather," and she felt quite glad to be going back to Fernieknowe. Sam, who was tired of sitting about by this time, looking sideways at the hens and the tortoiseshell cat, got up and shook himself violently. Mrs. Denholm returned with half a dozen brown eggs in the basket, and, promising to come and see her again soon, Millie started back down the road.

Sunlight lay warm on the slopes and in the more open hollows, but already the deep glens were filling slowly with shadows. In winter these glens were hardly touched by the sun at all, so that snow lay unmelted there for months at a time. The shepherd appeared on the skyline, a lean tall figure with two collies close at his heels, and Millie, who knew that no moving object would have escaped his keen glance, waved to him. He waved back, then vanished over the brow of the hill. Once more she was the only human being in sight, nor did she expect to see anyone else; but within a mile she met Martin Heriot, who, with a gun over his shoulder and a game-bag on his back, came striding down off the moor on to the road.

"Hullo! I didn't expect to see you here!" he exclaimed, lifting a disgraceful old felt hat from his head.

"I didn't expect to see you," said Mrs. Maitland, and they looked at one another in mutual surprise.

"I've been shooting," was his next remark.

"So I see," said Millie, who had recovered more quickly from her astonishment than he.

"I mean, I've been shooting partridges," he said, as if this made everything different. "Over at Dodburn, and I took a short cut home across the hill. But where have you been?"

"Up at Corselaw, seeing Mrs. Denholm," Millie said. "It's such a lovely day that I felt like a real walk."

"Let me carry your basket," he said as they walked on together.

"Be careful, then, because it has eggs in it," Millie said, relinquishing her basket.

"Eggs? Good Lord, you don't have to go all the way to Corselaw for eggs, surely?" he demanded.

"I don't have to, but I like the walk."

"I could always let you have eggs," he said. "You know that. You've only got to let me know when you want them."

Millie, who did not want to begin to argue about the awkwardness of asking her acquaintances for eggs or anything else, smiled and murmured, "Thank you, it's very kind of you."

"But I mean it," he insisted. "It's ridiculous for you to go short just because you have some silly scruple about asking."

"How did you know I don't like asking?" Millie was so surprised at his acuteness that the question was uttered before she could stop it.

"I *do* know," he said.

As this seemed so obvious that it did not need an answer, Millie made none.

"I can't see," he went on doggedly, "why you should mind asking me for eggs if you can trudge all the way to Corselaw to ask the shepherd's wife."

"I *don't* trudge," said Millie, stung by what seemed a reflection on the way she walked. "And asking Mrs. Denholm is quite different."

"I don't see why."

"Oh, dear!" In sudden nervous exasperation, Millie glared at him. "I don't think I can explain it properly, and I don't see why I should have to, but—if I were well-off and had plenty of everything, then it wouldn't matter asking people for favours because I should be doing it on equal terms. But because I'm poor, I *can't* ask. I have an unfair advantage, it's difficult to refuse me. It isn't pride and poverty, it's just that it wouldn't be *fair*. Asking Mrs. Denholm is another matter altogether; she is glad of the money, and I'm pleased to have the eggs. If she can't spare them she says so and there is no feeling on either side. Do you see?"

"In a way I do, but I think you're wrong," he said. "All this fuss about one or two eggs."

"It isn't only eggs—and if I have to say that word again, or hear you say it, I shall scream!" said Mrs. Maitland. "They are only a case in point. And now, please, if we are going to waste the rest of this afternoon in irritating arguments, I'd rather walk home by myself."

"I won't say any more about it," Martin Heriot said hastily.

Nor did he, until they reached the little gate which led down the path to the back of Fernieknowe. Then, as he handed over her basket, he said:

"I'd—I'd let you pay me for them, you know—"

"Oh, for goodness' sake!" cried Millie, half-laughing, half-annoyed. "Do forget about them! Good afternoon, Mr. Heriot. Come, Sam!" And she fled away down the steep path, Sam bounding after her.

Amabel came home for a night that week-end, and her mother said to her, "Would you like some fresh eggs to take back to Edinburgh, dear? I can let you have half a dozen."

"Oh, I'd love them, Mother. But are you sure you can spare them?"

"Quite sure," said Millie. "I'm—I'm rather off eggs just now."

Chapter 10

Though Mennan was only a small village, it was the centre of a large old parish spread over an unusually wide area. Because of its position it owned not only an excellent school, a handsome parish church, with a tall, grey steeple, a modest little building dedicated to the episcopal Church of Scotland and a tin chapel where a visiting Roman Catholic priest held services on alternate Sundays, but a commodious Village Hall, presented by a former laird in days when landed proprietors had the means to make such gifts. Every local function took place in the Blackburn Hall. To the Whist Drives, political meetings, concerts, jumble sales, dances, the activities of the Blood Transfusion Unit and the Civil Defence added a rather grimmer post-war touch; and it was there that the Mennan Branch of the Scottish Women's Rural Institutes held their meetings, on the last Tuesday of every month.

The noise of about fifty women of all ages talking broke on Millie's ears, as she followed Mrs. Gray's impressive bulk into the hall, in a deafening roar. As she looked at their faces, which were of an unhealthy yellow-green pallor, she wondered what had happened to them, and then saw that Mrs. Gray, usually ruddy and weatherbeaten, was the same colour.

"It's the lighting!" shouted her sponsor above the noise. "You look like boiled celery too. Surely you must have noticed it before? This can't be the first time you have been in the Blackburn Hall."

"I certainly never remember seeing a hall full of sick people," retorted Millie. "It is perfectly frightful."

"New strip lighting." Mrs. Gray sounded complacent. "It's been in for a couple of months now, and you've no idea of the difference it has made."

Millie thought she had a very good idea, but said no more. The new lighting was extremely bright, so it was probably better for everyone's eyes, and if they were all satisfied with the strange effect, so much the better.

Like an enormous queen bee in the middle of a swarm, Mrs. Gray was now surrounded by her committee, and Millie, feeling like a forlorn drone, was standing wondering what she ought to do, when someone gave her coat a hearty tug.

"Sit ye doon here by me, Mrs. Maitland," said a voice, as Millie, somewhat startled, looked round and down. Beaming up at her was the moon-face of Martin Heriot's housekeeper, Mrs. Wilson, surmounted by a plum-coloured beret. "They'll be beginning in a meenit, and ye'll maybe not get a good seat," she continued.

Millie sat down thankfully beside the ample form of this friend in need. "I feel a bit lost," she said. "This is my first time here, you see."

"Oh, ye'll soon get used with it. The Rural's real friendly," Mrs. Wilson assured her. "I just said when I seen ye come in, it would be the very thing for ye."

Wondering a little why "the Rural" should benefit her in particular, Mrs. Maitland returned the smiles and nods which she received from all sides. Now that she had time to look about her, she recognized nearly everyone by sight, even if she did not know their names. The friendly reception was very pleasant, she thought.

Now Davina was standing up just in front of the stage, welcoming new members, announcing future demonstrations, giving reminders about subscriptions now due, all in her brisk efficient way which yet was kindly. She then announced that this evening they had with them Miss Robertson from Middleton, who would show them the best method of plucking and dressing a fowl. Miss Robertson.

Up on the stage the demonstrator began to deal with a large hen, keeping up a running commentary as her fingers nimbly stripped it of its feathers. But Millie, though she tried to listen, and indeed was fascinated by the speed displayed by Miss Robertson, found her attention being constantly distracted. Mrs. Wilson and her neighbour on the other side, evidently a bosom friend, were conversing in sibilant undertones, and Millie could not help hearing at least part of what they said. She realized that they were stripping someone of her reputation as fast as the fowl was being denuded of its feathers.

"A painted Jezebel, no better!" was one remark which attracted her attention, and a few minutes later: "Why is she not with her husband? That's what I'd like to know!"

Who in the world could they be talking about, wondered Mrs. Maitland, to be enlightened when, under cover of a burst of clapping, as the demonstration ended, Mrs. Wilson said, "The only thing about *her* that's noble is her name!"

It was rather a shock to realize that Mrs. Noble had been the person discussed in such unfavourable terms. Mrs. Wilson and her friend had sounded quite worked-up, and Millie began to feel that the W.R.I. was a hot-bed of gossip and no place for her. And yet, at the same time, annoyed with her own lower nature though it made her, she felt considerable interest in the gossips' remark about Mrs. Noble's husband, for it had never occurred to Millie that the little woman was not a widow like herself.

"I wonder if they really know," she thought. "I do wish I could ask them—" and was ashamed of herself. Amabel had always insisted that the Rural meetings were only an opportunity and excuse for ill-natured talk, and her mother had always felt that this sweeping statement could not be true; but this evening she saw that Amabel had some grounds for what she said.

Mingled with Mrs. Maitland's disapproval of what she had overheard and of herself for wanting to hear it was some curiosity as to the necessity for having demonstrators at all. If the rest of the audience had been equally engrossed in conversation, was there any point in that capable woman's standing up on the stage neatly putting feathers into a box and trussing the corpse of her victim with such swift and practised skill?

It was with quite a shock that she heard her neighbour's voice in her ear asking: "Did ye enjoy the demonstration, Mrs. Maitland? She's good, isn't she? I'm a pretty fair hand with a fowl myself, but I can't equal that for speed." She was still clapping heartily. Mrs. Maitland's thoughts, which had seemed to last for so long, had occupied no more than a second or two.

"Oh, yes, it was very good—excellent—" she answered in some confusion, for it really did not seem possible that Mrs. Wilson had noticed anything.

"Maybe it's not quite in your line," Mrs. Wilson said kindly. "You'll get the butcher to dress your fowls, I expect. But for folk who kill their own hens or get one given them, it's a help to see how it's done."

"Of course it must be a tremendous help," Millie said, pulling herself together. "I can do it at a pinch, but I am not good at it, and it's a job I dislike very much."

"There'll be other demonstrations more in your line," Mrs. Wilson assured her. "We're to have embroidery and hair-styling and care o' the skin and all sorts later on."

Millie, quite overpowered by this mass of information rapidly hissed in her ear, could think of nothing to say but, "That will be very nice," while she wondered inwardly whether the hair and skin experts would have the effect of revolutionizing the appearance of Mennan's W.R.I. members.

"There's Mrs. Gray looking for you," said Mrs. Wilson, giving her a dig in the ribs, and Millie, glancing up, caught Davina's eagle eye fixed on her in a beckoning manner.

"Perhaps I should go and see if she wants me," she murmured, getting up from her hard wooden chair. "Thank you very much for letting me sit next to you."

She made her way towards Mrs. Gray through a swarm of women rushing about with large enamelled teapots and trays of scones and cakes, and found that lady, very much the President, being gracious to the demonstrator. When Millie reached her side, she turned on her with the demand, "Do you know anything about country dancing? Scottish, of course."

"Not very much," Millie said doubtfully. "I've done some of the better-known ones at times—Petronella and the Duke of Perth and—"

"Splendid! That's what we need. I want you to get them all up after tea," said Davina with terrible briskness. "Do them good to dance. They've been sitting quite long enough."

Millie could not help thinking that most of the members looked more suited for sitting than dancing, both in age and figure, but that was not her business, so she said nothing, and merely fixed her gaze enquiringly on Mrs. Gray's face, its usual ruddiness altered to a curious shade of orange by the new lighting.

"If one or two people like yourself will just start, we'll soon get them going, but they're slow to begin," Mrs. Gray explained. "So just pick a partner and form a set. I never can see why they are so bad about getting up to dance. They like it, really."

"Perhaps they'd rather talk to their friends," suggested Millie, thinking of Mrs. Wilson.

"They talk too much," Mrs. Gray said firmly. "Far better for them to dance. But have some tea. I brought a cup for you—"

She rummaged in a large basket and produced two plastic cups of a hideous blue, into which yellow-green tea was poured at once by a passing helper.

"Looks terrible, doesn't it?" she said chattily. "It's just the lighting. You'll see it tastes a' right. I ken. I made it."

After this recommendation Millie could hardly do less than take a cautious sip of the repulsive liquid, which did indeed taste all right, being boiling hot and freshly infused. The demonstration, or the heat of the hall, or both, had made her thirsty, so, though she did not really care for tea as late in the evening as this, she drank it gratefully and felt refreshed.

"Now, then, take your partners for Petronella!" called Mrs. Gray, who had been actively pushing chairs and benches to the side, and chivvying others to help her clear the floor. "And I want to see *everybody* dancing!"

Millie went obediently in search of a partner, and seeing the familiar face of Mrs. Denholm, invited her to dance.

Much to her relief the shepherd's wife rose with alacrity, and by shouting to various friends to join in, soon had a set on the floor.

"Just begin!" ordered Mrs. Gray, dashing past on her way to the piano. "The others will start if you do!" And she seated herself and rattled off the opening bars in grand style.

Capering about with Mrs. Denholm, short of breath and rendered more so by an idiotic desire to shriek with laughter, Millie could see no signs of anyone else joining the dance.

They remained seated round the room, some watching with indulgent smiles, some so deep in talk that they did not bother to watch at all. Mrs. Gray did not seem to be discouraged in the least. When Millie, with the others, sank panting on to chairs, she announced that they would *all* dance the Duke of Perth now; and so compelling was her look that the majority, evidently considering that resistance was useless, did creep reluctantly into the middle of the hall. Once on their feet they displayed astonishing energy, and called for more dances by name, until Millie felt as if her head would burst open and her feet fall off if she had to do another step.

"Well, that was a successful evening, wasn't it?" said Mrs. Gray with great satisfaction, when at last Millie was in her car and on the way home. "How did you enjoy it?"

"Very much, but if you are always so energetic I'm rather glad you only have meetings once a month," said Millie.

"Oh, sometimes we have community singing," said Mrs. Gray, sounding her horn loudly and unnecessarily as they went round a corner. "But they're better if they are kept on the go. They have plenty of time to talk scandal while they have their tea."

"Yes," thought Millie, "and while they are supposed to be watching demonstrations too!" Aloud she said, remembering what Mrs. Wilson and her friend had been talking about, "Davina, didn't you think that Mrs. Noble was a widow?"

"I haven't bothered my head about her at all," answered Mrs. Gray candidly. "Why? Did you hear her being discussed?"

"Yes, I did," said Millie. "It was horrid."

"I daresay Mrs. Wilson was a bit heated on the subject," Mrs. Gray said calmly. "In a way you can't blame her—and they don't really gossip more than any other gathering of women, Millie. But why should Mrs. Noble be a widow? Except a grass-widow!" She added with her loud cheerful laugh: "I believe she has a husband somewhere at a good safe distance—Malaya—Burma—I did hear, but I can't say I listened very attentively. What made you think she was a widow, Millie?"

"Well, she doesn't behave as if she had a husband anywhere," began Millie slowly.

"You mean the way she has been going about with Martin Heriot?" Mrs. Gray said, and sounded her horn again, this time at a rabbit which had darted to safety just in time. "Oh, there's no need to bother about *that*. I expect Martin knows she has a husband. He's no fool. But he's like a lot of men, he's quite pleased to have a pretty, well-dressed woman to take about when he wants some female society. Of course there has been talk—always is, in a place like Mennan where everyone knows everyone else—but I can't see much harm in it, myself. She certainly wouldn't be *my* choice if I were a man—or perhaps she would," Mrs. Gray said thoughtfully. It was plain that she was considering the matter with care and trying to be perfectly fair and honest, which was one of the reasons why her friends liked her and put up with her rather overbearing ways. "I daresay it's a rest to listen to her sort of feather-brained chatter, and she is very easy on the eye."

"Supposing she thinks she would like a change of husband?" said Millie. "I don't imagine she is as featherbrained as you say, Davina. I think she could scheme for her own advantage and do it very cleverly."

Mrs. Gray, stopping the car at Fernieknowe gate, laughed uproariously. "Well, if she is as clever as you seem to think, Millie, she will know better than to look for a new husband in Martin Heriot! Good heavens, he'd never dream of marrying her! Now here you are, and you won't forget next month, same day, same time, and bring a cup and something to eat. Good night, m'dear." There was a clashing of gears—Davina drove with absolute confidence and no care for her long-suffering car—and she was off, her headlights picking up the trunks and branches of the roadside trees and turning them to silver as she went.

Mrs. Maitland walked rather slowly up the steep approach to Fernieknowe, between the high banks where big clumps of ferns were already withering to brown. She was thinking over what Davina Gray had said, and finding it very sensible and reasonable. Davina had known Martin Heriot for a long time, and no doubt was quite right in thinking that he was just enjoying a pretty woman's society. Yet she was troubled, for she was not being sensible or reasonable. She would have preferred Martin to be in love with Mrs. Noble, even unhappily in love. That would have given some meaning to the affair. As it was, she felt a fastidious distaste at the idea of his making himself conspicuous with another man's wife simply for amusement, playing safely what should be a dangerous game. Of course it made Mrs. Noble conspicuous too; but Millie did not think that Mrs. Noble would have any objection to that.

"It all seems a bit squalid, to me," she said to herself, opening her door and groping for the light-switch. "I would never have thought *he* would do that sort of thing."

It was none of her business, of course, and her opinion of Martin Heriot mattered to nobody except a little to herself. All the same, she knew that he had sunk a little in her estimation, and the thought made an extremely disagreeable bed-fellow, keeping her awake for a long time after she had gone to bed that night.

CHAPTER 11

"MOTHER, how much longer are you going to keep Sam?" Amabel, home for the week-end, had followed her mother up the garden at the back of the house and now stood leaning against the sun-warmed trunk of an apple tree, alternately taking puffs at the cigarette in one hand, and bites from an apple in the other. Mrs. Maitland was working at her long herbaceous border, dressed in an ancient grey tweed skirt much frayed round its hem, an equally old blue jersey, and clogs.

When Amabel spoke, she straightened her back, and leaned on the fork with which she had been separating a large clump of Michaelmas daisies. "I really don't know," she said rather vaguely, looking round for Sam, and discovering hint stretched at ease on the path skirting the gooseberry bushes. "Why, Amabel?"

"Well, you don't usually have a dog for as long as we've had Sam, do you? He's—he's getting to be like your own, and I'm sure he thinks Fernieknowe belongs to him."

Mrs. Maitland pushed back an end of hair which had fallen over her eyes, transferring several earthy streaks from her hand to her forehead. "He *has* been here a long time," she agreed. "I'd forgotten how long. The weeks slip by so quickly that I haven't noticed. I don't believe his owner really wants him, you know—"

"Who actually is his owner?" Amabel asked.

"A cousin of Mr. Heriot's," said Mrs. Maitland. "That's all I know. She sends the money for Sam's keep through her lawyer. It's a shame to leave him here. He's a dear dog, and well-bred, and he ought to be getting some shooting, not hanging about doing nothing."

Amabel thought this over while she finished her apple. Then she threw the core away and said, "There's something funny about it."

"What do you mean?"

"Well, people don't usually just dump a valuable gun-dog for months on end and forget all about it," said Amabel. "Do they?"

"N—no. I suppose not," murmured Millie. "I'll miss him very much when she does decide to take him away."

"Do you know what I think?" said Amabel, in such a peculiar tone of voice that her mother stared at her. "I think you've got him here for keeps."

"But that's ridiculous!" cried Mrs. Maitland. "No one would do such a thing! Mr. Heriot's cousin will want him back when she's ready to take him. Perhaps she's abroad, or ill, or something—"

"Perhaps her name is Mrs. Harris," said Amabel. "In fact, I'm sure it is."

"Mrs. Harris?"

"There ain't no sich person," said Amabel.

"I wish you would stop talking in riddles and say what you mean, and let me get on with my border," said Mrs. Maitland.

"All right. I don't believe there's any cousin at all," Amabel said rapidly. "I think the dog was bought by Martin Heriot as a present for you. That's what I think, and if you give your mind to it, Mother, you'll see that all the evidence points that way."

"What *ab*solute rubbish!" said Mrs. Maitland, flushing deeply. "As if he would give me a present of a dog that cost as much as Sam must have! And then—all the paying for his board—does that look like giving me a present? Why should he give me anything? Especially something he knows I couldn't possibly accept. You really *must* be talking nonsense, Amabel," she ended rather piteously.

Amabel shook her neat glossy head. "No, I'm not," she said, kindly but very positively. "You just haven't been looking the facts in the face. I don't mean that you've deliberately turned a blind eye on them—"

"Thank you!" said Mrs. Maitland, with bitter meekness.

"But anyone except you would have seen through it ages ago," Amabel finished.

"Did you?"

"I've hardly been at home all through the summer," said Amabel. "Somehow I never realized that Sam was still here, and has been here without a break. But as soon as I gave my mind to it I did."

The remembrance of Mrs. Wilson and her friend gossiping at the W.R.I. meeting struck Mrs. Maitland like a blow. "In that case," she said with deadly calm, "I suppose everyone in Mennan is talking about it?"

"Oh, no, I don't think so. You aren't the sort of person people talk about," Amabel said reassuringly. "Don't take it madly seriously, Mother. I think it was rather nice of Martin Heriot to give you a present—silly, perhaps, to do it like that, but rather nice."

"Rather nice? Rather nice to make me look like a prize idiot?" cried Mrs. Maitland, roused to one of her rare rages, and thrusting the fork into the ground as if she were impaling Mr. Heriot on its prongs. "Then your idea of niceness and mine are very different, Amabel! Sam shall go at once. I won't keep him another day!"

She started off down the path towards the house, walking so fast even in her heavy clogs that Amabel had to run to catch up with her.

"Mother! Mother, what are you going to do?" she asked.

"Do? I'm going to take Sam back to his owner at once and end this—this farce of keeping him for a cousin who doesn't exist!" said Mrs. Maitland shortly.

"Oh dear!" For once Amabel was at a loss. "I wish I hadn't said anything about it. I—I thought you'd be amused, and a little touched. I never thought you'd be angry."

"Amabel, I know you are a clever young woman, but there are times when you talk like a fool," said her mother. "Touched, indeed!"

"Well, surely you aren't going to Wardlaw looking like that? There's mud on your face and hands, and—"

"I don't care in the least."

"And you can't possibly walk in those clogs. They'll blister your feet."

"Very well, then I shall change," said Mrs. Maitland. "But it's no use talking to me in that reasonable way as if you were a nannie and I a spoilt child. As soon as I have changed I am taking Sam to Mr. Heriot."

Amabel fell back. Her mother, usually so easy to persuade that everyone was right but herself, had suddenly turned adamant, and Amabel realized that the best thing she could do was to leave her alone. Too late she wished that she had not yielded to her freakish and rather unkind sense of humour which had prompted her to speak of her suspicions about the dog. She was right, but that did not seem to make it any better, and she began to perceive that always being right was an indulgence and could be very misleading. So she stood on the path watching her mother's slender retreating figure, rigid with indignation, until Sam, roused from his peaceful slumbers by their unexpected movements, bounded past her and, overtaking Millie, seized her hand gently in is black velvet mouth. Amabel saw her mother suddenly withdraw her hand, and as suddenly put it on the big dog's head, and she wondered if Millie's anger would really carry her to the point of parting with Sam. . . .

Millie Maitland, with Sam still at her heels, clumped into the scullery by the back door, kicked off her clogs, and went upstairs to her bedroom. Even the few moments which it had taken her to traverse the garden had convinced her that she would do better to confront Martin Heriot looking less like Madge Wildfire. There was a certain amount of moral support to be had from wearing a respectable suit and powdering one's nose.

So it was dressed in the blue tweed which Amabel had given her for her birthday and with a much more lavish application of lipstick and powder than usual that she set out for Wardlaw twenty minutes later. She had considered putting on a touch of rouge, but a glance at her pink cheeks decided her against it. She did not want to arrive looking as if she were in a high fever, but she had forgotten how quickly the flush of temper ebbs, and she had not allowed for the distress which the thought of losing Sam made more acute with every step she took. The first mile was covered at a very brisk pace indeed, but Mrs. Maitland found herself walking more and more slowly, and she could hardly bear to see Sam bounding ahead, or turning to run back and look up at her with his honest, loving eyes.

"What a fuss to make over a dog!" she said scornfully to herself, knowing even as she said it that it was treason.

Everything conspired to make her feel more wretched, the bright sunshine touching the autumn leaves to gold and copper and crimson, the blue sky reflected back from puddles in the rough road, Sam's obedience and evident wish to please her. When she met Davina Gray bicycling furiously in the opposite direction, towards the village, she could hardly reply to her loud cheerful greeting. And when Davina said unexpectedly, "That dog does you credit, Millie, he looks so fit," it was almost more than she could bear. If it had not been for the thought of facing Amabel, she would have turned back, she thought; but of course, even if Amabel had not been there, her own self-respect would have forced her to go on. The situation was an impossible one. She could not keep Sam if he really did belong to Martin Heriot.

Composed, but very pale, she reached the big comfortable farmhouse facing south over its rolling fields, and rang the bell. She had a dignified request to see Mr. Heriot all ready for Mrs. Wilson, or whoever should come to the door, and had embarked on it: "I should be glad to see Mr. Heriot for a moment—" before she realized that it was Martin Heriot himself standing there with a welcoming smile on his brown face.

"Come in," he said. "You couldn't have chosen a better time, for I'm just having tea. Mrs. Wilson!" he shouted. "Send Elma in with another cup for Mrs. Maitland. She's come to tea."

"No, no!" protested Millie, ready to weep with nervous vexation, for how was she to conduct the kind of interview she had intended over cups of the culprit's tea? "I really don't want tea, thank you—"

"Nonsense, of course you want tea. You look a bit tired," he said solicitously, and he took her arm and led her into the house. "You've never been to Wardlaw yet, and you can't refuse to drink a cup of tea with me."

Short of a free fight with someone greatly her superior in physical strength, there seemed nothing Mrs. Maitland could do but go in, and as Sam dashed joyfully ahead of them, having no reluctance to entering the house, she gave in without unnecessary fuss. The room into which he brought her was long and low, running forward to a bow window looking to the front, and with three more windows in a row breaking the wall opposite the door. Very few women are proof against the interest held for them by other people's houses; a bachelor's sitting-room in particular excites feelings which range from despairing pity to wild envy, according to his means and taste.

Mrs. Maitland had come on a most disagreeable errand, she had entered this house against her will, but once seated in one of the deep armchairs beside a wood fire which burned on a wide stone hearth, she could not keep her eyes from looking about the room, appraising its contents, taking in every small detail of fabric and colour. A set of coloured hunting prints on the plain cream-papered walls, carpet and curtains of a deep red which had faded slightly so that it exactly matched the chrysanthemums glowing in a pewter, chair-covers of oatmeal rough-surfaced linen, all blended harmoniously. Even the big writing-bureau bulging with papers and the table between the windows, where books and periodicals were strewn, did not spoil the effect of a room used for living in and not for show. Near the fire a smaller table carried all the paraphernalia of tea, silver glittering in the sunlight which streamed in on it from the western-facing windows, china sparkling. A covered dish set down close to the burning logs was being sniffed at hopefully by Sam. It was very plain that Mr. Heriot was well served by Mrs. Wilson and Emma, a rosy-cheeked young creature in blue print dress and white apron, fresh as a daisy, who came in and set a cup and saucer on the tea-tray and fled out again overcome with shyness.

Since it had developed into a social occasion, Millie Maitland decided that she must behave accordingly, and delayed the purpose of her visit until she had eaten one of the delicious hot scones and drunk her tea out of what she saw with pleased surprise was a Rockingham cup where gold arabesques curled and twisted on a soft grey background. To her relief, Martin Heriot did not seem to expect her to pour out, for he did it himself as a matter of course, almost emptying the teapot at one go into his mammoth blue and white cup after he had supplied his unexpected guest.

The tea was deliciously refreshing, and Millie drank it gratefully, but she felt miserably ill-at-ease, and all the more so because Martin Heriot showed not a trace of guilty discomfort. With the idea of making conversation, for the pauses seemed endless, Millie said, "What an attractive room this is!"

"D'you like it? I'm glad," he said. "My cousin planned it for me and got it done—except for the old prints, of course. They were my grandfather's."

"Your cousin?" Fury rose suddenly in Millie like a wave, almost choking her. How dared he sit there munching seed cake and drinking tea, and blandly mention cousins?

In a voice like small pieces of icicle falling on glass she heard herself say, "The cousin to whom Sam belongs, I suppose?"

"Er—no. Not that one," he answered, looking slightly, but only slightly, discomposed.

"You seem to have quite a number of cousins," continued Mrs. Maitland.

"Oh, come! Two isn't a great many," he said. "Most people have dozens!"

Mrs. Maitland refused to be side-tracked into a discussion about the numbers of cousins people had or had not.

"The one who owns Sam is the cousin I am interested in," she said. "I think it is time she took Sam home. In fact, that's what I came to see you about this afternoon. I should like to leave him with you now, and you can arrange to send him to her, as I know neither her name nor her address."

This, she was glad to see, really did shake him. He stared at her in blank dismay. "What's wrong?" he asked. "Has Sam been making such a nuisance of himself that you can't stand him? I thought he was pretty well-behaved by now—"

Sam, who had enjoyed a dish of milky tea out of the slop-basin and was lying quietly before the fire, raised his head when he heard his name, and put it on one side as he tried to puzzle out what this was all about. Mrs. Maitland found she was quite unable to look at him and remain firm. So she kept her own head turned away.

"No. He is very good," she said. "But he must go home."

"You don't—it's not—you're not doing this because people have been talking about me for taking Mrs. Noble out to dinner?" He was staring straight at her now, as if accusing her of being narrow-minded, as if he were the judge and she a guilty creature.

"Certainly not!" she said emphatically. "It is nothing to do with me what you do or whom you go about with. And I think," she added, "that we'd better stop beating about the bush like this, Mr. Heriot. You *must* know why I am saying that I can't keep Sam."

"I'm damned if I do!" he burst out. "I don't understand it at all!"

"Suppose I asked you who Sam really belonged to, would that help you to understand?" asked Mrs. Maitland, still icy.

"A—ah!" He drew a long breath. "So that's it. You've tumbled to it?" He still had a guilty look, but now there was a mischievous glint in his eye as well. "I must say, I rather wonder that you didn't sooner than this—"

Mrs. Maitland gazed at him stonily. So he thought it was rather funny, did he, and evidently expected her to think so too. . . . He was still talking.

"Yes, it's true enough. Janet bought Sam on impulse, and found she couldn't be bothered to look after a pup. Janet's like that, so—"

"Janet?" said Mrs. Maitland.

"Yes. My cousin Janet. So she gave Sam to me, and you know I was busy at the lambing, I really hadn't time to train him—"

"Then *why*," asked Mrs. Maitland, conscious of such a flood of relief that it almost made her angrier than ever. "*Why* did you tell me he belonged to your cousin? Why all the mystery about paying for his board?"

"Well, for a bit I thought Janet might change her mind and want him back," he said. "And then, what with hay harvest and all the rest of it, I honestly couldn't be doing with a young dog. And I could see he was happy with you, and you seemed to like having him, and I was pretty sure if you knew he was mine you'd begin to wonder what I was playing at, leaving him with you at Fernieknowe."

"But I met you not long ago coming back from shooting," said Mrs. Maitland. "If you have time to shoot, you could have a gun-dog, and Sam would train very easily."

He stirred uncomfortably in his chair. "I'd better just tell you the whole thing," he muttered. "I like coming to Fernieknowe, but you're too busy to have people dropping in without any real reason for calling, so I felt—I thought—I mean, of course it was all right if I came to see how the dog was getting on."

"Of all the bird-witted, idiotic ideas I have ever heard," said Mrs. Maitland slowly and clearly, "I think this is the peak. Do you really mean to say that you worked up this mystery for no other reason?"

He nodded rather shamefacedly.

Mrs. Maitland began to laugh, and laughed until tears were pouring down her cheeks, no longer pale. When at last she could stop, and had taken out a handkerchief and dried her eyes, she said, "But we still haven't settled about Sam. You *ought* to have him here—"

"No. He's far better with you. Look here, let me take him when I go out with the gun," said Martin Heriot eagerly. "That's an idea! He'll board with you and go shooting with me. How about it? He's happy with you—"

"Yes, he is," agreed Mrs. Maitland. She looked from the dog to his owner and back again. "And I should miss him dreadfully. Very well, I will keep him for you, but he is *your* dog."

"Whose else would he be?" asked Martin Heriot in some surprise, and Mrs. Maitland blushed.

"Well, I mean, he isn't your cousin's dog," she murmured rather confusedly, and got up to go.

"I can come and see him whenever I like, of course. That's in the agreement."

"Oh, yes, of course. Good-bye, Mr. Heriot, and thank you for giving me tea," said Mrs. Maitland, now restored to her normal pretty, rather diffident manner, "and for settling this question. It—it really was worrying me quite a lot."

He walked to the gate with her, and when they reached it stood looking down at the top of her plain felt hat which only came up to the level of his shoulder. "The other business," he said suddenly, "I've felt you rather disapproved of it. Did you?"

Millie Maitland was too honest to pretend to misunderstand him. "I've told you already it was none of my business," she said evasively, "and I do not try to interfere with other people's business."

"A lot of talk about nothing," he said with impatient resentment. "Why should a woman live like a hermit just because her husband happens to be abroad? There was no harm in my taking her out. She was bored to death living alone."

He seemed to expect an answer, and at last Millie said: "If you were the husband in such a case, would you like to think of your wife going out with other men? I think that's the point."

"If I had been fool enough to marry a woman like that I'd be darned glad to know she was going about with someone like me," he said grimly. "I'd know it kept her out of mischief, at least."

"Well—perhaps. I don't really understand how men look at things," said Millie.

"No, and I don't understand how women do," he replied.

"Women are really much simpler than men on the whole," said Mrs. Maitland. "There are a few who reason everything out and argue it academically, but most of us just go by our feelings."

"Do you call that simpler?"

"Oh, dear me, yes! Much simpler," said Millie. "I *must* go—"

"But even if you disapprove of me I may come to Fernieknowe?"

"You will have to come to get Sam when you want to take him shooting," said Mrs. Maitland, avoiding the issue. "Goodbye, Mr. Heriot."

Amabel, too uneasy to make tea for herself, was prowling about upstairs in and out of each room which had a window looking to the back and the little road across the moor to Wardlaw. As she played the ancient game of "Sister Anne, Sister Anne, do you see anybody coming?" she continued to tell herself that of course she wasn't in the least worried, that she hadn't had tea because it was too much trouble to make it, and that her mother would very soon be back, and Sam with her.

It was only when she saw the slender upright figure in misty blue walking towards Fernieknowe at a good pace, with the black dog bounding ahead of her, that Amabel admitted to a feeling of intense relief.

"Thank goodness!" she thought. "I was really afraid she was going to leave Sam behind. But I wonder how he managed to talk her round."

By "he" she meant Martin Heriot, not Sam, though it struck her that Sam's wordless affection probably carried more weight with her mother than any amount of pleading from Sam's owner.

She waited upstairs until she heard Mrs. Maitland's light step in the hall, and then called over the banisters: "Is that you, Mother? I'll come down and make tea."

Millie looked up; her face under the brim of her blue hat looked surprisingly young in spite of her grey hair. How pretty mother is! thought Amabel without envy, for she admired a more classic type of good looks.

"I've had tea at Wardlaw," said Mrs. Maitland. "Don't say you've waited for me!"

"Not exactly," Amabel admitted truthfully. "I didn't really want any, and it's too late now, don't you think?"

At this rate, they might go on babbling about trifles for ever, Mrs. Maitland thought, so she said, "I've brought Sam back with me."

"Oh—good! I'm awfully glad, Mother," said Amabel.

"How did you arrange it? I mean—" she floundered and added hurriedly, "Don't tell me if you'd rather not."

"Sam belongs to Mr. Heriot. He was a present from his cousin," Mrs. Maitland said in a clear voice.

"So there really *is* a cousin?"

"His cousin Janet found she didn't really want a dog so she gave Sam to Mr. Heriot," Millie said. "But he's to go on boarding here—"

"What on earth for?" asked Amabel.

Mrs. Maitland had been expecting this question, and she had an answer ready. On the way home she had suddenly realized that of course Martin Heriot wanted an excuse to come to Fernieknowe; it was the best arrangement he could make for seeing Amabel, or at least of hearing of her from her mother. How he reconciled this with his squiring Mrs. Noble all through the summer, Millie did not know. If at some future time Amabel wanted an explanation, then he would have to give her one. In the meantime, he still had a good reason tor visiting the Maitlands. So Mrs. Maitland now answered readily.

"Oh, he really hasn't time to look after Sam properly, and I think he was afraid I'd miss him. Sam is going to go out shooting with Mr. Heriot, of course."

She had been so glad both to keep Sam and to leave his owner free to come to Fernieknowe that she had not stopped to consider how very thin this explanation sounded. Only after she had spoken did it occur to her that if Amabel pressed the point there was nothing more she could say in defence. To her great relief, however, Amabel, who had her own reasons for letting well alone, appeared satisfied.

"Oh, I see," she said. And then, beginning to come downstairs, "Mother, let's have a glass of sherry."

"I thought that bottle you brought with you was to be kept for a special occasion?"

"Well, in a way, I think this is quite special enough for us to open it," said Amabel. "Sam would say so."

Mrs. Maitland laughed and yielded. After the tempest of anger and distress, followed by violent relief, which had shaken her that afternoon, she felt that sherry would be very nice.

As Amabel handed a glass to her mother a few minutes later, when they were both in the drawing-room, she said, "Mother, I'm sorry I upset you this afternoon. I didn't really mean to. I wish I hadn't said anything—"

Mrs. Maitland looked at her, saw the unusual softness in her fine eyes, and decided that for once she could speak like a mother to her daughter.

"My dear child," she said, "it entirely depends on your motive. If you said what you did in good faith, because you were afraid I was being made a fool of, I think you were perfectly right. But if you were only exercising your—your not very kind sense of humour, then it might have been better if you had kept quiet. Of course I *had* to know, but I daresay I would have thought it out for myself in time. But you would find life much pleasanter if you tried to be kind sometimes instead of clever, and in any case, surely the cleverness that hides itself is the best sort, like art is to conceal art, you know. Now we won't talk about it any more."

She took a sip of sherry. "What a good judge of sherry you are!" she said. "This is delicious."

It happened to be South African, and Amabel opened her mouth to say so, adding something about her mother's untrained palate; then, almost without knowing why, she checked the words on her tongue, and, instead, said mildly, "I'm glad you like it, Mother."

Chapter 12

When a gentle but persistent knocking at the back door announced the fourth interruption of a busy morning, Mrs. Maitland raised her floury hands from the baking-bowl in which she was rubbing fat into flour.

"I shall never get done to-day, never," she said with calm despair. "I might have known it would be like this when I dropped those spoons."

She was a firm believer in the superstition that to drop a spoon meant an unexpected visitor, and experience had usually proved her right.

"Be quiet, Sam, *please*!" she added, for Sam had discovered that he was the owner of a fine bass voice and believed in exercising it at every opportunity.

Shutting him into the kitchen, where he went on barking, Mrs. Maitland went to the back door, and on opening it discovered one of those old men with suspiciously pink noses who go about trying to sell a pathetic selection of very large blunt needles, very coarse thread, plastic hairslides in a variety of hideous colours and designs, and combs.

"Good morning," said Mrs. Maitland, giving one quick practised glance at his wares, which he was sorting in a cardboard attaché case with tremulous hands. "I'd like a comb, please—

nothing else to-day. But if you'll wait here a minute I'll make you a cup of tea, and a piece."

They knew each other quite well, for the old man called at regular intervals. Mrs. Maitland always bought a comb, and he never failed to try unsuccessfully to persuade her to buy something else as well. The transaction was carried out with good humour and each side considered itself lucky: Mrs. Maitland because she resisted his petitions to buy safety-pins or elastic, the old man because he charged two-and-three-pence for the comb, which meant that he had enough for a drink—also, he got his tea and a substantial sandwich, so he may be considered to have made the better bargain.

Mrs. Maitland returned to the kitchen, where she put the comb on the dresser, pulled the kettle forward on the hotplate, and admonished Sam. Then she cut two mighty slices of bread, spread them with margarine, and after a look round the larder shelves, decided that there wasn't enough cheese, and she would have to spare some meat off the weekly ration, which had been a small bit of roast mutton. Just as she made the tea, footsteps could be heard in the hall, and Pat Ross's voice calling, "Are you in, Mrs. M.?" produced a fresh outburst of barking from Sam.

"A spell of peace and quiet in a large city is what I need," thought Mrs. Maitland, at the same time shouting, "Come in, Pat. Shut up, Sam!" in one breath and exactly the same tone.

Pat appeared in the doorway, hugged Sam, who rose and put his forepaws on her shoulders, and said, "Have I disturbed you in the middle of baking, Mrs. M.?"

"Not exactly," said Mrs. Maitland, pouring strong tea into a large enamelled mug which she kept for her back-door callers, and adding a lavish measure of sugar and milk. "Just smack Sam and sit down for a minute until I've given this to my old man."

"Do you have many people round asking for tea and selling things?" asked Pat, when Mrs. Maitland came back to the kitchen after giving the old man his two-and-threepence and telling him to leave the mug and plate on the doorstep.

"They come in waves," explained Millie, washing her hands in the scullery and coming back to the neglected baking. "About this time of year they are on their last round before they disappear for the winter. I think they must hibernate in workhouses, or whatever they call workhouses nowadays—and then in spring they come out again and take to the road."

"It must be a dreadful life," said Pat.

"It would be to us, but they seem to like it. And of course they are free of any responsibility except the next meal and enough money for a drink," said Mrs. Maitland, weighing sugar and adding it to the mixing-bowl. "Did you come for anything special, Pat, or just to see me? And where's the baby?"

"Sleeping in his pram, with Mrs. Miller keeping an eye on him," said Pat. "Oh, Mrs. M., he's got *four* teeth now, you can see them when he smiles!"

Mrs. Maitland was delighted to hear of Master Ross's progress, but she did wonder a little if Pat had bicycled to Fernieknowe simply to talk about it. But it was never any use trying to hurry people, she knew, so while she transferred the contents of the bowl to a cake-tin lined with greased paper and put it in the oven, she regaled Pat with an account of the morning's interruptions.

"First there was a man who wanted to buy false teeth, old jewellery, silver, sovereigns—and he wouldn't believe that I had none to sell him! And then it was the laundry, and then someone from the R.S.P.C.A. asking for a subscription, and then the old man—"

"And now me," Pat broke in with a rueful laugh.

"Oh, but you don't count as an interruption, Pat! I'm always glad to see you, and besides, I don't have to stop doing anything when you come," said Mrs. Maitland.

"I'm afraid you won't be so glad to see me when I tell you why I've come. It's to ask you to do something," said Pat.

"Oh, dear! What?" asked Mrs. Maitland.

With an all-too-familiar sinking feeling she listened while Pat poured out her errand. It seemed that the local Scouts and Guides (Pat had been Captain of the Guides Company until her marriage) were putting on a show before Christmas, and urgently required help with their costumes. Waving aside Mrs. Maitland's protests with a biscuit which she had taken from a tin placed at her elbow, Pat continued. This time, she said, her eyes blazing with enthusiasm, her dark hair wildly on end, *this* time they were going to do something worth while! A scene from *A Midsummer Night's Dream*—"Bottom and Titania, and we can hire the ass's head if we can't make it ourselves"—scenes from *As You Like It*, the usual camp-fire songs and country dancing, and to wind up, as it would be the Coronation next summer, a grand tableau with Britannia in the middle, and various historical and symbolic figures grouped round her. "What do you think of it, Mrs. M.?" demanded Pat breathlessly.

What Mrs. Maitland thought, apart from several things which would not bear being spoken aloud, was that if they must have Shakespeare, it would be a great deal easier to do scenes from Julius Caesar, because togas could be produced from old sheets; but in face of Pat's eager eyes she only said feebly, "Very nice, Pat, but—isn't it a bit ambitious? They are only children, remember—"

"Oh, we'll manage the acting all right—if they will only learn their words," said Pat with sublime confidence. "What's worrying me is the *clothes*."

"Well, if you want me to sew, of course I'll do it," Mrs. Maitland promised. "As long as you tell me what you want. I'll run the things up for you on the machine." Miles of machining, she felt, would be preferable to having to take an active part in the production.

But though Pat thanked her, she did not seem entirely satisfied. "The thing is, we'll need to collect stuff to make the clothes out of," she explained earnestly, taking another biscuit and biting into it with an abstracted air which Mrs. Maitland felt was unjust to the biscuits—she had made them herself, and they were very good. "Old dresses and curtains and things," she specified. "People often have lots put away that they don't need—"

"I'm sorry, Pat, but I haven't anything like that," said Mrs. Maitland very firmly. "My scrap-drawer is absolutely bare just now."

"Oh, I didn't mean that!" cried young Mrs. Ross. "You aren't the kind that hoards things—"

"Then what exactly do you want? For I can see there's something," said Mrs. Maitland.

Pat drew a deep breath. "It's—will *you* ask Mrs. Noble if she can let us have some things? I know she's got lots, because her daily woman told my Mrs. Miller that there were trunks and trunks full in her box-room! Only—no one will go and ask her—"

"Have you asked her yourself?" said Mrs. Maitland.

"I will, if you won't, but she always looks at me as if I were an untidy schoolgirl," Pat confessed. "I'm sure she wouldn't give me a *thing*! But you—"

"I really don't feel that I *can* go and ask her," began Millie. "I've never even spoken to her since that awful afternoon she came to tea! Wouldn't Mrs. Gray—?"

"Not a hope!" said Pat. "She refused point-blank, and I've tried every single person I can think of before coming here." She spoke brusquely, and Mrs. Maitland knew that she was disappointed.

"Very well, I'll go," said Mrs. Maitland suddenly. "But you realize that Mrs. Noble is pretty certain to be as unhelpful as she can, and that, once I've seen her, it's no use your going."

"Mrs. M., you really are an absolute angel!" said Pat, springing up and throwing her arms round Mrs. Maitland's neck. "It is wonderful of you! I'm sure Mrs. Noble will do it for *you*!"

Mrs. Maitland did not share this happy assurance, but she repeated that she would do her best, adding, "'Angels can do no more.'"

"Oh, it will be all right now!" Pat said blithely. "And you'll help with the sewing, Mrs. M., darling."

"I won't do anything at all if you've made me let my cake burn," retorted Mrs. Maitland, opening the oven door and peering in. "No, it's doing quite nicely—a fruit cake to send to Amabel for her birthday," she explained.

"Lucky Amabel. I say, Mrs. M., I've eaten all your biscuits! How awful of me!"

"Go home to your child," said Mrs. Maitland. "It must be almost time for his dinner. As for you, I shouldn't think you will want any lunch. That tin was more than half full." Feeling as if, much though she liked her, she could not bear another moment of her young friend's society, Mrs. Maitland almost pushed her, still mingling thanks and apologies, out of the house, and went back to her neglected jobs.

On the principle that it was always better to do a disagreeable thing quickly and get it over, Millie decided to go and see Mrs. Noble that same afternoon.

It began to rain, quietly and relentlessly, just before she sat down to her simple meal—soup, cauliflower cheese and biscuits, and apples from the garden—and, from the signs by which Millie gauged the weather, it was on for the rest of the day. Mist had come rolling low over the hills, blotting out all but their lowest slopes, and there was no wind to blow it away.

Obviously a waterproof was the only sensible wear, and Mrs. Maitland's was badly in need of cleaning and re-proofing. "I must buy myself a new one," she murmured to herself for perhaps the fiftieth time, as she pushed her arms into the sleeves. "No, Sam, you can't come. I'll take you out as soon as I get back." Trudging downhill into Mennan she felt that the rain had at least spared her the problem of what to put on. Nothing in her wardrobe, so largely home-made, was fit to be seen beside Mrs. Noble's superlative clothes, but a waterproof was almost like uniform, correct for the occasion at least, no matter how shabby.

Mrs. Noble had bought a neat little house about half a mile on the other side of the village from Fernieknowe. This she had christened "Cherry Trees", but it was still known as "Logan's" to everyone else, that having been the name of the original owner and builder. If it had ever been called anything else, the name had long since been forgotten, nor did it seem very likely that it would become known as Cherry Trees, no matter how hard Mrs. Noble tried. A fine beech hedge, now clad in its winter livery of sober russet, half hid the house from the road, and beside the gate two very small wild cherry saplings testified to the appropriateness of its name. Mrs. Maitland gave them a compassionate glance as she passed. They had the drooping air of growing things planted by someone who does not care for a garden. It seemed to Mrs. Maitland that they would not survive very long. Perhaps Mrs. Noble would put in lilacs or laburnums then, and call her house after *them*!

Shivering slightly in her streaming waterproof, she stood on a snowy doorstep and put her finger on the brightly-polished bell. There was a narrow strip of flower-bed under the windows on either side of the door which would have looked lovely filled with chrysanthemums; but probably the only flowers that Mrs. Noble admired were orchids. . . . Millie Maitland, as she waited rather impatiently for someone to answer the bell, thought that she seemed to stand on other people's thresholds on tiresome errands far too often. She had not wanted to go to Wardlaw, and she wanted even less to come here to Logan's—or Cherry Trees, as she must remember to call it to Mrs. Noble. Bother the woman, why couldn't she come to the door? Just as she pressed the bell again, the door was opened by a tall young woman in tweeds the colour of the beech hedge, long slim legs in sheer nylons and shining brown pumps as glossy as a newly-peeled horse chestnut.

"Hullo!" said this vision. "D'you want to see Mrs. Noble?" And without waiting for Millie to reply, she called over her shoulder into the warm, flower-scented hall: "Roxana! Oh, Roxana! There's someone to see you. I told you I'd heard the bell!"

"What a shattering bore!" Mrs. Noble's voice could be heard with devastating clearness, and too late Millie realized that she had arrived in the middle of a party.

"If Mrs. Noble has people here I'll come back another time," she said hastily.

"Good Lord, no. It's only a game of bridge, and we've just knocked off for tea," said the tall young woman. "Come in, and don't let Roxana worry you. She always talks like that."

Miserably conscious of her bedraggled state, Mrs. Maitland allowed herself to be led through the hall and into a drawing-room which to her dazed eyes seemed full of smart women, though actually there were only three, two strangers and Mrs. Noble herself, who came forward languidly to meet her.

"Oh, it's Mrs. Maitland, isn't it?" she said. "How dreadfully wet you are! Won't you take off your waterproof?"

"I'm so sorry," murmured Millie, looking at the dark patches made by her wet garments and squelching shoes on the white carpet. "I really shouldn't have come in when I'm so wet—your carpet—"

While Mrs. Noble was saying with chill politeness that it did not matter in the least, she was interrupted by a well-bred yell from one of her friends, who all looked to Millie alike: tall, slim, wearing beautifully-cut suits and strings of pearls.

"Mrs. Maitland!" this one shrieked. "But you're the wonderful woman who saved my father's old Border terrier when everyone said he was dying! You must be, aren't you? The dog-woman?"

Far from flattering though it sounded, Millie had to admit that she *was* the dog-woman, and found to her honest amazement that the three strangers instantly accepted her as someone of note.

"Simply too amazing with dogs!" they were saying. "Everyone *raves* about you!"

In this atmosphere, Mrs. Maitland lost her nervousness, and turned to Mrs. Noble with new composure.

"I really won't keep you a minute," she said. "If I may just tell you why I've come—"

In the fewest possible words she made her errand plain; Mrs. Noble, with her friends all exclaiming that of course she had masses of old curtains, they were sure, promised to look through her trunks and send what she could spare to Fernieknowe.

"But you'll help with the costumes too, Roxana," they urged. And to Millie: "Roxana is really marvellous about clothes, Mrs. Maitland. She could dress all your Scouts and Guides so that they look like a West End production!"

Millie doubted this very much, but did not say so, and when she left, refusing a rather lukewarm offer of tea, and laden with eager requests from the three young women to take their dogs whenever they went away from home, departed thankfully from Cherry Trees.

"Well, I *hope* Pat will be satisfied," she thought doubtfully as she walked homewards in the steadily falling rain. "She's got her material, but whether she will be so pleased when she hears that Mrs. Noble—and apparently all her friends—are going to help to dress the show, I am not so certain! I have a feeling that there is trouble ahead."

Chapter 13

November winds blew the painted glory of October from the trees, rains beat the bracken on the hillsides to a sodden dark brown. Only the spruce plantations showed deep green against the pale grass fields, and under trees to which one or two withered leaves still clung, moss was brilliant as emeralds. Mrs. Maitland, walking through a small wood with a bull-terrier on a lead, paused to admire these soft green cushions of moss, which a pale wavering sunbeam striking through the bare branches had suddenly lighted. Moments like these made November beautiful, she thought, and gave the lie to those who talked of it as a grey dreary month.

Button, the bull-terrier, an amiable but stupid beast—and what could you expect of a dog but stupidity if you saddled him with such a name?—Button gave a tug at the lead and yawned loudly. He had no opinion whatever of moss as an object of interest, its infinite variety of delicate detail, of tiny fronds like ferns, of hair-thin stems rising a quarter of an inch in height and crowned with minute bubbles which made them into green notes of music, meant nothing to him.

"All right, I'm coming," said Mrs. Maitland resignedly, wishing it were Sam who was with her and not this pink-eyed moron, good-natured though he was. Sam was always interested in his surroundings, stopped if you stopped, looked where you were looking; but Sam was out shooting with his owner to-day. Having to keep Button on the lead because of his incurable passion for chasing and if possible, killing hens, ducks, cats, sheep and cattle, Mrs. Maitland found that, by walking slowly enough to let him enjoy the wayside smells, she did not need to think of him at all. So as she went up the sheep-track between the trees, with a burn chattering over stones in the hollow on her left, she was thinking about what Pat Ross had said to her on the telephone just before she came out.

"I'm ringing up about the clothes for our show," Pat had said, in an oddly hesitant, apologetic voice. "You know you promised you would help to make them, Mrs. M.—"

"Yes, I did." How reluctantly she had admitted it, Millie remembered—and what a shock it had been when Pat went on, more hesitatingly than ever:

"Well—it was terribly kind of you, but well—I don't think we'll need to bother you now after all."

"Why, Pat? Isn't the show coming off?"

"Oh, yes, it's coming off all right, in the second week of December. But—well—Mrs. Noble seems to think she can manage the clothes without troubling you, Mrs. M. And of course you *are* very busy, and she has so little to do, and—"

"But that's splendid, Pat!" Millie had answered, trying to sound whole-heartedly pleased and to keep the hurt surprise out of her voice. "I'm sure she will do it exceedingly well. Aren't you delighted that she is willing to help you?"

"As long as *you* don't mind!"

"Mind? Of course I don't mind!" Millie Maitland had said quite convincingly.

"Oh! Well, then, I suppose it will be all right," Pat had replied, and then she had rung off before Millie could say anything more.

"There's something odd about this," Mrs. Maitland said to Button, who stared at her in blank bewilderment. She had not had a classical education, but some quotation from Latin about fearing gifts offered by the Greeks came into her mind, and she wondered just what Mrs. Noble's reason for taking on a job like making costumes for a number of the local children could be.

"Now you're just being a cat!" she said firmly, and Button stared at her again, this time with dejection in every line of his foolish good-natured face, for her voice had been sharp.

"Not you, Button," Millie added, and gave him a pat. "There's no need for you to look like that."

When they reached the upper end of the wood they went through a gate into a narrow track, overgrown with rough grass, Between high walls, and here it was safe to let the bull-terrier run free for a mile.

As she unclipped the lead and he bounded off, Millie thought, "All the same, cat or no cat, I'd like to know why Pat is so dismal about this business." And she determined to carry the oddments of material she had collected round to the Rosses' house next day, and see for herself how the land lay.

Rummaging in all the cupboards and drawers for bits and pieces took longer than she expected, as it inevitably does, and by the time she had given the dogs their walks and food, and swallowed a hasty cup of tea herself, Mrs. Maitland found that it was almost six o'clock and quite dark. The prospect of trudging down to the village and then another half-mile to the house which the young Rosses had made out of a row of three small cottages and continued to call Hillend Cottages, was not alluring; but when Mrs. Maitland saw the dimensions of the bundle she was going to carry with her, she thought that perhaps it was just as well it was dark. Even a tinker's wife, she felt, would find it cumbersome, and as to its appearance, the less said about *that* the better!

It was a cold evening, but Mrs. Maitland reached Hillend feeling hot and rather cross. If Pat had started to bath the baby she would just hand the bundle to Jack without going in and wait for another day to find out what, if anything, was worrying Pat. When she felt like this she was incapable of judging anything coolly and clear-headedly.

But it was Pat, looking flushed and agitated, who answered her ring, and said, as she peered out into the dark porch with eyes dazzled by the light: "Who is it?"

Mrs. Maitland changed her mind with the speed of lightning, and walked firmly into the hall, where she put down the bundle on a chair. Then she said, "Only me, Pat. I've brought the bits and pieces along, as there is no need for me to keep them at Fernieknowe."

"Oh!" said Pat, her clear forehead wrinkled in a perplexed frown. "Oh, that was—that was very kind of you, Mrs. M. You shouldn't have bothered, really—"

"What on earth is the matter with you, Pat?" asked Mrs. Maitland crossly. "I haven't got the plague! Aren't you going to ask me in? And anyhow, why aren't you bathing the baby?"

"We're in a—a bit of a muddle," began Pat helplessly. "Roxana's here, looking over stuff, you see—but—of course, do come in—"

"Roxana?" Mrs. Maitland's eyebrows rose.

"Roxana Noble," said Pat, flushing. "She's asked us to call her that—"

"I see. And the baby?"

Pat seemed to become her normal self quite suddenly. "Good heavens!" she cried. "It's long past his bath-time—and there's his bottle to heat, and—" As if in answer an angry wail came drifting downstairs.

"Go and bath him," said Mrs. Maitland, giving her a little push. "I'll see to his bottle and bring it up. Is that all he has?"

Pat was already flying up the stairs. "A rusk—in the blue tin—dresser—" she called over her shoulder without slackening speed.

A tinkling soprano laugh trickled from the sitting-room, followed by Mrs. Noble's voice.

"How *amusing*, Jack! Do go on," it was saying.

"Roxana at work," thought Mrs. Maitland grimly. She decided that the baby's bottle could wait for a few minutes, and picking up the disreputable bundle, pushed open the sitting-room door and marched in.

"Well, Jack," she said. "Oh, good evening, Mrs. Noble. You *have* been busy. I've brought along a few things I collected for Pat."

Glancing about her with apparent casualness, she took in the disorder of Pat's neat little room. Every chair but one was occupied by open boxes, from which streamed a motley jumble of materials of all sorts and colours. Ribbons and lace and tangled strings of beads were heaped on tables and covered the top of the piano, while trails of old curtains lay about the floor to trip the unwary.

On the only chair left empty of what looked like the last relics of a rummage sale, Mrs. Noble leaned back in charming exhaustion, her long lashes casting shadows on her rather pale cheeks.

"More remnants?" she murmured faintly. "It is really *most* kind of you, Mrs. Maitland, but, you see, we have so much—"

"Roxana has been here all day helping Pat to sort it," Jack broke in. He was hovering restlessly about the cluttered room, catching his feet in draperies and shaking them free. "I was just going to take her home. I say she has done enough for one day. Don't you, Mrs. M.?"

"Quite enough," said Mrs. Maitland emphatically, thinking it was not surprising that Pat looked so worried if she had had the little Noble woman turning her house upside down for hours on end.

"Where *is* Pat?" Jack asked suddenly.

"Putting the baby to bed, of course," Mrs. Maitland said. "It's after six, and that reminds me, I said I would heat his bottle and take it up. Otherwise I'd help you to clear up all this mess."

Then, as Jack stared blankly at her and a certain rigidity rather spoiled Mrs. Noble's pose, she went on cheerfully,

"But it won't take long if you both do it—" and hurried from the sitting-room before either could find breath to reply.

Blandly smiling, Mrs. Maitland proceeded to get his bottle ready for the son of the house and take it up the steep little stair to the room where Pat had just laid him, a rosily blinking cherub, in his cot.

At sight of his supper, he grinned, displaying two teeth, and stretched out hands like starfish to seize it. His mother and Mrs. Maitland watched approvingly while the milk went down in the bottle. Pat's face had lost its distraught expression. She gazed in adoration at her son's round cheeks as they reddened with the effort of imbibing. Only when he suddenly fell asleep over the last drain, and his hands loosened their passionate grasp, did she murmur, as she took the bottle gently from him:

"Oh, dear! I quite forgot Roxana, waiting down there with all that stuff to put away! I must hurry—"

"I shouldn't, if I were you," said Mrs. Maitland. "Just leave it to them. They can manage perfectly well without you."

"Them?"

"Well, I expect Jack's doing most of it," admitted Mrs. Maitland. "I can't quite see Mrs. Noble really getting down to a job like that."

Pat looked at her. "Mrs. M., how *could* you?" she said, and laughed, though quietly because of the baby. "How naughty of you—"

"Nonsense! Who made all that mess, I should like to know? And why is your house being turned into a shambles and not hers?"

"Now, be fair," Pat implored. "After all, she's doing it to help me, and it's difficult for me to go over to Cherry Trees, so she has to come here. Once we've looked everything over and got it sorted out there won't be so much lying about."

"I should hope not." Mrs. Maitland was unimpressed.

"Mrs. M.," said Pat, "it's been *the* most awful day! What with having to give her lunch and tea, and look after young Jack, and try to keep all that stuff in some kind of order, I could have *cried*! But what am I to do? She *is* helping me, after all!"

"Do you like having her to help you, Pat?" asked Mrs.. Maitland bluntly. Then, seeing the look on Pat's face: "There, don't tell me. I can see for myself!"

"It's all so difficult," Pat began. "You see, Jack thinks it is wonderful of her, and if I said I didn't want her, it would sound— it would seem—"

"Yes, I see. You needn't explain. But Jack—I thought Jack couldn't be bothered with her?"

"Nor he could—until she came here the other evening and was so friendly and anxious to be of use and save me trouble," Pat said miserably. "And—she *was* very nice, Mrs. M., she really *was*."

Mrs. Maitland was saved having to find an answer by the appearance of Jack, who came tiptoeing into the room.

"Asleep, is he?" he whispered. "That's fine. Pat, you'd better come down and say good night to Roxana and then I'll drive her home. She's dead beat."

"And what about Pat?" Mrs. Maitland wanted to ask, but told herself sternly to keep quiet and not make mischief. If Jack couldn't see for himself that his wife was tired out, it would not improve matters for someone else to tell him so.

"I'm just coming." Pat still lingered beside the cot, as if inviting Jack to join her, but when he turned to the door she straightened the small blankets with a gentle touch, and followed him out to the little square of landing, where Mrs. Maitland had already gone.

"When will you be back? It's just to know when to start getting supper, Jack," said Pat, putting a detaining hand on his arm.

"Oh, I'll be back in a few minutes," he said. "I'll just have to help Roxana in with some of the boxes she's taking home with her, that's all."

"Good, then I'll allow about half an hour," said Pat.

"You'll allow half an hour? Look here, Pat, what the dickens do you mean? I'm not a child to be told how long I can stay out!" said Jack with that irritability which is induced by a slightly guilty conscience.

"I only meant the *supper*, Jack!" Pat's voice was rather shaky and she took her hand from his arm as if she had been stung.

"Oh—well! I don't like to be timed as if I were an egg you were boiling," he said, trying to turn it off as a joke, but without much success.

"An egg boiled for half an hour?" Mrs. Maitland asked, and laughed. "I can't believe that Pat's cookery is as elementary as that." She was talking nonsense, and knew it, for at all costs Pat must be prevented from crying.

Jack snatched at the rope she had thrown him. "Pat's a darned good cook," he said. But Pat, with her head high, was walking downstairs.

"We'd better not keep Roxana waiting," was all she answered, and made for the sitting-room, leaving them to follow.

Mrs. Maitland longed to tell Jack that he was a great clumsy booby and had better be home within half an hour, but resisted the temptation again, with a heroic effort.

The sitting-room, she was glad to see, looked several degrees less chaotic than when she had left it. True, it was nowhere near being tidy, but at least the larger items like old curtains had been thrown in a heap into the darkest corner, and everything else had been rammed into the boxes and taken off the chairs. Mrs. Noble, who had obviously redone her complexion while they were upstairs, was now perched on the arm of a large chair, looking anything but dead beat, Mrs. Maitland thought. Her coat of soft dark musquash was draped round her shoulders, and from it her yellow hair and small, beautifully made-up face rose with excellent and no doubt carefully studied effect.

"Oh, here you are, at last!" she said. Perhaps she was speaking to Pat, but it was certainly Jack at whom she looked.

Pat, however, answered with a composure which Mrs. Maitland found admirable. "Sorry, but young Jack has his routine and it can't be hurried or shortened," she said. "I know, because I've tried, and it just doesn't work. Babies are like that."

Mrs. Noble only answered with a vague, sweet smile which somehow managed to convey that she was too frail for motherhood but would have loved to have a baby; that she admired Pat and envied her; and that to someone of Pat's coarser fibre a baby was not in the least a wingless cherub but simply a job . . . and the net result of this was to make Mrs. Maitland want quite violently to take her by her fur-covered shoulders and shake her until the little white teeth rattled in her pretty head.

The tiny silence was broken by Mrs. Noble, who yawned as daintily as a kitten, patting her mouth with a little gloved hand, and murmuring that she *was* so sorry.

Jack said, "I'll bring the car to the door, Roxana. I won't be a minute," and hastened away on his errand.

When he had gone, Mrs. Noble said to Pat: "I'm going to take some of these red curtains home to try the effect with other colours, Pat dear. I won't be able to come to-morrow, because I shall be going to the meet at Templeton Bridge, but the next day I'll be over *quite* early, about eleven, and we'll have a long, busy day. If you'll just sew up all that we cut out"—she waved a hand carelessly towards a huge pile rather apart from the rest—"then we shall really be getting on."

Pat looked dismayed at the task set her. "That's rather a lot—" she began in a worried voice.

"Perhaps you'd like me to help?" suggested Mrs. Maitland.

"That's so *very* kind of you," Mrs. Noble said swiftly before Pat could answer, "but you see, Pat and I have it all arranged. It would be difficult to explain it to anyone else. And Pat is so clever, I know she can do it—just put them together *quite* roughly, you know"—this to Pat. "We don't need fine sewing for a thing like this."

Jack put his head round the door. "Coming, Roxana? I've got your stuff in the car. Good night, Mrs. M. Be home soon, Pat."

Mrs. Noble smiled at Mrs. Maitland, gave Pat a swift peck of a kiss on her unready cheek, and swept out.

"Well!" observed Mrs. Maitland, as the car could be heard retreating from the gate. "Well, of all the—"

"I know, but that doesn't make it any better," said Pat, and burst into tears.

"It's *not* that I'm jealous, Mrs. M.," she sobbed. "I *despise* wives who are jealous, but I'm so tired. It makes such a lot of work when Roxana is here all day, and Mrs. Miller is beginning to grumble because of the mess, and having to do so much extra cleaning, and oh! I *wish* we'd never asked Roxana for an inch of ribbon!"

Mrs. Maitland did not know how to comfort her, because of course the poor child *was* jealous; all her other worries came from this, that Jack had fallen under Mrs. Noble's spell.

"Great dolt!" said Mrs. Maitland aloud, and Pat's sobs changed to hysterical laughter.

"If you m-mean Roxana!" she gasped. "I d-don't think that's a very g-good description of her!"

"Well, lets try to forget Roxana," said Mrs. Maitland. "In the first place, whatever she says, I am coming here to-morrow while she is gallivanting at the meet, to tidy some of this rubbish, *and* to sew. You can tell me exactly what to do and she won't be any the wiser."

"But it seems so awful, after I rang you up and said we didn't need you," said Pat, still sniffing dismally.

"Never mind about that—and do blow your nose, Pat, I hate to hear people sniffing—don't you see that the sooner we get the costumes made, the sooner you'll get rid of her?" said Mrs. Maitland. "Once they are finished she won't have any excuse for spending so much time here."

This had not occurred to Pat in her state of bewildered distress, and she reacted to it as Mrs. Maitland had hoped.

She dried her eyes and blew her nose, announced that she was sorry to have been such an idiot, and gratefully accepted her friend's offer to come and sew.

"I'm going home now. You'd better bathe your eyes—hot and cold water alternately is the best thing," said Mrs. Maitland practically. "And powder your nose. And if Jack's late for supper don't wait for him, but have your own and keep his hot for him."

"I will, Mrs. M.," Pat promised, and she waved good-bye cheerfully from the door as Mrs. Maitland set off on her walk home.

But Millie did not feel as confident as she had appeared to Pat. Though she was quite certain that Jack Ross was far too fond of his wife to let himself become involved with any other woman, he could hurt Pat and spoil her trust in him by a temporary infatuation such as Mrs. Noble might easily prove. Millie did not want Pat to be hurt; she did not want the Rosses' happy marriage to be clouded even slightly by something which could and should be avoided. There was enough trouble for people in life without extras of this sort she felt.

The difficulty was to know what to do. Obviously she could hardly set up as a rival to Mrs. Noble—and at the absurdity of the thought an unwilling laugh bubbled up inside her, to be followed immediately by a gust of anger against Jack, all the more violent because she really liked him so much.

"What *damned* fools men are!" she exclaimed aloud to the darkness, and was horrified to be answered by a deep voice full of mirth.

"Is that a generalization, Mrs. Maitland? Or are you thinking of any man in particular?" asked Martin Heriot, falling into step beside her.

Chapter 14

Millie gave a little shriek. "I wish you wouldn't creep up to me in the dark and give me such a fright!" she said petthishly and unreasonably.

"I'm sorry if I frightened you, but as this is the first time I have encountered you in the dark it's not fair to talk as though I made a habit of it," he protested with annoying good humour. "Besides, you were talking—"

"I was talking to myself," said Mrs. Maitland coldly.

"Bad thing to do, especially when you make the sort of remark I overheard just now."

"I had a great deal to provoke me this evening," Mrs. Maitland explained.

"You must have. I've never heard you swear before," he said, chuckling.

"Swear? Oh, dear, so I did. But it's quite true. Men *are* damned fools—sometimes."

"Of course they are—sometimes," he agreed. "So are women. Am I allowed to ask who roused you to such a pitch against men?"

"No, I don't think you are," said Millie. She spoke in her usual gentle manner, but with a firmness which he recognized as final. Her spurt of anger seemed to have died down, and he thought she walked as if she were tired.

After they had gone a few yards in silence, he said, "You're worried about something. Can't I help you?"

She shook her head, forgetting that he could not see her, and presently he spoke again.

"It's—there's nothing wrong with Amabel, I hope?"

"Oh, no, no! Thank you very much, but she is quite all right—and so am I," said Mrs. Maitland hastily. "I *am* a little worried about something, it's true, but probably I am making a mountain out of a molehill. The trouble is that if one falls awkwardly over a molehill, one can get hurt. Not desperately, of course, but enough to be very unpleasant."

Martin Heriot listened attentively to this rather breathless and muddled statement, finding that it added up to something quite sensible, as many of Mrs. Maitland's rambling remarks did.

"I rather agree with you," he said gravely. "And I am glad it is someone else's molehill that you are trying to level, and not your own. I wish you good luck with it."

"That is really kind of you, and if it *were* my own molehill, I would ask you to help me," Mrs. Maitland assured him.

They had reached the open gate beyond which the steep drive wound up to Fernieknowe.

"Will you come in for a minute? Amabel left some sherry when she was here last," said Millie.

He hesitated, for he would have liked to sit for a little by her friendly fire, but, "Not this evening, I think," he said. "You're tired, aren't you?"

"I am, rather," said Mrs. Maitland in an astonished voice.

"Ask me another time," he said. "And—don't wear yourself out with digging, will you?"

"Digging?" she echoed.

"At the molehill, I mean. Good night." And he walked off towards his own house.

Mrs. Maitland listened to his footsteps growing fainter along the road, and then went slowly up the hill. She liked him for not having asked her any more questions, and she liked him for having been considerate of her tiredness.

"He would flatten out a molehill with one bang of a spade," she thought. "He would be a very good person to go to if one needed help."

She went to bed very early that night, but her sleep was broken and restless, and she dreamed that she was digging madly at a molehill the size of a mountain with a very small trowel, while hundreds of moles with yellow hair and pretty little faces like Mrs. Noble's kept on putting back the earth she had dug away. And she woke from this with a strangled yelp, to find Sam, whose interpretation of the term "parlour boarder" was very liberal, standing at her bedside poking her anxiously with his cold nose. It was twenty minutes past three.

"It's all right, Sam. I was only dreaming," she said. "Go back to your basket."

Sam retired, and after turning round once or twice, was asleep again. But Millie remained obstinately awake, wondering what could be done to stop Mrs. Noble from hurting Pat. No solution occurred to her, and at last she switched on the light, took up the detective novel which she found the most soothing type of literature, and read until she fell asleep with her spectacles on her nose and the light burning wastefully.

Morning, which is said to bring counsel, brought none to Mrs. Maitland, except that she would have to hurry with her housework and dog-feeding if she wanted to make any time for sewing at Hillend Cottages. Fortunately Pat had no objections to the dogs, so Millie, with Button on the lead and Sam gambolling rather ostentatiously ahead, set out, feeling heavy-headed and stupid after her disturbed night.

She had barely reached the first houses in the village when Mrs. Gray, on her bicycle, overtook her and jumped off with the vigour characteristic of everything she did.

"Good morning, Millie!" she said briskly. "Now what is this I've been hearing about the Scout Concert?"

"Good morning, Davina," said Millie, pulling Button to an unwilling stop. "I don't know what you have heard—" ("But I can guess," she added inwardly.)

"Perfectly ridiculous," said Mrs. Gray. "You needn't stop. I'm in a hurry and we can talk as we go along. I am told that Mrs. Noble has taken it upon herself to act as wardrobe mistress and is refusing everyone's help. Says that she and Pat Ross can do the whole thing."

"Yes, I believe that is quite true."

"It must be put a stop to *at once*," said Mrs. Gray. "Pat has no time to do all that, with a baby to look after. Why aren't you helping? Weren't you asked?"

"Well, yes, I *was* asked," Millie admitted. "And then told—very nicely, Davina, mind—that I wouldn't be needed after all. Exactly as you heard."

"But do you mean to say you are going to leave it at that?" cried Mrs. Gray. "And let that wretched little interloper run things just as she likes? Aren't you going to do anything about it?"

"It's rather difficult—" began Millie, wishing that dear Davina would not talk so loud and so hist, wondering how in the world she could prevent her from rushing in impetuously and making matters much worse for Pat.

"I see no difficulty about it, and I am going to take steps immediately," said Mrs. Gray magnificently.

"What can you *do*, Davina?"

"I can get one or two people who aren't as weak-kneed as *you*, my dear Millie, and take them along the next time Mrs. Noble has a sewing-meeting. A sewing-meeting! I can just see it. Pat sewing like a slave and that woman lolling in an easy-chair with a cigarette stuck in her mouth." Mrs. Gray sprang on to her bicycle again. "You'd better come too," she shouted as she began to pedal on.

"No, thank you, Davina. Nothing would induce me to!" Millie shrieked after her, and thought she heard the words "weak-kneed" borne back on the chill November air.

The picture drawn by Davina of Mrs. Noble's "sewing-meeting" was so true to life that Millie could not help laughing, but she was too worried to laugh for long. Should she tell Pat of the rescue-party which was being organized on her behalf, or not?

After some consideration, which brought her to the green gate of Hillend Cottages, where Master Ross slept placidly in his pram outside the door, she decided to say nothing about it. This might be, and no doubt was, weak-kneed, but it seemed to Millie Maitland useless to disturb Pat even more. Let Davina descend upon them without warning, and she would probably rout Mrs. Noble. . . . As to the wisdom of Davina's action, she was very dubious indeed, but one might as well hope to stem the tide of molten lava flowing from a volcano in eruption, as stop Davina once she had made up her mind to do anything.

So she spent a peaceful though busy day turning the handle of Pat's sewing-machine, with a pleasant break to have a picnic lunch in the kitchen, and frequent interludes of admiring young Jack, and went home in the evening without having so much as mentioned Mrs. Gray's name.

Afterwards she blamed herself severely for this, and wished that she had told Pat, but by then the mischief was done. Besides, she could never be certain about what she ought to have done for the best, and at first Davina's tactics seemed to have borne excellent results.

It was Davina herself, flushed with victory, who came to see Mrs. Maitland and tell her what had happened.

"We just walked in," she said, flinging her gloves and scarf on to one chair and herself into another, in Millie's drawing-room. "And I said we had come to sew, as we were all members of either the Scouts' or Guides' local association, if not *both*, and—"

"Was it at Hillend?" asked Mrs. Maitland.

"Of course it was at Hillend," said Mrs. Gray impatiently. She hated being interrupted. "Catch Mrs. Noble allowing *her* precious drawing-room to be mucked about! Well, we went in, and there they were, Mrs. Noble with a cup of tea and a cigarette in a long ivory holder and Pat sewing away for dear life—reminded me of that poem by Browning or Kingsley or somebody about stitch, stitch, stitch, you know—" ("Hood," murmured Millie unheeded.) "Though it wasn't in poverty, hunger and dirt—but you never saw such a mess! We had to clear great piles of stuff off the chairs before we could sit down, and the floor was inches deep in threads and pins and snippings—"

"But, Davina, what *happened*?" almost screamed Mrs. Maitland, unable to endure the suspense any longer. "Tell me what happened, and never mind the mess!"

"I *am* telling you, if you wouldn't keep on interrupting me," said Mrs. Gray.

"You aren't! I want to know what the other two—Pat and Mrs. Noble—were doing while your party was clearing chairs and sitting down to sew!"

"Oh! Oh, well, I was just coming to that," said Mrs. Gray. "Poor Pat sort of twittered round helping to move things and saying how good it was of us to come. The little woman just sat and glared, like a thundercloud. I must say," added Mrs. Gray with the air of one making a magnanimous concession, "that we had her at a disadvantage, because she hadn't expected us. But she might have had the *savoir faire* to make me best of it, one would have thought."

"So *then* what?"

"Then I said—quite nicely, you know, Millie—that we would have come to sew long before that if only we had been asked," said Mrs. Gray. "And she threw her cigarette end at the fire— it fell on Pat's nice rug that I gave her for a wedding present, and burned quite a hole before we found where the smell was coming from and put it out—and said with that horrid little tinkly laugh of hers that she had *quite* thought it was understood *she* was running the costumes for the show and had all the help she required. And *then*"—Mrs. Gray was breathless now with her own eloquence—"*then* I said that it was absurd for two people to try to do so much when others were willing to take their share, and that it wasn't the way we are accustomed to doing things in Mennan."

"That was a broadside with a vengeance," said Millie, half horrified, half admiring. "Did it sink her?"

"I don't know what you mean, but she said that if her arrangements were going to be interfered with and upset there was nothing for her but to withdraw," Mrs. Gray said. "I told her that of course we had no intention of interfering with any work she was actually doing herself—I knew that was pretty safe, for I was sure she hadn't put a stitch into anything! And then she got up out of her chair and announced that as all her work was of an organizing and advisory nature, she could do no more. And of course, she finished up, as we did not need *her*, we wouldn't need any of her materials, and she would take them away with her at once, if Pat would be so kind as to ring up Corsar and tell him to send his taxi for her."

"Oh, no, Davina! Surely she couldn't be so mean!" cried Millie.

"Couldn't she? She was, and in five minutes off she went, with the taxi stuffed full of curtains and things. And we just turned to and did quite a lot of sewing," ended Mrs. Gray.

"How did Pat take it?" asked Millie anxiously.

"Well, she was rather shaken," admitted Mrs. Gray. "We could hear her trying to smooth things over in the hall, but she didn't manage to do it. I think once the little woman had gone, she was really relieved—and no wonder! She had far too much to do. Now we've got a proper work-party laid on. We are going to meet at Netherton the day after to-morrow, and at Miss Kennedy's early next week, and then at Hillend again. What about helping us, Millie?"

"Of course I will. You'd better come here instead of going to Pat's again," said Mrs. Maitland. "She has had more than her share already."

"Good. I hoped you would say that, and by then we should have the things more or less ready," said Mrs. Gray. "Dear me, how thirsty I am!"

"No wonder," said Millie. "I'll make us a cup of tea."

Mrs. Gray might have carried matters with rather too high a hand, but there was no doubt that she was a hard worker as well as an excellent organizer. The sewing-parties were hives of industry, and in spite of Mrs. Noble's having removed all her contributions, there seemed to be no lack of materials. Gradually the garments took shape and were completed, and each costume with all its appropriate details was laid out on the billiard table at Netherton, a useful piece of furniture now very seldom used for its original purpose.

Pat brought young Jack with her to Mrs. Gray's and Miss Kennedy's houses, where he behaved in the most exemplary fashion while his mother sewed. She appeared to be quite cheerful again, and as she said nothing about Mrs. Noble to Millie, that lady refrained from mentioning her.

But on the afternoon of the final work-party, to be held at Fernieknowe, she arrived looking pale and subdued, and Millie determined to have a word with her before she left.

"There! I think we've really done the lot!" said Mrs. Gray triumphantly at half-past five, when the last garment had been neatly folded and put into a large suitcase, already bulging. "I'll get the children along to Netherton one evening to have a grand trying-on, and then we'll be ready for the night. Thank you all, everybody."

She drove off, taking one or two of the others with her; the remainder drifted away, thanking Mrs. Maitland for her good tea, and only Pat was left, slowly putting her thimble and scissors into her chintz sewing-bag.

"Now, Pat," said Millie, "I can see that something is wrong. Do you want to tell me about it?"

"I—don't—know," Pat said, with a pause between each word, and there was a strange look in her eyes, a doubtful look, which worried Mrs. Maitland more than tears.

But she answered in as matter-of-fact a tone as she could.

"Well, don't, of course, if you'd rather not. Perhaps it's a mistake to be too confiding. I didn't mean to pry."

She made this last statement with a little smile, conscious of its absurdity, but there was no answering smile, no eager disclaimer from Pat, and a most uncomfortable silence fell, which neither seemed able to break.

At last Mrs. Maitland, feeling acutely distressed and hurt, turned and began to collect the scattered remains of tea on to the tray which still occupied a low table near the fire. After a minute Pat picked up a cup and saucer and brought it over.

"Don't bother, Pat," said Mrs. Maitland in a stifled voice. "I can manage, and I'm sure it's time you went home."

"Oh, Mrs. M.!" Pat burst out miserably, "I can't just go like this. I *must* ask you something—"

Well, thought Mrs. Maitland, anything would be better than that doubting silence.

"What is it?" she asked.

"I *must* know—was it you who told Mrs. Gray that Roxana Noble and I were doing the costumes ourselves, and got her to come and—and upset everything?"

Mrs. Maitland stared at her. "No, it certainly wasn't," she replied at once. "I don't know who *did* tell Davina, but you know how things get about in a place like this. Does it matter very much how she found out?"

"Not as long as *you* didn't tell her," said Pat. "Roxana is sure it was you, but I didn't really believe it. Only—only, when you've been at all these sewing-bees, and you knew about it, and then you didn't come with Mrs. Gray that afternoon she burst in on us, I couldn't help beginning to wonder—I feel ashamed of myself!"

"I don't know why you should be," said Mrs. Maitland honestly. "Because I did wonder if it wouldn't be a good thing to tell someone and see if we could stop Mrs. Noble making a slave of you and a pig-sty of your house. But I would never have chosen Davina. There's too much iron hand and not enough velvet glove about her methods. It may interest you to know that she called me weak-kneed for not joining her rescue squad!"

"Then you *did* know she meant to do it?"

"I knew she was going to do what she called 'taking steps'," said Mrs. Maitland, "but as I didn't know what the steps were, and couldn't have stopped her in any case, I said nothing to you. Would it have been better if I had?"

"Oh, I don't know. It's all such a mess," Pat said wearily. "Roxana is a martyr now, you see, and Jack thinks she has been badly treated, and he's furious with me for allowing it."

"I see," said Mrs. Maitland. And indeed she did see all too clearly that Davina, with the best intentions, had put a weapon, well-sharpened, into Mrs. Noble's ready hand, which the little woman had lost no time in using.

That it had been turned against herself Millie Maitland did not care. She was not vulnerable, and one could support irritation; but Pat was a different matter altogether. She could be hurt; she was hurt already, and Mrs. Maitland realized with dismay that the molehill she had spoken of to Martin Heriot was a very large one. . . .

"This is a very troublesome business," said Mrs. Maitland.

"I'm so sorry about it. I told Roxana you had nothing to do with it," said Pat unhappily.

"Good gracious, you don't suppose I care what that little woman with hair like a chicken in an Easter egg thinks about me?" cried Mrs. Maitland, and had the satisfaction of seeing a wavering smile on Pat's face.

"Now, wait. You mustn't go yet. I want to think," she went on, sitting down and pointing to another chair, on which Pat obediently sank.

There was another silence, but this time a friendly one. Pat took a cigarette and lighted it, and through puffs of smoke watched Mrs. Maitland, who appeared to have gone into a kind of sibylline trance.

"Have you any relations?" she demanded suddenly.

Pat stared at her. "Why—?" she began in astonishment, for it seemed to her that dear Mrs. M. was behaving very oddly.

"Never mind why, just tell me."

"I have an aunt and uncle in Natal," began Pat obediently.

Mrs. Maitland shook her head. "Too far," she said. "Any more? In the British Isles, for choice."

"There's Aunt Eleanor at Bournemouth—"

"That would do beautifully," said Mrs. Maitland. "Doesn't she ever ask you to go and stay with her? I'm sure she must be longing to see young Jack—"

"She has asked me, yes. I'm her god-daughter," said the bewildered Pat. "But I can't get away, of course—"

"Now that these costumes are finished you have nothing more to do for the Guide concert, have you?" asked Mrs. Maitland, pursuing her own train of thought.

"No, nothing—"

"Then you must write to your Aunt Eleanor at once—no, don't write, send her a telegram and say you want to go and stay with her and take the Baby. Poor old thing, it's a shame to neglect her," said Mrs. Maitland warmly. "You can go by night, in one of those nice new third-class sleepers, they are just as comfortable as the firsts, I'm told, and young Jack will sleep all the way, and you will have no bother at all—yes. That's what you must do, Pat."

"But, Mrs. M., I *can't*! How can I leave Jack?" cried Pat.

"Jack? It will do him a power of good to be left. It's just what he needs."

"But *now*? It would be like running away and leaving Roxana to—"

"Call it a strategic withdrawal," said Mrs. Maitland, smiling. "I don't think he will find the fair Roxana much of a substitute for you, Pat, once you're away. Besides, if you stay here you will lose your sense of values altogether. Now at a nice distance like Bournemouth you will be able to see things in their proper perspective again."

"Do you really mean it? Do you really think I should?" asked Pat.

"Yes, I really do think so. You go home and send off that telegram before you can change your mind. Promise me you will, or I'll send it for you from here!"

Pat rose and buttoned up her coat. "Very well, I'll do it," she said. "But—I hope you're right, Mrs. M. You see, it means—rather a lot to me."

"I know I'm right," said Mrs. Maitland with calm and comforting certainty.

Chapter 15

Mr. Ramsay was giving Amabel Maitland dinner at his club. The great high-ceilinged dining-room was lighted only by the mild radiance of shaded candles in silver candlesticks set on the small tables, so that the effect was of a vast space of shadowy corners dotted with little islands of brightness. Occasionally, when a coal flickered to flame in the enormous fireplace under the Adam mantelpiece, the prim rosy face of the club's founder, painted by Raeburn, swam into sight, smiling discreetly from the heavy gilt frame; but for the most part the portrait was invisible except by daylight. Georgian Silver, smooth with generations of careful polishing, winked on the glossy damask, elderly waiters moved soundlessly over the thick carpet, intent on the ritual of service. The few diners spoke in low voices, nothing so indecorous as a burst of laughter was ever heard. It was a serious business, dinner at the club, where the port and claret were fabulous and the cooking inspired.

Millie Maitland would have been overpowered by the hushed atmosphere and the almost religious devotion of the waiters. Though she appreciated good food, she preferred to eat it in gayer surroundings, and even an orchestra did not spoil her enjoyment. To her daughter, however, Mr. Ramsay's club represented the ideal place in which to be given dinner. The huge dim room, the silent service, so smooth and yet so swift, the little pool of mellow light which seemed to enclose them in a comfortable intimate seclusion—she liked it all more every time he brought her here. She felt and looked her best, she knew, and the knowledge gave her a warmth of manner which became her vastly. All her normal sharpness was discarded with the coat she took off when she entered the pillared doorway. Millie would have been surprised if she could have seen her *farouche*, difficult Amabel so like her name, smiling and appreciative of the care Mr. Ramsay took over his choice of dishes for her; and her acquaintances in Mennan, especially Mrs. Gray, would have been staggered.

It was of Mennan that the two were talking. Amabel had been home for two nights, and Mr. Ramsay was asking her how she had found her mother.

"Very well indeed, and absolutely bursting with energy," said Amabel. "She has taken to all sorts of village activities, the W.R.I., you know, and helping with some concert that the children are doing—all sorts of things that she never seemed to have time for before. I believe it is really a relief to her not to have me living at home."

Mr. Ramsay took a sip of the claret which a waiter had just reverently poured into his glass, nodded in approval, and observed, "I hope she is looking after herself properly, and not trying to live on tea and buns as I believe far too many women do when they are alone."

"Oh, no. Mother isn't like that," said Amabel. "Of course she doesn't bother with anything elaborate in the way of cooking, but she always has at least one reasonable meal a day. Even if I go down unexpectedly I never find her eating tea and buns."

She spoke cheerfully, and no one would have guessed that Mr. Ramsay's solicitude about her mother was not entirely to her liking. Even to herself she did not admit it, putting it down to selfishness in wanting all his attention. Millie made friends so easily, much more easily than she did, and this one friend she would like to keep for herself.

"Did you see anything of your farming acquaintance, that big burly fellow who came to supper that first week-end I stayed at Fernieknowe?" was Mr. Ramsay's next question.

"Martin Heriot? Oh, yes," said Amabel. "Mother is keeping a dog of his, and he comes over quite often to see him. Would you call him 'burly', exactly? He is tall, of course, and broad-shouldered, but burly always sounds rather lumpish, I think, and Martin Heriot isn't that."

"I had no intention of calling him lumpish, my dear Amabel," said Mr. Ramsay with his small wry smile. "I do not think that the adjective burly implies any such thing. But I will look it up in *Chambers's Dictionary* when I get home, and if I am wrong, I will withdraw it."

"Thank you," Amabel said quite gravely. "I haven't got a dictionary, so it would be kind of you to let me know."

Mr. Ramsay took a neat little leather-bound notebook out of a pocket and wrote in it. "Not that I am in any danger of forgetting," he explained, "but, as you know, I always make a note of anything I wish to remember."

"What have you written?" asked Amabel.

He looked at her for a moment, and then read out: "Look up 'burly' in *Chambers* and let A. know."

"Thank you," said Amabel again. "It is nice to know someone who takes so much trouble over little things like that."

"You said that just like your mother," remarked Mr. Ramsay unexpectedly.

"Did I? Mother is good at saying graceful things. I'm not."

"But she means them," he pointed out. "They are never said simply for effect."

"Oh, no! Of course they aren't," said Amabel. "That's why they are so pleasant—because she does mean them. But—somehow—I can't get my tongue round them!"

"Perhaps it would be out of character for you to make pretty remarks, Amabel."

"How dreadfully disagreeable that makes me seem," said Amabel.

"Downright, that's all," he assured her. "You don't always consider other people's feelings before you speak." Then he smiled at her hurt look.

"You brought the matter up," he said. "But I am not in the mood for lecturing you, and this isn't the time or place. When I see you on business, Amabel, I say unpleasant things to you if need be, but this evening I am your host—and your friend, I hope."

"I hope you are, too," said Amabel, recovering her composure. "This is very excellent mutton," she added, changing the subject firmly.

"I'm glad you like it. Now tell me more about Mrs. Maitland. I suppose she is busy with dogs, as usual?"

"Oh, yes. Dog Hall is living up to its name," said Amabel. "Sam is there, of course—Martin Heriot's Labrador, you know.

He is more or less a permanency. And there was a very stupid bull-terrier, and a little Cairn, and a Pekinese, just to add variety."

"Good heavens!" murmured Mr. Ramsay in a tone of horror. "It always seems to me quite incredible that your mother should be able to manage all these animals."

"You talk as if she were a female lion-tamer," said Amabel. "But I do agree that no one, looking at Mother, would ever take her for a doggy woman. However, as I told you, she is so fit and energetic that she has had time to spare from the kennels—" she broke off and looked at him rather oddly.

"Are you being mysterious, by any chance?" asked Mr. Ramsay.

"Yes, I am, and don't say it is out of character, please. I want to rouse your curiosity. You will never guess what Mother has been up to."

"Up to?"

"Yes. Up to," repeated Amabel.

"Well, are you going to tell me? I take it her activities, whatever they are, haven't put her on the wrong side of the law?" he said.

"No, she hasn't done anything illegal. But she has deliberately encouraged a young woman to leave her husband!"

"My *dear* Amabel! I sincerely hope that this is intended as a joke?"

"Well—only temporarily. I mean, the girl has only gone on a visit," said Amabel. "But it was Mother who made her go. We have a siren at Mennan, you see, a little creature, very attractive, with beautiful clothes and yellow hair—"

"And blood-red nails?" he asked, with a glance at Amabel's own shining but uncoloured ones.

"Sometimes they are blood-red, and sometimes they are purple, and sometimes almost orange," Amabel told him, and he shuddered.

"And you say this—this siren is attractive! With hands finished off at the tips like that!"

"She *is*, most attractive," said Amabel. "And she has had her claws ready to snatch any man she fancies, and to scratch any woman she doesn't."

"Ah! I begin to see. She has snatched, or attempted to snatch, the husband, and scratched the young woman you are talking of."

"You have got it in one," said Amabel. "How fast the legal brain works! But Mother happens to be fond of Pat Ross, that's the wife—she is much more the kind of daughter Mother ought to have than I am—and so she decided to put a spoke in the siren's wheel."

"Sirens don't have wheels. Your metaphors are shockingly mixed," said Mr. Ramsay.

"Never mind about that. The point is that *Mother* stepped in and foiled the siren. She told me all about it," said Amabel with a reminiscent smile, "because her conscience was beginning to bother her about it."

"Surely even your mother couldn't be conscience-stricken over a woman who paints her finger-nails purple and orange?"

"Toe-nails as well," said Amabel. "But not purple and orange together. That would be going a little too far. No, of course Mother doesn't care a bit about the siren. What was troubling her was that she was wondering whether perhaps she hadn't simply encouraged Jack Ross—I mean, empty house, no home comforts, wife and child away. It's enough to make any man seek consolation in a siren's company.

"And has he sought it?"

"The difficulty was to find that out. Even Mother could see that it would hardly do to ask Jack himself!"

"Hardly," said Mr. Ramsay drily. "But at the same time I should not have thought that there would be any difficulty in finding out whatever happened in a small place like Mennan, where everyone is interested in his neighbour's affairs."

"It's a strange thing," said Amabel, "that if one really *wants* to know about something, one never hears it being discussed. Then, you see, Mother hates gossip, and so people very seldom tell her any. She was completely stuck. She didn't dare even to ask Mrs. Gray, partly because she was afraid of starting a rumour when perhaps Jack had had enough sense to keep clear of his siren, and partly because it would have looked so odd if she, of all people, began to talk about her neighbours—oh, dear, I don't think I'm putting this very well!" She broke off with a slight frown of perplexity. "Does it make sense to you?"

"I can unravel it," said Mr. Ramsay gravely. "Go on with the story—but first, will you have pudding or a savoury?"

"Savoury, please," Amabel said promptly, and earned an approving look from her host. The chef's genius came to its finest flower in his savouries, and far too often ladies who dined at the club chose a sweet.

It was on the tip of Amabel's tongue to ask in her downright manner why Mr. Ramsay was so interested in this tale of purely local affairs. Then, remembering that it concerned her mother, she thought she understood the reason, and swallowed the question like a rather bitter-tasting pill.

"Mother was really worrying about it, I could see," she went on obediently, while the waiter flitted away to bring their savoury. "So I said I would try to find out what was happening for her."

"It doesn't fit in with my estimate of your character to try to think of you indulging in gossip, Amabel."

"No. I knew I couldn't manage it by gossiping to any of the women," said Amabel. "I never can find anything to say to them anyhow."

"What did you do, then?" he said.

"Oh, I asked Martin Heriot. It was much the easiest way. I didn't have to hedge or hint, you see. I just asked him point blank."

"Indeed?" Mr. Ramsay's eyebrows shot up.

"Mm," said Amabel, nodding.

"And did he answer your question?" asked Mr. Ramsay.

"Well—no. Not directly. He was rather sticky about it," admitted Amabel. "He wanted to know why I asked him, and said it was none of my business, and a lot of other things like that. I must say I find men very hard to understand."

"Men," said Mr. Ramsay, "find themselves at the same disadvantage where women are concerned."

"I can't see why," retorted Amabel. "Women are quite logical, except that you have to allow for sentiment sometimes."

"Quite so," said Mr. Ramsay with feeling. "But we are getting away from our original subject, which was whether the deserted husband had or had not flown back to his siren. If Heriot—quite properly, in my illogical masculine opinion—refused to tell you, how did you discover the answer? Or did you give it up?"

"There was no need for me to give it up, because of course I discovered it from Martin," said Amabel. "As soon as he began muttering about not giving young Ross away, and telling tales out of school, and all that, I realized that Jack *must* be in the siren's clutches."

"I see. That was the logical conclusion to come to, and I have no doubt you are right," said Mr. Ramsay. "I hope Mrs. Maitland is not very much distressed."

"She is, rather, but I told her to leave things alone now. I don't believe Jack Ross has really a thought to spare for any woman but Pat, and he will very soon sheer off if the siren shows her claws," said Amabel. "It's far better that he should get her out of his system while Pat isn't there to be hurt by seeing it happen, and I told Mother so."

"H'm," was Mr. Ramsay's only comment.

"I can see that you don't approve of our interference," said Amabel rather defiantly.

"I must say that I deplore your sex's passion for meddling in other people's affairs," he said. "It doesn't so much surprise me in your mother, because she lets her heart run away with her head; but I did not expect it from *you*, Amabel.'

"I had to find out, for Mother," said Amabel. "I suppose it was rather awful of me to ask Martin like that, especially as he had a fancy for the siren himself."

"The devil he had!" exclaimed Mr. Ramsay, startled out of his usual precise legal manner. "Really, Amabel! And you asked *him*, of all people! I should have thought your own feelings would have stopped you—"

"What have my feelings to do with it?"

"I thought you liked Martin Heriot."

"So I do."

"And I thought he—liked you," pursued Mr. Ramsay. Amabel, on the point of saying heartily, "Good Lord, the poor fool is crazy about Mother and hasn't the sense to know it!" caught an unexpectedly anxious glint in his frosty grey eyes, and changed her remark to a prim and colourless, "I hope he does."

"Ah, well. Shall we have coffee beside the fire in the ladies' library?" said Mr. Ramsay, and rose to pull out Amabel's chair for her.

But something seemed to have gone wrong with the evening, and even the splendid fire in the small room which they had all to themselves did not cheer things up. Much earlier than usual Amabel said she had a busy day before her to-morrow, and thought she ought to go home to bed; and Mr. Ramsay did not demur. He saw her to the door of her offices, where she lived in a neat little flat on the top floor, made certain that she had her latch-key, stood on the step until she had opened the door, and then, with a brief, "Good night," lifted his hat and walked away.

"Oh, dear!" said the efficient and logical Miss Maitland, for his retreating figure danced about in that peculiar fashion that figures do when seen through eyes full of tears.

Chapter 16

To say that Mrs. Maitland was distressed by the result of her plotting was an understatement. She was appalled when Amabel told her that, as far as she could make out, Jack Ross must be spending a good deal of time at Mrs. Noble's little house. It took all Amabel's powers of reasoning to argue her mother out of rushing straight to the telephone and ringing Pat up to summon her home from Bournemouth by the next train. Having reluctantly given her promise to Amabel that she would leave things alone, Millie's hands were tied, though she was far from being convinced that Amabel was right.

Partly with some vague unformulated idea of doing penance, partly to take her mind off, she spent the next few days in an orgy of out-of-season spring cleaning. Not only did she turn out every room in the house, but she included the kennels in her fury of scouring and scrubbing, to the great discomfort and indignation of their occupants, who infinitely preferred a slightly doggy aroma to the smell of disinfectant which now pervaded them. The only person who enjoyed it was Sam. He dashed up and down stairs, removing dusters and tins of polish, hiding brushes, and delightedly unrolling rugs which had just been rolled up. Angry spiders, which had counted on sleeping out the winter in various dark corners, found themselves rudely awakened, and scuttled madly to and fro seeking shelter; and a hibernating butterfly, dislodged from the top hem of a curtain in Amabel's bedroom, fluttered its wings feebly and died of shock.

When it was all over, Fernieknowe glittered with spotless purity, and Millie was too exhausted to care what happened to the young Rosses. This state of numb indifference would not last very long, however, and she was already wondering what to do next to take her mind off, when Mrs. Gray rang her up.

As always, she came to the point without delay.

"About the carols, Millie," she said briskly.

"Carols? What carols?"

"Good gracious, Millie!" Mrs. Gray sounded a trifle annoyed. "Surely you haven't forgotten that the W.R.I. are getting up a choir to sing carols at Christmas? You were there when I gave it out."

"Oh, yes, so I was. I remember now," Mrs. Maitland said with a guilty start, and added rashly, "but what have they to do with me?"

"Do pull yourself together, Millie! You sound half asleep," said Mrs. Gray's voice, resonant even on the telephone, and making it vibrate with her indignation. "I want you to sing in the choir, of course. Alto. You can read music, can't you?"

"Yes. At least, I used to be able to," said Mrs. Maitland. "But, Davina, I—"

The feeble protest she was about to make was ignored. "Splendid. I knew I could count on you," said Mrs. Gray. "We are having a practice to-night at the Hall, so I'll call for you at seven-fifteen, sharp. Good-bye for now."

There was a crash as Mrs. Gray slammed her instrument down, and Millie was left holding her own receiver until the voice of exchange patiently reiterating, "Number, please," recalled her to her senses. Then she said, "I'm sorry, I don't want anyone," and replaced it in its cradle.

Little though she wanted to sing carols with the W.R.I., and gravely though she doubted her ability to read and keep to the alto part, Mrs. Maitland realized with gratitude that here was something to occupy her mind. If Davina intended to conduct the choir herself, as seemed all too probable, there would be neither time nor opportunity for thinking about anything except carols.

"A blessing in disguise," she thought, as she waited at the gate that evening and heard Davina's approach, heralded by the usual lavish use of the horn and grinding of gears when the car drew up.

Unfortunately, when they passed Hillend Cottages, Jack Ross was just turning out or the drive in his car, and Davina, as she sounded the horn, said coldly, "Off to visit Mrs. Noble again, I suppose. What can Pat be thinking of, to leave him to get into mischief like this?"

Mrs. Maitland's guilty conscience stung her into replying more sharply than she usually spoke. "Surely Pat ought to be able to trust her husband enough to go on a visit, Davina. If she has to stay at home all the time to watch him, their marriage isn't likely to prove very successful—or very happy."

"I wouldn't trust St. Anthony alone with that horrid little woman!" Mrs. Gray retorted.

"You are probably making a fuss about nothing," said Millie, in a confident tone, which belied her inward feelings. "There's always so much *talk* in Mennan over the most unimportant things that happen! And you thought nothing of it when Martin Heriot was going about with Mrs. Noble, Davina."

Mrs. Gray experienced the same sort of shock that a wolf must know if a sheep were to turn and bite it. She rallied immediately and answered, "That was *quite* different, Millie, and you know it!" But she was conscious that her words, though true, were lacking in vigour and incisiveness. Before Mrs. Maitland could say anything more she went on hurriedly: "Martin is an older man, a bachelor, and much better able to look after himself than Jack Ross."

As Millie's opinion of Mr. Heriot was that he needed someone to look after him, but she was oddly reluctant to say so, she struck out in a different direction.

"All this discussion of other people's affairs is a thing I dislike very much, Davina," she said. "I do wish we could talk about something else."

Then she wondered if fire from heaven would strike her dead for daring to outface Davina Gray in this bold and unprecedented fashion.

Mrs. Gray had her faults, but she had always prided herself on being able to take plain speaking in the same spirit as she gave it. Allowing her feelings only the relief of sounding her horn several tunes as she tinned into the parking space beside the Hall, she said, "Very well, Millie. I know you don't like gossip, so I'll say no more." And on a generous impulse she added, "I daresay if everyone interfered with their neighbours' business as little as you do, there would be nothing to gossip about."

"Oh, dear!" thought Mrs. Maitland miserably, following her friend through the draughty passages which led to the Hall. "How smug I must seem to Davina, and how dull! And it isn't even true that I don't interfere!" She had a sudden longing to say to Davina's solid back: "If you only knew it, *I'm* responsible for Pat's being away. It is my fault that Jack is seeing so much of Mrs. Noble!" It would be an enormous relief even to see Davina's shocked reactions to it, but of course she could not do anything of the kind. She must suffer the alarming results of her well-meant advice alone.

Walking along deep in depressed thought, Mrs. Maitland had not realized that they had reached the door into the Hall, or that Davina Gray had pushed it open and then come to a sudden standstill, until she had collided with that lady's solid back.

"So sorry—" she murmured in a dazed voice, straightening her hat which the bump had pushed askew.

"Millie!" hissed Mrs. Gray. "Do you see who is there?"

Mrs. Maitland peered round her shoulder, and saw who was there—or at least, understood what her friend meant; for of course there were about a dozen women standing forlornly round the piano, but among them, with the new lighting turning her yellow hair to a strange orange-pink, was Mrs. Noble.

"Of all the infernal impudence! And she's not even a member! I'll soon see about this!" muttered Mrs. Gray.

But before she had taken more than one menacing stride into the big chilly hall, Millie had grabbed her by the sleeve.

"No, Davina! Stop!" she said in an urgent squeak. "*Don't* send her away!"

"Don't send her away? Are you mad?" demanded Mrs. Gray.

"If she's here practising carols with us, she can't be with Jack Ross!" whispered Millie. "You must encourage her, Davina! Think of Pat! Think if it were your own Susan's husband—"

"Consider anything, only don't cry," said Mrs. Gray unexpectedly, and was so pleased at her aptness that she nodded. "All right," she agreed. "But don't expect me to be cordial to her!"

The mere idea of Davina being cordial to anyone she disliked was enough to make Mrs. Maitland laugh hysterically.

The group at the piano heard her, and turned. Little Miss Kennedy, who had been sitting on the piano-stool, rose and came flittering, bat-like, across the floor towards Mrs. Gray.

"Ah, Davina, and Mrs. Maitland too! Both altos, are you not?" she cried. "This is indeed splendid. We have been waiting for you, and now we shall begin at once."

"I don't think I am late, am I, Beryl?" said Mrs. Gray.

"In*deed*, no, Davina! As ever, the *soul* of punctuality! It has just gone the half-hour. You see I have persuaded Mrs. Noble to join us," said Miss Kennedy happily. "She has such a good soprano that, although not yet a W.R.I. member, I felt we were fortunate to have her in our little choir."

"She can join now," remarked Mrs. Gray. "You'd better get her subscription from her to-night, Beryl, as you are treasurer." She stalked up to the piano and said a general "Good evening" to the others.

Mrs. Maitland wondered how Miss Kennedy, who was obviously in command, would ever succeed in conducting a choir which contained so formidable a personality as Davina Gray, especially Davina in her present war-like mood, restraining herself with the utmost difficulty from telling Mrs. Noble that she was not wanted.

It soon appeared that music really had charms to soothe the savage breast, and Miss Kennedy at the piano was quite different from Miss Kennedy away from that instrument. Millie, allowing her roving brain to picture the little mousy creature transformed into a dictator by going through life seated on a piano-stool, was rudely brought to her senses.

"The altos," Miss Kennedy was saying in a tone of reproof, "must really sing up."

And at the same time Davina, who had been booming away next to her, muttered in Millie's ear, "Do *sing*, Millie! You're not making a sound!"

After this Mrs. Maitland gave her undivided attention to business, and as she had a pleasing voice and the ability not only to read music but to keep to her part, the practice went a great deal better. However little they liked to admit it, Mrs. Gray and Mrs. Maitland knew that Mrs. Noble made all the difference to the sopranos. Her voice, of a slightly metallic quality which would have been harsh as a solo, sounded very well when blending with others, and she soared to the not very high top notes without difficulty.

As she stood there with her music in her hands, her pretty mouth open, showing pearly teeth and a pink tongue like a kitten's, she looked, for all her modernity, like one of Melozzo da Forli's angel-musicians; which, considering her real character, thought Mrs. Maitland, was most unfair.

Throughout the practice she continued to wear the demure look of a cat which has stolen cream and seen someone else blamed for it. And at the end, when Miss Kennedy announced that they were shaping very well, and dismissed them with a warning that there would be another meeting early in the following week, Mrs. Noble's complacency was explained.

"I hope," said Mrs. Noble, "that we are not singing our carols on the night of December the fifteenth, because if so I shall not be there. It's the date of the Hunt Ball, you see." She spoke in her clear tinkling voice, but it rang like a challenge in the ears of Mrs. Maitland and Mrs. Gray.

Under the buzz of comment which greeted this announcement, the eyes of these two ladies met, full of foreboding, and the words "With Jack Ross, of course!" shimmered on the air between them until Millie was surprised that they were not audible and visible.

Miss Kennedy, reduced to her normal twittering self, piped up, "Then your husband will be home in time for it, Mrs. Noble? Really, how delightful!"

"Oh," said Mrs. Noble, negligently. "No, Miss Kennedy, I don't think Arthur will be here until several days after the ball. His ship is due on the thirteenth, but he will have to go and stay with his old mother before he comes north."

Millie Maitland's heart, which had soared at Miss Kennedy's question, sank again until she felt it must be somewhere in the soles of her shoes. It was quite obvious to her that Mrs. Noble would be going to the Hunt Ball with Jack Ross. Something, she thought vaguely, would have to be done about it, but at the moment she was quite unable to think what. All she wanted was to go home and creep into bed with two hot-water bottles and a "whodunit".

For a wonder Davina evidently felt the same. She was saying: "Let's get out of here, Millie. I can't bear to stay in the same room as that poisonous little reptile any longer!"

They drove home in silence except for Davina's horn, until they reached the gate at Fernieknowe. Then Mrs. Gray said, "You know, Millie, Pat really *ought* to come home."

"Yes, I know. I think so, too," Mrs. Maitland replied. "I will write to her to-morrow."

She went to bed with a heavy heart, blaming herself more than ever. What a mess and muddle she had made by her efforts at putting things right! If Mrs. Noble went to the ball with Jack Ross the whole neighbourhood would be talking about it, for it was too blatant to pass unnoticed. In a place like Mennan young husbands did not escort other men's wives to the Hunt Ball, the social highlight of the year. Of course Pat could put a stop to it by coming home. Mrs. Maitland was sure that Jack would never think of going and leaving her; but then, Mrs. Maitland did not want Pat to come home and find that he had arranged to go to the ball in her absence. Why was Mrs. Noble's tiresome husband lingering with his mother when he ought to be here looking after his wife? Once again Millie spent a broken night and rose in the morning unrefreshed, and with the letter which must be written to Pat hanging over her.

It took a long time to write, and when at last it was finished, Mrs. Maitland was not very pleased with the result. She had not mentioned the ball, hoping that something might happen even now to prevent Pat from knowing. She said that she thought Jack had been left alone for long enough, and that Pat had better come home before the trains were too crowded with Christmas holiday traffic. It was a dull letter, but it would have to do. Millie stuck down the envelope and stamped it, put Button on his lead and called Sam, and rushed out to post it before she could change her mind about it.

Coming back she met Martin Heriot, who turned to walk with her.

He seemed rather distrait and had less than usual to say for himself, but Millie in her present mood had no heart to speculate about this as she would have done normally.

It was with extreme surprise, therefore, that the cause for his constraint was revealed when he blurted out, very red in the face: "I've got a couple of tickets for the Hunt Ball. Would you—I suppose you wouldn't—would you come to it with me?"

"Oh, no!" cried Mrs. Maitland, to whom the mere sound of the words "Hunt Ball" was unwelcome. "I mean—thank you *very* much for asking me, but I'd rather not." An idea sprang into her head, and without giving herself time to think, she added impulsively, "Take Mrs. Noble instead. Oh, *do* take her!"

"But I don't want to take her," he said, annoyed. "In any case she couldn't come with me. I got a couple of tickets for her and her husband. She asked me to."

"Her husband!" Millie laughed bitterly. "It's Jack Ross she's going with—"

"But that's nonsense. I had to give the names to the secretary, they are very sticky about that, and I certainly gave them as Mr. and Mrs. Noble. She couldn't possibly be going with Jack. How on earth did you get hold of such an idea?" he asked.

"Well—" now that Millie came to think of it, she suddenly realized that she had no proof at all that Mrs. Noble *was* going with Jack. It had been no more than a suspicion in her mind and Davina's, which dread had made a certainty. So much for womanly intuition. Millie felt a fool.

"Well—" she said again, and remembered. "Mrs. Noble said, last night at the choir practice, that her husband wouldn't be here in time for the ball."

"That doesn't mean she is going with Jack Ross," he said, putting his finger on the weak spot at once. "No, you're barking up the wrong tree there. If her husband isn't going, she won't be. The ticket is for a couple, and has their names on it."

"Then why do you suppose she led us to believe that Jack Ross was taking her? She really wanted us to think that," said Millie.

He smiled. "Feminine spite, I expect. She knew it would cause a flap among the Mennan ladies—and you see, she was right."

"How queer. Imagine *wanting* to make people dislike you," Millie murmured. "But I *am* glad it isn't true!" She turned a face radiant with relief, to look up at him. "I was so afraid—what an idiot I am! Please forget what I said, will you?"

"All right. But will you go with me?"

"Oh, no, I couldn't. If you really want a partner, why don't you ask Amabel? She could easily get down for it. I haven't got a dress," said Millie. "Honestly, I would much rather not—"

As if a woman of my age wants to go gallivanting off to balls, she thought. It would be different if Maurice were alive and *we* were taking Amabel. But to go with Martin Heriot—the mere idea was absurd—and to have to squander money she had not got on a dress, gloves, evening shoes . . . ! And she added aloud, "Early to bed with a cup of Ovaltine and a book is much more my line, let me tell you!"

"Do you think Amabel would like to go?" he asked rather gloomily.

"Yes, I am sure she would. She doesn't get enough light relief from her job—and she happens to be a beautiful dancer," said Amabel's mother fondly.

"I'll write and ask her, then," he said, without enthusiasm.

"Yes, do. I'll give you her address."

"Oh, I've got it, thanks," he answered, and even his subdued manner could not take away Mrs. Maitland's pleased surprise at this piece of news, which seemed to her the most hopeful sign of their mutual interest in one another she had yet seen.

She said good-bye to him with a warmth induced by her almost motherly feeling towards him, and then, as he walked away, hoped she had not been gushing. It was really very difficult, dealing with reserved creatures like Amabel and Martin Heriot....

"I wonder what Mrs. Noble will do about a partner for the ball?" she said to Davina, on whom she had called at Netherton some days later to assure her that they had been mistaken about Jack Ross and the little woman.

"She'll get some fool to go with her, you may be certain," was Mrs. Gray's curt reply. No one likes to be made a fool of, and she liked it even less than most.

"As long as it isn't Jack Ross," Millie said peaceably. "Pat will be home on Saturday, Davina. I had a letter from her this morning."

"I wonder if she and Jack are going to the ball?" said Mrs. Gray, instantly diverted, as Millie had hoped she would be.

"I think they are. Martin Heriot is taking Amabel, and they may join up and all go together," said Mrs. Maitland, and awaited a candid expression of Davina Gray's astonishment.

It bubbled out of her at once, irresistibly, like water welling up in a spring. "Martin and Amabel! Well—that *is* a surprise, I must say, Millie! I didn't realize he knew her well at all. And so he's taking her to the ball, is he? *Well!*"

Then she added hastily, to cover up her amazement: "No reason why not, of course, Millie. I didn't mean that. Only somehow, one never thinks of Amabel at a ball."

"I know," Millie said calmly. "It would be a very good thing if she went out more often, and she is extremely fond of dancing."

Mrs. Gray wanted to know what Amabel was wearing, and Millie was able to tell her that Amabel had bought a very well-cut black dress for the occasion, also long black gloves, and that she was going to wear gold shoes.

Satisfied on this point—had she been expecting to be told that Amabel was going to the hall in a tailor-made suit, Millie wondered?—Mrs. Gray nodded her approval. "I'm sure she will look very distinguished," she said. "Oh, must you go already, Millie? And I hope she and Martin have a really good time."

Mrs. Maitland, half-way to the door, thanked her friend sedately and said she was sure that they would.

"Be *sure* to find out from Amabel who that horrid little Mrs. Noble goes with, and let me know," was Mrs. Gray's last earnest remark. "Though I *hope* she won't be there at all!"

Millie laughed, promised, and set off on her walk home over a road ringing with frost. She was quite certain that Mrs. Noble would find a solution to the problem of a partner for the ball; and at the same time thought that far too much importance was being given to this, which was, after all, only a dance. Nothing else seemed to be talked of just now, and she herself had behaved as if it were a matter of life or death that Pat Ross should come home to go to it with her husband.

"One really ought to have some sense of proportion," she told herself severely.

Chapter 17

Yet when Amabel arrived on the afternoon of the ball, displaying merely a composed pleasure at the prospect, her mother was unreasonably irritated.

"Aren't you glad to be going, dear?" she asked as they sat lingering over a final cup of tea by the fire.

"Of course I am, Mother, or I shouldn't have told Martin I would go," replied Amabel, opening her fine eyes more widely than usual at Mrs. Maitland's tone. "But surely you don't expect me to be in a girlish flutter about it!"

The thought of Amabel in a girlish flutter about anything made Millie laugh a little, and give up the attempt to find out if her daughter felt any of the excitement she refused to display about going to a dance with Martin Heriot.

When Amabel, looking tall and extremely elegant in her new black dress, had driven off with her escort, Mrs. Maitland sat by the fire, feeling most unaccountably like Cinderella. In vain she reminded herself that she had been asked and had refused because it was so much more fitting that Amabel should go. Her toes twitched with longing to be skimming over a shimmering expanse of shiny parquet once more. Even the tunes she had danced to in the nineteen-twenties, forgotten for all these years, went tinkling through her head with maddening persistence. "For I'm just wild about Harry," she hummed, almost feeling a man's arm round her waist, a man's hand holding hers. Maurice's, it should have been . . . but Maurice did not fit into the picture any longer. Even his gay, easy-going ghost seemed to be laid for her now.

"Why, you silly elderly *fool*!" exclaimed Mrs. Maitland, jumping up and alarming tie peacefully slumbering Sam by her violence. "You ought to be ashamed of yourself. Go to bed at once!"

Scolding herself with rather unnecessary severity, she had a very deep hot bath, piled up her pillows behind her, and settled down to read until she felt sleepy. The book, which was a light-hearted Regency romance, full of snuff-boxes, high play, pairs of blood-chestnuts and lovely young women, did not seem as amusing as she had hoped, though it was by one of her favourite authors, and in that author's best vein. She envied Sam, curled up in his basket and dreaming, to judge by his twitching toes and small strangled yelps, of the chase. It must be wonderful to be a dog, with that capacity for sleep, untroubled by the tiresome thoughts and useless wishes that kept poor humans wakeful. Even the recollection that Amabel would probably be annoyed if she came home and found her mother awake, as if waiting for her, could not send Millie to sleep. She dozed uneasily, the book slipping from her hand, only to be wakened by her reading-lamp; she read a few quite meaningless sentences and dozed again. . . .

"Mother! Are you awake?" Amabel's voice, Amabel's face, unusually animated, peeping round the door which she had gently opened, brought Mrs. Maitland to her senses with a sudden start. The book slid to the floor, and Sam got up, shook himself, and yawned reproachfully.

"Oh, Mother! I believe you were asleep, but your light was on, so I thought I'd look in." Amabel did not sound cross, Millie thought with relief. She did not know that her strangely defenceless look, as she drooped among the pillows, with the light shining on her tired face, had moved Amabel to unwilling tenderness.

"No, I'm not asleep, dear. Did you have a good time?" asked Millie, sitting upright.

"Lovely, thank you. I've made some Ovaltine. Will you drink a cup if I bring it in here?"

It seemed very cosy to Mrs. Maitland to be sipping her hot drink, with the electric fire wastefully blazing, and her daughter perched on the arm of a chair telling her about the ball. Often and often she had pictured a scene like this, but never before had Amabel been willing to play her part in it.

Now, however, she answered her mother's questions readily, and added comments of her own.

"Oh, yes, Mrs. Noble was there, with a young cousin of her husband's, down from Oxford," she said. "I suppose that's how she got over the difficulty of the tickets, because of course this young man's name is Noble, too. Martin was furious about it!" She laughed. "I must say I thought it was rather clever of her—"

"I knew she would manage it all right, somehow," murmured Millie. "And the Rosses, Amabel? Did Pat look nice?"

"I've never seen her look so well," said Amabel. "Sort of cloudy dead-leaf brown, she was wearing, with *miles* of material in the skirt. . . . It made her hair shine and her skin as white as milk. She really was lovely, Mother, and Jack was absolutely doting!"

Amabel's voice, as she said this, held none of its customary scorn for what she scoffed at as "sickly sentimentality". It was half-laughing, but wholly indulgent.

"I *am* glad," said Mrs. Maitland, with a sigh of heartfelt relief, "I'm very fond of Pat, and I have been so worried about her and Jack."

"Well, you needn't be, any more," Amabel assured her. "I wish you could have seen them to-night, dancing together. I believe, you know, that you were very wise to tell Pat to go away. I'm sure Jack missed her and is more in love with her than ever now she is home again." Then she glanced quickly at Mrs. Maitland, who was staring with a rapt expression at the thin curl of steam rising from her cup.

"Don't let success go to your head, Mother," she said. "I mean, you were lucky this time. It mightn't work if you tried it again."

With immense dignity her mother said. "It was hardly *luck*, Amabel, I mean, my judgment—"

"Judgment, my foot! You know very well it was luck and you've been on pins and needles in case it went wrong!"

"Well, dear, we won't discuss it. Tell me what Mrs. Noble was wearing and if she looked nice," said Mrs. Maitland.

"Mother, you *are* funny when you're being dignified—your chin goes up in the air, and your eyebrows climb away up too, until they nearly disappear in your hair!"

Not even her pleasure and surprise in Amabel's new mellowness could prevent Mrs. Maitland from feeling indignant at this remark.

"I daresay," she said coldly, and suddenly realizing that she had jerked her chin up as she spoke, stuck it down again until it was in her neck.

"Oh, don't do that!" Amabel was laughing openly. "It looks rather sweet when you stick it in the air!"

"I can't think what has come over you to-night," complained her mother.

"Perhaps it's the champagne, though I only had one glass," said Amabel. "Or perhaps Mr. Ramsay is right. He told me, the last time I saw him, that I was *mellowing*, and that I was one of the people who mature rather late. He was quite as serious about it as if he were discussing claret laid down by his Club! Do you think that's it, Mother?"

"I really *can't* think at four o'clock in the morning, and if you aren't going to tell me about Mrs. Noble you'd better go to bed!" exclaimed her exasperated parent.

"I *will* tell you. I mean to tell you, but you mustn't rush me! You know you want to hear, if it's only to pass it on to Mrs. Gray!" cried Amabel, putting down her empty cup on Mrs. Maitland's dressing-table, and stretching her long bare arms above her head with a yawn. "Goodness, how sleepy I am! Well, you will be rejoiced to know that Mrs. Noble was in girlish white tulle, and did *not* look her best. White doesn't suit her, which is odd, with her yellow hair, but it doesn't. I'm not being catty, and of course it was a beautiful dress, only somehow instead of making her look young and innocent, it just made her more serpentine and predatory than ever. You could see the young cousin was fascinated by her. A lot of people were wondering if she would make a dead set at Jack, and upset Pat, and she did give him a sort of smile that *hinted* things—you know what I mean. Pat saw it, she was meant to, of course, and do you know what she did? You'll never guess—"

"Well, tell me, tell me! Don't keep me waiting," said Mrs. Maitland breathlessly.

"She went straight up to Mrs. Noble," said Amabel, "and said—not loudly, but so that everyone round about could hear—'It was so kind of you, Roxana, to keep my husband from being too bored and lonely while I was away seeing my godmother. He told me how good you had been to him. Thank you very much.' Talk of spiking people's guns, or taking wind out of sails, Mother! You know, for a moment I was almost sorry for Mrs. Noble. She couldn't think of a thing to say, and after Pat had smiled and turned away, she was still speechless."

"I think that was wonderful," said Millie dreamily. "I would never have believed that Pat could have done it. That has certainly settled Mrs. Noble as far as Jack is concerned."

"It was the high spot of the whole evening," Amabel agreed, and uncoiled herself from the chair-arm. "I *must* go to bed, and leave you to get some sleep, Mother."

"But wait just a minute, Amabel! You haven't told me how you enjoyed it, or who you danced with, or anything!" cried Mrs. Maitland.

Amabel had reached the door, and paused there on the point of opening it. "Yes, I did enjoy it. I had a very good evening," she said.

Mrs. Maitland made one more attempt to detain her. "Does he—Martin Heriot—dance well?"

"Fairly, nothing great. He's like a good many hunting men, a bit apt to take you round as if you were a horse he was putting at a difficult jump," said Amabel. "But I danced with lots of other people, Mother. Your child wasn't a wallflower."

"I didn't expect you to be," Said Millie.

Amabel opened the door, yawning openly. "I will say that Martin looks after one very nicely, she said. "Good night, Mother, or rather, good morning. Do go to sleep now."

The door shut gently but firmly behind her. It was quite plain that she was not going to tell her mother anything more.

Millie, in spite of her relief about Pat, fell asleep feeling vaguely dissatisfied. Amabel, though she had been so much gentler and more confiding than usual, had not let her know the most important thing of all in Mrs. Maitland's estimation. She left for Edinburgh after a late breakfast without giving any clue as to her feelings about Martin Heriot, but with a promise to be home on Christmas Eve for a few days.

"I'm afraid I shall miss your carol singing. What a pity," she said, as she kissed her mother good-bye. "I hope it will go very well and be a great success."

"I hope so," said Millie in a rather dispirited voice. "We are practising hard enough."

Amabel looked at her, seemed about to say something, changed her mind, and left to catch her train.

"Now *why*," said Mrs. Maitland aloud, while she drifted about the house dusting and tidying before going out with the dogs, "*why* couldn't I ask Amabel about herself and Martin Heriot? I could ask Pat anything, but when it comes to one's own only daughter, it seems that a mother is afflicted with dumbness!"

Chapter 18

The last few days before Christmas were spent, by all except the provident few who are always well organized, in frantic buying of presents and cards, in discovering that they had, as usual, forgotten someone, in tying up parcels and standing in queues in the village post office to send them away, and in untying parcels which arrived for them at all sorts of odd hours, "postie" being "fair run off his feet wi' the Christmas rush".

Mrs. Maitland attended the final choir practices, made a handsome cake stuffed with the fruit which she had been slowly accumulating for several months, and covered it with almond paste and royal icing. She had few people to give to, and little money to spend on them, so they did not present any great problem. For Amabel she had two pairs of nylons and a book which she knew her daughter wanted, and she had knitted a pair of gloves for Davina Gray, a coat for the Ross baby, and socks tor Mr. Ramsay. She had never given Mr. Ramsay anything at Christmas before this year, but somehow after his having stayed at Fernieknowe she wanted to. She would have liked to knit a pair of socks for Martin Heriot, but decided against it. If Amabel liked to give him a present, that was a different matter, and much more suitable. Mrs. Maitland wondered if Amabel *had* bought him something, and if he had a present for Amabel.

It was the evening of the carol singers' final performance, if performance were the proper word for singing in church. They had sung at a special meeting of the W.R.I., and at the carol service in the Parish Church; and now they were to sing in the little Episcopal Church with its battered tin roof, on which heavy rain fell as noisily as a shower of gravel.

Mrs. Maitland had refused Davina Gray's offer of a lift because she said it was such a beautiful night that she would enjoy the walk to Mennan. This was the truth, but not the whole truth. Davina, since the Hunt Ball, had been showing so much interest in Amabel, and her conversation so succeeded in linking her name and Martin Heriot's, that Mrs. Maitland felt she could not bear another dose of it just yet. When Amabel came for Christmas, the day after to-morrow, perhaps she and Martin would settle their affairs one way or another, and then, thought Millie, Davina may talk about them until she is hoarse, and welcome. But of course, once there was an engagement, she probably wouldn't want to talk about it, for it would have lost all its speculative interest.

For herself, Millie was sick of speculation. She felt restless and unsettled as she locked the front door and put the big key in the pocket of her tweed overcoat, which it weighed down in a fashion ruinous to the hang of this garment.

The night was very cold and still, and brilliant with stars. Mrs. Maitland hurried down the hill into Mennan, clasping her music and Davina's present wrapped in holly-sprinkled paper. There was no sound except her own footsteps on the road. The infinite remoteness of the myriad pinpoints of light so far above, each wheeling in its appointed orbit, seemed to reproach her for worrying over her little troubles. Usually she found the thought of all these other worlds rather frightening, but this evening their calm indifference was a comfort. Suddenly she felt sure that everything would be all right; there was no need to reason it out, she simply knew it, and in this mood of faith she reached the church and slipped quietly into her place among the choir, next to Mrs. Gray.

The little church was full. Not only was there a good turnout of its own small congregation, but friends who belonged to the Parish Church had come as well to hear the carols. After the service people gathered in groups outside, exchanging greetings, telling one another how much they had enjoyed the singing, and what their plans were for Christmas. Mennan showed its friendliness to the greatest advantage on such an occasion, and in spite of the cold air Mrs. Maitland felt warm and cheerful while she talked to her neighbours.

Finding herself beside Mrs. Noble, who was muffled in a fur coat and had her hand tucked through the arm of an exquisite young man with an air of weary suffering, Millie spoke to her in her friendly way, in case she might be feeling a little out of things.

Mrs. Noble introduced the young man as her husband's cousin who was spending the Christmas vacation with them, and turned to answer some remark addressed to her.

This left Mrs. Maitland and the gorgeous youth staring at each other in silence until, feeling that she ought to say something, she asked rather timidly, "How did you think the altos sounded?"

"*Were* there any altos?" he drawled in languid amazement, and moved away, leaving her feeling like a pricked balloon.

"Well!" said Mrs. Maitland aloud, divided between mortification and laughter. "Well, really—"

"Insufferable young brute!" growled the voice of Martin Heriot close at hand. "What he needs is a kick in the pants—and how I'd like to be the one to do the kicking," he added with a wistful note in his voice.

"I'm afraid you will have to deny yourself the pleasure," said Mrs. Maitland, now laughing outright. "This is hardly the place, is it? Besides, it's Christmas-time. You must let him off. He is very young and probably thought he was being clever."

Martin Heriot cast a longing glance at the young man's elegant back view, and then turned to Mrs. Maitland.

"How are you getting home?" he asked.

"Walking. Davina Gray offered to drive me, but I wanted to walk. It is a splendid night, isn't it?"

"I'll walk home with you," he said. "Let me take your music."

Mrs. Maitland handed over the bundle of paper-covered music, rather dog-eared now after all their practices, and they walked away along the village street.

They did not talk, but he was a silent person, and Mrs. Maitland did not find it necessary to make conversation. She walked beside him, with the tunes of the carols she had just been singing still following each other through her head, and was considerably surprised when he said haltingly:

"I'm in a bit of a fix. I was wondering if you could help me out—"

"Of course I will, if I can."

"Well," he said, more slowly than ever, "I want to ask someone to marry me, and I don't know just how to set about it. I'm not sure what she feels, you see."

Mrs. Maitland's heart gave a funny little jump. Dancing with Amabel at the Hunt Ball had evidently brought him to this decision. She answered in her quiet way, "I think, really, the best thing to do is to ask straight out, and not beat about the bush."

"Do you?" he said. "Do you? I'm glad of that. Will you marry me, Millie?"

Mrs. Maitland's feet continued to carry her forward quite mechanically, but her head was going round and round and her brain seemed unable to make sense of what he had said.

"Will you?" he repeated, taking her nearer arm in a gentle but firm grasp. "You must have guessed, surely, how I feel about you, Millie?"

Forced by his hold to slow her pace, Mrs. Maitland found enough breath to gasp out, "Certainly *not*!" and added wildly, "I never heard of anything so—so ridiculous in all my life!"

"There's nothing ridiculous about it," he said, and she thought she could detect a slightly amused tremor in his voice. "Why do you suppose I've been coming to Fernieknowe so much all this last year?"

But the misery of remembering that she had innocently imagined Amabel to be the reason for his visits almost overwhelmed Millie. "Don't say any more!" she cried through the choking sobs that constricted her throat. "You make me feel *sick*!"

She had hurt him now, she knew, and felt the savage pleasure which the gentlest creature knows when roused by its own pain. His hand dropped from her arm.

"If that is the case, I'd better leave you," he said. "Good night."

He walked away quickly, and Millie stood listening to his footsteps growing fainter along the iron-hard road. She was so completely shattered that she still felt nothing but the satisfaction of having hurt him, and this hot glow carried her home so fast that she was almost running. It was while she stood on her familiar doorstep, panting and fumbling for the key in her pocket, that the fine warmth of rage suddenly left her.

Tears were blinding her as she got the door open at last, and crept into the dark house, pushing away Sam, who had rushed to welcome her. What a fool she had been, what a thick-headed, dull-witted *fool*! It was interfering again that had caused this even though her interference had not gone beyond wishful thinking. Had not Amabel warned her not to play providence, in case her luck did not hold? Poor Amabel, who had never so much as looked twice at a man until she had met Martin Heriot. . . . And of course he had every excuse for thinking that she, Millie, had encouraged him; she *had* encouraged him, though it was for Amabel's sake.... How sordid the "eternal triangle" drama was when the characters were one man and two women, and the women were mother and daughter!

With all this churning confusedly in her aching head, Mrs. Maitland switched on the light in the kitchen and sank into the comfortable sagging embrace of her old basket chair.

What was to be done about Amabel, who must never, never know that Martin Heriot fancied himself to be in love with her mother! "I don't know *what* to do!" said Mrs. Maitland aloud, the slow hot tears dripping on to her coat, which she had forgotten to take off. "I don't, indeed! I hope I shall never have to speak to that wretched man again—and oh! he's gone off with my music!"

This trifle, in her overwrought state, was the very last straw to her burden, and she cried until she could cry no more, while Sam whimpered unhappily, at a loss to know what had happened to her.

Sam! He must go now, of course. It was quite impossible for her to keep him any more. She would ring up Wardlaw and tell Mrs. Wilson that Mr. Heriot must make other arrangements for his dog at once. What the house would be without him now she dared not allow herself to think.

The telephone roused her from her dreary brooding over Amabel's unhappiness and her own loss of Sam, and she went out of habit to answer it. Only when she had lifted the receiver did it occur to her that it might be Martin Heriot at the other end of the line. It was not. In a way it was almost worse, for it was Amabel....

"Good evening, dear," said Mrs. Maitland in a hoarse croak which she hardly recognized as her own voice. "How are you?"

"I'm all right, thanks, but *you* sound queer," replied Amabel, whose ears were sharp. "Have you got a cold?"

"Oh, no, dear. No. The—the line must be bad, or perhaps it's just all that carol singing," said Mrs. Maitland, improvising rapidly.

"Oh, good. Listen, Mother. I've just discovered that Mr. Ramsay is going to be all alone over Christmas, so I wondered if I might bring him down with me to Fernieknowe?" Amabel sounded oddly diffident. "I know he'd love to come."

Mrs. Maitland, suddenly realizing the advantage of having a third person with them to act as a buffer state in her distraught condition, said as heartily as she could, "Yes, do ask him, Amabel. Christmas is no time to be all alone."

"I wondered if you'd ask Martin Heriot round for a drink on Christmas Eve? We'll arrive in time for tea, and—"

"NO!" cried Mrs. Maitland violently before she could stop herself.

"But, Mother, why not?" asked Amabel's voice in astonished tones.

"I'm sorry, dear. I didn't mean that for you. I was—I was speaking to Sam," said her distracted parent, lying like a trooper out of desperation.

"Oh, I see. Well, will you ring Martin up?"

"He's sure to be going out somewhere already," objected poor Mrs. Maitland, torn between distress at Amabel's calm confidence and rage at her quite reasonable suggestion. "I don't think he—"

"No harm in asking him. He can only refuse," Amabel said blithely. "But I think he'll come."

This was too much for Mrs. Maitland. "There are the pips, dear," she said hastily. "Good night!" And she put me receiver down as if it were red-hot. When Amabel arrived, she would have to pretend she had been too busy to remember about asking Martin Heriot, she decided. She really felt that she could not endure to speak of him any longer to a blissfully ignorant Amabel.

A letter, which had evidently been dropped in by hand, lay on the mat inside the front door the next morning, and Sam, who loved to feel useful and important, brought it to her with pride.

Mrs. Maitland took it from him and opened it listlessly. It was from Martin Heriot, and was very brief.

> "I hope you will keep Sam," it began, without any preamble. "His home is really with you, and it seems a pity that he should be unhappy. Yours, Martin Heriot."

For an instant, looking down at the satin-smooth black head and the kind intelligent eyes, Mrs. Maitland weakened. Then she shook her head. If only for Amabel's sake, Sam would have to go. He could not stay here to be a continual reminder of his owner. She went straight to the telephone and asked for Martin's number in a steady voice.

It was the housekeeper, Mrs. Wilson, who answered, and on Millie's asking for Mr. Heriot, informed her that "the master" had left by the early train and would not be back before the New Year. Millie, feeling that every man's hand was against her, asked without much hope whether Mrs. Wilson could undertake to look after Sam. But no, Mrs. Wilson was very sorry, she would like fine to oblige Mrs. Maitland, but she was going home herself, and the house would be shut up, and she wished Mrs. Maitland a merry Christmas and a happy New Year.

"The same to you, Mrs. Wilson," said Millie automatically as she replaced the receiver. A merry Christmas indeed! The irony of it! When she remembered her calm certainty of the evening before that everything would be all right, she could have screamed with hysterical laughter.

On one thing she was determined. Amabel's Christmas should not be spoiled. Amabel was to have if not a merry, then at least a quietly happy Christmas. Later on, Millie thought, she could write and tell her in a discreetly veiled way, that Martin Heriot was not likely to marry. She could do something, but not now, not yet. So as she made Amabel's room and the spare bedroom ready, she practised laughing gaily, until a passing glimpse in a mirror of her pale face twisted into a Medusa-like smile decided her to leave it alone and hope she would feel more her normal self by the next day.

Unfortunately it is only the very young who can cry themselves sick and spend two miserable days and almost sleepless nights without showing very marked traces of it. The lines on Mrs. Maitland's little round face were unobtrusive as a rule, but the afternoon of this Christmas Eve they were deeply engraved, and the shadows under her eyes looked like bruises. Her rosy colour had faded; even her hair had lost some of its springy curl. She tried the effect of a little rouge, but it stood out in patches over her cheekbones, and in the end, thinking it only drew attention to her shadowed eyes, she rubbed it off again.

If Amabel had seen her first by day she would have been horrified, but it was dark when she and Mr. Ramsay arrived, and as Mrs. Maitland had wreathed the electric fittings in holly and ivy the light was dimmer than usual. Even so she exclaimed as she kissed her mother:

"You've been doing too much! I can see that."

"There has been a lot of to-ing and fro-ing lately, with the carol singing and W.R.I. Christmas party," said Mrs. Maitland, her pale cheeks flushing slightly. "Don't fuss, dear." And she turned to greet Mr. Ramsay with friendly warmth.

There was a difference in Mr. Ramsay, hard to define but quite easy to recognize. Mrs. Maitland noticed it as soon as she shook hands with him. He seemed younger, his eyes were less frosty and his smile not so dry. He had brought a surprising quantity of luggage with him, but this was explained when he begged Mrs. Maitland to accept "a little wine", which he had carried, each bottle tenderly swathed in many wrappings, in a large travelling-bag.

His hostess's eyes widened as he brought out bottle after bottle: "the Club claret, Mrs. Maitland, is a very fine wine and I am sure you will like it"—"two bottles of Niersteiner—a good year"—"champagne, for Christmas Day, though I am not particularly fond if it, it seems appropriate to the occasion," and finally, two bottles of Amontillado.

Mrs. Maitland, who could barely distinguish port from Graves except by the colour, thought claret nasty sour stuff, and recognized champagne because it was "fizzy", was touched by the thought he had obviously given to choosing the wines, and thanked him with sincerity. At least, she hoped, Amabel would appreciate them, though where she had acquired a palate her mother did not know.

Presently it appeared that she might have gained this knowledge of wine by dining with Mr. Ramsay, for they both spoke of it as if it happened quite frequently.

Millie, if she had not been engrossed in Christmas preparations and the fear that at any moment Amabel was bound to ask her whether Martin Heriot was coming in for a glass of sherry, could hardly have failed to mark her daughter's manner towards

Mr. Ramsay. But it was only much later that she remembered it and wondered how she had not noticed that mingling of deference to his opinions and indulgence for his little oddities, so unlike Amabel as a rule.

By the time the dreaded enquiry came, just as they were finishing tea, Mrs. Maitland had worked herself into such a state of nerves that she almost welcomed it.

Amabel received the news that Martin Heriot had gone away for Christmas with equanimity.

"It's a pity," she said, cutting another piece of the Christmas cake for herself and beginning to eat it with hearty appetite. "But after all, we are quite happy without him. Mother, I don't believe you've ever made a better cake."

Happy was hardly the adjective poor Mrs. Maitland would have chosen to describe her own state of mind, but she was so relieved to see Amabel taking the news of Martin Heriot's absence with calm composure that she did feel a little cheered.

After all her forebodings the Christmas holiday was a quiet, contented three days. Mr. Ramsay, she realized, was largely responsible, less for his laughter-provoking efforts to wash up and lay the table than for the stimulation of his dry witty talk and his unexpectedly soothing silences.

Mrs. Maitland found that it did not fidget her to have him sitting in the kitchen while she baked or cooked, as he seemed to like doing. She heeded him as little as Sam, though as a rule she hated people "underfoot" when she was busy.

Then, he handled Davina Gray so well when she dropped in to see them on Christmas morning after church, holding her in conversation, drawing Amabel into the talk, so that she and Davina, who normally glared at one another like two dogs thirsting for a fight, were suddenly exchanging views on what they had read recently in the most friendly way. Not only that, but he did not give Davina a chance to mention Martin Heriot, as she undoubtedly would have but for him. Altogether, Millie decided, when the morning came for him and Amabel to go back to Edinburgh, Christmas had not been too bad. She had managed to put up a sufficiently good pretence of cheerfulness to escape any questioning by her daughter. Now if Amabel, who seemed so much less allergic to men than before, could only meet someone else and forget about Martin Heriot, all would be well.

"Except that *I* shall never forgive him. Never!" said Mrs. Maitland to herself with a lamentable lack of Christmas spirit.

Chapter 19

THE New Year brought a sudden change in the weather. Overnight the frost vanished, a wind blew from the south-west and brought rain with it, rain which fell with a sort of savage steadiness for almost a week, with an occasional pause to allow a brief glimpse of the pallid sun, and to gather fresh energy for each succeeding downpour. There was an apparently inexhaustible supply of water in the weeping heavens. The hills were swathed in mist, which lay in impenetrable folds on their crests and crept half-way down their flanks, eddying and at times thinning to show slopes seamed with the silvery threads of innumerable tiny runnels, all leaping to join the larger streams, and all swollen by melting snow as well as rain.

Mennan Water went roaring down the valley below Fernieknowe, past the village, running a turbid red-brown, and the low-lying marshy meadows beside its banks were sheets of water where cattle stood disconsolately in the flood and bellowed for their lost grazing ground.

To Mrs. Maitland, who at the moment had no boarders in her kennels, and only Sam in the house, the forced confinement indoors was particularly trying because she was feeling so restless and unhappy. Cabin'd, cribb'd, confined, only dashing out for a few bleak minutes twice a day to air Sam, with the obliging shops sending supplies to her before she even asked them, with the house painfully empty and tidy, even all the arrears of mending made up, she moped and fretted. No one ventured out except from sheer necessity, even Davina Gray rang up to say in a snuffling voice that she had caught a heavy cold and was in bed. Millie felt cut off from all her world just when she would have welcomed a little society. And when Sam, also feeling the effects of too little exercise, and perhaps missing his shooting expeditions with his owner, came and clawed at her knee with a sharp and heavy paw, she spoke to him so harshly, pushed him away so petulantly, that he gave her one look of grieved bewilderment and crept with drooping tail to sanctuary under her bed.

This shocked Mrs. Maitland out of her ill humour as nothing else could have done. Remorsefully she went upstairs to her bedroom and tried to coax Sam out; but it was not until she had gone on her knees and beseeched him with every endearment in her vocabulary that he would leave his lair. Even then his wary glances, though he forgave her at once with true dog magnanimity, reproached her. At last, anxious to make amends, she said desperately, "I know, Sam. We'll go out for a real walk and get soaked, and then I'll dry you when we get home. We'll go down to the bridge and look at Mennan in flood."

This met with instant approval. Up went Sam's tail, his eyes sparkled, and he proceeded joyously to impede Millie's endeavours to struggle into her heavy wellingtons by every means known to him, and they were many, for he was a dog of ingenious imagination and infinite resource.

Finally, however, Mrs. Maitland succeeded in arraying herself in boots and waterproof, tied a scarf over her head, took Sam's lead, and plunged out with him into gale and pelting rain.

Battling down the road, the south wind, unseasonably warm, unseasonably damp, blowing violently in her face, Millie laughed aloud. She felt happy for the first time since the night of the carol singing which had ended with Martin's unwanted proposal, and Sam, hearing the sound, turned his head to look sagely at her. "I knew this was what we needed. I knew this would do you good," he seemed to say.

Millie laughed again. "Clever boy!" she cried.

The last shreds of withered leaves, torn from the trees, went whirling past her, and she made wild futile snatches at them, remembering her firm belief as a child that each one caught meant a happy day, or a present, or a wish come true. She had forgotten which, but they all amounted to the same thing more or less, and were all as elusive as the leaves fluttering almost into her hands and then whisking away out of reach.

The wind was rising, and as it rose the rain slackened. Presently she could see a shred of blue sky between the hurrying clouds. It widened, and a diffident gleam of sunshine fell palely on the marshy ground to her right, turning the hazels and willows which marked Mennan's normal course to a lovely silvery gold. To-day the bushes stood in water and the rushy fields were submerged. A heron, missing his usual fishing preserves, flew over with wild harsh cries towards a thick plantation of dark spruce firs. Scores of small birds, chaffinches and sparrows, rose from the leafless hedges where! they had been searching for possible berries and haws, and went twittering along the road in front of her, dipping up and down. Millie passed the rather tumbledown farm where an old, old collie crept out, as always to growl a feeble challenge at Sam, who growled back and was rebuked by Mrs. Maitland.

Growls and rebukes alike were purely conventional and meant nothing serious; the formalities had been observed and both dogs parted satisfied.

They were a mile below the village now, the bridge was beyond the next bend, a few hundred yards ahead, and soon Millie was standing on it, her arms folded on its mossy stone coping, staring fascinated at the wild dirty brown flow.

On the upstream side all the water from the flooded meadows was guided and gathered into a high-banked channel faced with stone, and it roared savagely through this and poured under the stout old bridge, lashing at the masonry as if enraged by its narrow confines. An uprooted tree was bobbing down through the fields, carried as lightly as a twig by the swollen river. It was hard to believe that on other days Millie had stood there and seen this same Mennan Water babbling mildly over its bed, every pebble on the bottom visible. Deafened and yet soothed by the noise, she watched the fitful progress of the tree towards her, wondering if it would negotiate the bridge or become jammed athwart the channel; but some obstacle appeared to have stopped it farther up, and she turned to the other side to look downstream.

Here the river widened to a big pool with an ugly swirl, then made a sweeping bend round a piece of higher ground. Twigs, leaves, broken baskets, a hen-coop, and the body of a sheep with all four legs sticking straight up into the air, all the wreckage collected on the water's passage to and through the village, whirled round and round this pool in giddy circles before being swept relentlessly on towards the sea.

Millie saw, rather to her dismay, that Sam had got bored with waiting on the road, and was down at the waterside nosing among the long wet grass, too close, she thought, for safety. She hoped he was not going to indulge his craving for drinking running water here and now.

"Sam!" she called sharply. "Come here, sir!" only to realize that he could not possibly hear her voice above the noise made by the river and the wind. "Sam!" This time it was a scream shrill with terror. The ground, sodden with much rain, undermined by the flood, had given way, and she saw him fall into the raving water.

Sam was a powerful swimmer like all his breed, and he had a great heart, but no dog could prevail against that current. He gave one despairing yelp; guessed at rather than heard, she saw his straining head and the whites of his frightened eyes. Then, paddling bravely but uselessly, he was swept away downstream.

The farm was too far; there was not a soul in sight to help, and Millie did not waste time in looking or shouting. Somehow she flung herself over or through the hedge into the field, and was running madly for the bend, her heavy rubber boots dragging at her feet, her breath coming in sobs. "Oh, Sam! Oh, Sam!" she cried inwardly, in a wordless agony. If she could save enough time by cutting across, would she reach the far side of the bend before he was carried down?

After that it was all a nightmare that went on and on, a nightmare of plunging far out into the angry river, staggering, sucked at by its hungry force, and seeing Sam, his head still bobbing above the water, whirled down towards her; of snatching at him, missing him, falling to her knees, of somehow struggling up again only to see him beyond her reach. . . . Running again, cumbered by soaked clothing, kicking off her waterlogged boots, heedless of cuts and scratches and the pain of her unprotected feet. There was nothing in all the world but roaring water and a drowning dog who looked to her for rescue and looked in vain. This time she could not get to the next bend before him, and though she still staggered on, falling and rising again, she knew it was hopeless. She was too slow and Sam was almost done; he could not last much longer now, but while he lived and struggled, she must struggle too.

A hand grasped her arm, she had been dragged to a standstill, she was being shaken violently, a man's voice was shouting in her ear, but she could not hear what he said.

"Sam—save—" she said in a croaking whisper, leaning against the arm that held her, unable to stand alone any longer, yet still straining wildly.

"He's all right. He's all *right!*" the voice said, slowly and loudly, so that she was able to make sense of the words, and then to realize that they had been repeated many times already. She was shaken again, but gently. "He's all right. Look—"

Millie did not need to look. A wet heavy body crashed against her trembling legs, there was an overpowering smell of water-weed and river mud, and a soft whimpering, as if Sam were begging forgiveness for having fallen in. . . . She fell to her knees again in the dank grass, but now her arms were round Sam, dripping and shivering, but *alive*; she was hugging him while he madly licked her face and hands and his own soaking body alternately.

She had forgotten everything but Sam, until a voice spoke again above her bent head. "Look here, you know, you really ought to be getting home," it said. "Change those sopping things and have a hot bath and a hot drink—"

Millie recognized the voice this time. It was Martin Heriot's.

She looked up—it seemed a very long way up from her present lowly position—and saw him frowning down at her.

"Yes, of course. Yes, I suppose I should," she said dazedly. "How stupid of me. I ought to get Sam home and dry him—"

"Sam's all right. He'll be none the worse, and more or less dry by the time you get him to Fernieknowe. But you're wet through—"

"I suppose I am," said Millie, and suddenly a thought struck her and she looked at him more attentively. "You—you must have pulled Sam out!"

"There was nothing to it. He'd been brought up against a great pile of driftwood and most likely would have got himself out, given time," said Martin Heriot. "It was quite easy for me to get hold of him. But you—good God! You might have been drowned, plunging in the way you did! I saw it all from the top of the hill over there and dashed down as fast as I could. I shouted, too, but you never heard. I thought you were gone, that time you fell in the water. . . . Here, let me give you a hand up. You must be stiff as a board. . . ."

Rising with his help, Mrs. Maitland found herself not only stiff but numb with cold. "Don't bother about me any more. I can manage quite well now, thank you," she said with chattering teeth. "It will warm me up to walk fast."

"Walk fast?" he echoed grimly, and she saw that he was staring at her feet. "You'll have the devil of a job to walk at all. Do you realize that you're practically barefoot and cut to ribbons into the bargain?"

He was only too right. The thick woollen stockings which she wore inside her wellingtons were nothing but shreds, and her bruised and scratched feet showed through them.

"I—I had to kick off my boots," she said. "They were so heavy. I couldn't run in them. They should be somewhere near the bridge, I think."

Martin was pulling a scarf from round his neck, and a large silk handkerchief from one of his pockets.

"These will be better than nothing in the meantime," he said, busily folding. "Now don't argue, it's a waste of time. We can't stand here in this wind and rain. Lift your foot a minute. That's right. Now the other—"

As Millie obeyed in silence, he slipped the improvised bandages into place, and tied them firmly about her ankles.

"Is that a little better? Can you manage to walk as far as your boots now, do you think? And then we'll see if you can put them on. I'd bring them to you, but I don't think you ought to stand here any longer. You must keep moving somehow."

He looked so anxious, his brows were drawn together in such a worried frown above his big nose, that Millie, in spite of her chill discomfort, grew hot with the remembrance of how she had last parted from him.

"You—you're being so kind!" she said. "I don't deserve it. I—I want to ask you to forgive me for being so rude to you. Couldn't we go back to—to before that evening and be friends?"

"No. I'm afraid we can't do that," he said. "But we'll forget about it for just now. Can you walk all right?"

Millie swallowed the unreasoning disappointment which made her want to weep. "Yes, thank you. My feet feel wonderful in these mufflings," she said shakily. "But I'm afraid it will ruin your scarf and that nice handkerchief—"

"Good Lord, what do *they* matter? Here, take my arm—"

"Now in one of those romantic out-of-date novels," thought Mrs. Maitland, to take her mind off their slow and painful progress through the field and make her less conscious of his support—"the hero would have swept me up into his strong arms and lightly, as if I were a feather, gone striding back with me to his lonely farm, gazing masterfully over my head into the distance with eagle's eyes under beetling brows. There ought to be a riding-whip somewhere about, too. . . . How much more difficult it is in real life! Martin is a big, strong man, but it would take him all his time to carry Sam, let alone *me*! It's a pity the people who write these stories don't sometimes try things out to see if they work. Perhaps it's wishful thinking? They are usually written by women. Or possibly by little anaemic men who can hardly carry a loaf of bread—"

In spite of this diversion of thought, it seemed to Millie miles to the bridge, but they reached it at last, picking up the sodden boots on the way. Once at the road, there was an exceedingly unpleasant struggle to put the boots on, which almost reduced her to tears of pain and rage. "Ugh!" she exclaimed, angrily, as with a final effort she succeeded in cramming her foot into the second. "They look and feel like those horribly squashy black slugs!"

"They do, you know," he agreed, his gaze carefully on the offending wellingtons, for he knew that she would rather believe he had not seen the tears in her eyes. "But the point is can you walk home?"

"Oh, easily!" said Millie, hoping that she sounded more cheerful than she felt. "Only, do please let us go the other way, and not through the village!"

"Come on, then." He took her arm again in a firm hold and started with her along the road. Sam, subdued but apparently none the worse otherwise, plodded at their heels. Fortunately they met nobody, though by this time Millie, with all her energy concentrated on putting one foot in front of the other, would hardly have noticed if they had. She remembered very little of the rest of that trudge back to Fernieknowe. Her one ambition in life, it seemed to her, was to get home and send Martin Heriot away before she broke down. Somehow she succeeded, though it was not easy, for he did not want to leave her alone.

"I'll bring Mrs. Wilson over in the car," he said. "You ought to have someone with you."

"No, thank you so much. I couldn't bear to have Mrs. Wilson—or anyone," said Millie.

"I'll ring up Davina Gray, then, she's a friend of yours—"

"Oh, heavens, no! Davina is the *last* person—think how she'd talk! Besides, she is in bed with a bad cold," said Millie hastily. "I shall be quite all right, really! I'll go to bed at once—"

He still lingered on the doorstep. "Promise me you'll get the doctor, then. Or shall I ring him up for you?

"No, no! Please don't! I'm perfectly capable of ringing him up for myself!" cried Millie. "If you will please just let me go in and take off these wet clothes—"

That argument worked. With a last reluctant glance at her he turned away. Millie stumbled into the house and shut the door, then sank down on the first seat she could find, the lowest step but one of the stairs.

Her feet were burning, her head was hot, and yet she was shaking with cold. It was extremely odd. She sat wondering about it in a detached sort of way, and crying quietly until Sam, distressed by her tears, and impatient to be dried and fed, clawed urgently at her knee, and roused her to full awareness. All in a moment she realized everything; Sam's narrow escape, her own soaked condition and the feet that she had never properly thanked Martin Heriot. She found time to be sorry for this as she limped stiffly about, rubbing Sam down with his towel and feeding him, but Martin did not want her thanks. No doubt he didn't feel like forgiving her for the way she had refused his proposal. She had behaved very badly; she could see that now; it was not his fault if he did not care for Amabel, and she could not make him care. In, her mood of unusual clearsightedness, induced, if she had known it, by delayed shock, she acknowledged that she did not think she really wanted Martin to marry Amabel.

But all these considerations faded from her overwrought mind as shock and bodily pain began to make themselves felt. Unless there happened to be a drop of brandy in the medicine chest, she was going to have a very bad chill indeed; and that, with Amabel in Edinburgh and Sam to look after, would be exceedingly awkward. The little brandy bottle, however, had only a drain left in it, not enough to be any good, and she was wondering vaguely if blackcurrant tea would help when she remembered the rum which had been bought for the Christmas pudding's sauce. There was plenty of that, and much as she loathed it, Mrs. Maitland poured out and drank a stiff dose. The fiery stuff burned her throat as she swallowed it, but it certainly induced a most comforting warmth of body and an energy which lasted until she had filled two hot bottles, dragged off her clothes and crawled into an almost boiling bath.

There the lethargy which threatened to overcome her was kept at bay by the pain of her torn feet. Perhaps it was a blessing, though very well disguised, since she had no wish to be drowned in her bath, Millie thought philosophically as she tied up her cuts and scratches. After all, and no matter that it was only about seven p.m., bed was a better place to sleep.

She drank another tot of rum, and thinking that her room now smelt like a pub, fell into heavy slumber with Sam snoring beside her feet.

"Bother! I promised to ring up Doctor Wingate, and I've forgotten! Oh, well, I'll do it in the morning," was her second-last waking thought. The very last was that she could never part with Sam now, she must buy him from Martin Heriot, however little she could afford it.

And about the same time that she fell asleep, Martin Heriot, tramping restlessly about his sitting-room, decided that Amabel ought to know about her mother's adventure.

He lifted the receiver and put a call through to Edinburgh.

Chapter 20

There was a gentle, almost a timid, knock at the back door, and Amabel, opening it, found Martin Heriot on the step, with a large basket in his hand.

"How is she?" he asked.

"Mother? Oh, she's much better, thank you, Martin," said Amabel. "Do come in for a minute, won't you? I'm making an egg-flip for her and I don't want the wretched egg to go all unwhisked again."

He came into the kitchen, walking gingerly, as if afraid to put his feet down.

"Why are you walking like Agag?" demanded Amabel, whirring away at the egg-beater.

"I—I don't want to disturb her."

"Good heavens! Mother can't hear a sound that we make down here! Her bedroom's at the front of the house," said Amabel.

"I know. That's why I came to the back door," said Martin. He put his basket on the table. "I've brought a few things. Is there anything I can do?"

"Well—I don't know that there is," said Amabel. Then she looked at him and relented. "Unless you'd take Sam for a walk? He lies up there and I can hardly get him out of Mother's room, and I haven't time to give him a proper run, poor thing."

He brightened. "Yes, I'll take him. I can come over every day and take him out," he said. "Or would you rather I had him at Wardlaw altogether while she's ill?"

"I would," said Amabel frankly. "I'm forever falling over him, but Mother would have a temperature if I suggested it. She can't bear him out of her sight for long. Between the two of them I don't know if I am on my head or my heels! Wait here while I take this stuff up to her, and I'll bring Sam down."

In a few minutes she came back, hauling an obviously unwilling Sam by the collar. "Here he is," she said rather breathlessly. "Don't keep him out for very long, will you?" Amabel watched the two going up the path between the bushes of rhododendron to the gate on to the moor road with a puzzled expression.

"What *has* been going on?" she wondered aloud. "I must get to the bottom of this."

She picked up the basket brought by Martin Heriot and took it into the big old-fashioned larder with stone shelves round three sides of it. On this cold morning it was like an ice-house.

"Butter," said Amabel, unpacking neat parcels. "Grapes—heavens, he must have sent to Edinburgh for those! More eggs ... and oh, dear, *another* fowl!"

Already two plump fowls reposed on a dish on the shelves, beside a large bowl full of eggs. During the week that had passed since Amabel had hurried down from Edinburgh after Martin Heriot had telephoned to her, and had found her mother with a high temperature and a cough, offerings had poured in to Fernieknowe.

There were flowers, not only in Millie's room, but all through the house, besides the more practical proofs of affectionate regard for her which filled the larder. Amabel had always known that her mother was well liked in Mennan; she was almost overwhelmed by the evidence now before her eyes. She had laughed a little over Mrs. Gray's bowl of jellied chicken-stock, clear and stiff, and the note accompanying it in which Davina had written "to save you the trouble of boiling the fowl and with love and best wishes for your mother's speedy recovery". It was quite plain that Mrs. Gray mistrusted Amabel's ability to make really good chicken broth!

But all the same, Mrs. Gray, though she was still kept to the house by her cold, had turned to and made this for her friend. Amabel appreciated that. Still more did she appreciate the shepherd's wife, Mrs. Denholm's walking all the way to Fernieknowe to bring half a dozen eggs, with apologies because there were not more; and old Miss Kennedy's little jar of home-made bramble jelly, and someone else with honey from her own bees, and Pat Ross's soft Shetland wool bed-jacket. . . . There was no end to the stream of presents, all given with affection and goodwill.

Amabel learnt a great deal in that week, not only about the kindliness which underlay the surface love of gossip in Mennan folk, but the amount of hard work involved in keeping a house even moderately clean and tidy. A very real respect for her mother was planted and took root as she toiled to produce something approaching the results which Millie achieved without making heavy weather of it. She made a vow to herself never again to accuse Millie of "fussing" about preparations for guests, for she was quite sure that the smallest extra added to the household chores would drive her mad.

She was not being quite fair to herself, for she had not taken into account that she had Millie to look after besides the house, and for a day or two Doctor Wingate had been afraid that the chill might develop into congestion of the lungs.

But however short of perfection Amabel fell as a housewife, she proved an admirable nurse. Quiet, quick and deft, she obeyed the doctor's orders to the letter, and succeeded in making her mother obey them too. Further, she had the gift of being able to anticipate her patient's needs just before the patient herself became aware of wanting something. Mrs. Maitland, at first more distressed than relieved to have her at home, very soon missed her if she was out of the room for more than a few minutes.

Millie had been tired and depressed before her alarming adventure with Sam, and this, added to shock and feverish chill, made her so limp that she was content to lie still and be waited on, for the first time in more than thirty years. Having to depend on someone else was good for her, and it was equally good for Amabel to be in charge.

She was one of those who are at their best with someone to look after. From the moment when she had walked into her mother's room and seen the pale face with spots of high colour over the cheekbones, the too-bright eyes, heard the short dry cough, the affection which had lain dormant in her heart all her life had shown itself with less and less reserve.

Millie had always known that her daughter was capable, so her skill in nursing was not surprising, but that Amabel should be so tender, so like her name, in fact, seemed almost a miracle.

"How glad I am that we called her Amabel," thought Millie. "It's worth being ill to know she's really like this underneath."

Doctor Wingate was surprised too, and lost no time in telling everyone that Amabel Maitland was nursing her mother as if she had been born to it. "Yes, and being so gentle with her that it's difficult to believe she's the thorny creature we know," he added in answer to Mrs. Gray's anxious enquiries.

Davina, being Davina, of course retorted: "And about time she was, too!" but thought it over, and went on in her honest fashion: "I daresay Millie was wrong in always trying to do everything for Amabel. I'm sure I told her so often enough. Perhaps we've all been too hard on the girl, though her manner is enough to put anyone's back up!"

"Well," Doctor Wingate repeated, "you ought to see her now. She's like a different being."

"I *would* be seeing her now, and Millie too, if you weren't such an old woman, fussing over me and keeping me in the house," responded Mrs. Gray at once. She was a very bad patient, as might be expected.

"Old woman I may be, but you will *never* be if you don't do as I tell you," said the doctor composedly. "You'll stay indoors for another three days yet. Mrs. Maitland is better without visitors just now in any case."

"What worries me is how Amabel is feeding the poor thing," said Mrs. Gray restlessly. "She's no cook."

"She'll manage. I am willing to bet that she'll learn enough cooking to feed her mother all right," said the doctor, and went off leaving Mrs. Gray fuming but helpless.

It would have comforted Amabel to know that Doctor Wingate's new high opinion of her capabilities extended to her cooking, as she stood in the larder looking at fowls and eggs and wondering what to do with them. Up to the present, while Mrs. Maitland had wanted nothing but hot milk, tea, egg-flips and tiny pieces of thin bread and butter, she had managed, and Mrs. Gray's chicken broth had come in very handy. But now that the doctor said she ought to eat more solid food because she required feeding up, things were going to be more difficult.

"I *could* ask Mother," she thought, eyeing the chickens dubiously. "But I'm not going to. It would be enough to spoil her appetite if she had to tell me how to cook everything! No, I must do it myself. . . . I suppose if I put one of these birds in a pot with a lot of water, and boil it . . . ?"

Martin Heriot brought Sam back and found her poring over an enormous *Mrs. Beeton's Household Management*, which Mrs. Maitland's mother had been given as a bride at the beginning of the century.

"What are you studying?" he asked, and Amabel gave a guilty start.

"It's Mrs. Beeton," she confessed. "I was really only looking up to see how to boil a fowl—but she's fascinating, Martin! I've never read her before, and I just couldn't stop! Listen to this: 'In the country the summer-houses, garden seats and chairs are also under her charge.' Who do you think 'she' is? The *cook*!"

"Good Lord! Imagine expecting a cook to do that," said Martin, duly impressed.

"And there are some lovely recipes," Amabel went on. "Here's one called 'To Clean Ribbons', and the ingredients are half a pint of gin, half a pound of honey, half a pound of soft soap and an eighth of a pint of water!"

"I thought it was a cookery book—"

"Oh, it's far more than that. It has everything you can think of in it—First Aid, Legal Advice, Duties of the Wet Nurse and the Coachman—"

"Did you discover how to boil your fowl?" asked Martin Heriot. "And by the way, the one I brought you is for roasting."

"Oh!" said Amabel rather blankly. "Bread sauce and stuffing? Oh, dear!" Then she brightened. "Never mind. Dear Mrs. Beeton will tell me what to do."

"Well," said Martin, "I don't know much about cooking, but if that pot bubbling like mad has a fowl in it, it's boiling too fast—with all deference to Mrs. Beeton."

"That isn't Mrs. Beeton, it's me. I don't know how it is, but everything either cooks far too quickly or doesn't cook at all, when I'm doing it," said Amabel, hurriedly turning the gas lower under the big pot.

"It smells all right, anyhow," he said, and picked up his empty basket. "I'd better be off. You won't want to be kept away from your mother too long."

"Mother's sleeping just now. In a day or two she will be seeing people," said Amabel, on her way to the door with him. "And I'm sure she would like to see you. I'll ring you up, shall I?"

"I don't think she will want to see me," said Martin. "So don't do anything about it, Amabel."

"Oh!" Amabel could think of nothing more to say until he was going down towards the gate. Then she called after him: "Martin! Thank you so much for all the lovely things you brought!"

He turned. "Oh, it's nothing. I'll come round again and bring what there is, and take Sam out for you," he said, and walked on.

"Now *why* does he seem so certain that Mother won't want to see him?" murmured Amabel. "It's all most mysterious."

She returned to the kitchen and made a fish custard with Mrs. Beeton's help, then arranged a little bunch of Martin's grapes on a plate and took them upstairs.

Millie was awake, and wanted to know who had been in, and where Sam was.

"It was Martin Heriot," Amabel explained, plumping up her mother's pillows. "He brought you a whole basketful of things. We have enough provisions now to stand a siege! These grapes are from him. He took Sam for a walk."

"Oh! That was very kind of him," said Millie. She stirred restlessly and looked at the grapes on the bedside table near her hand. "I don't think I want these, dear. You eat them."

"I thought you liked grapes. You enjoyed the ones Mr. Ramsay sent," said Amabel a little reproachfully.

Mrs. Maitland lay still for a moment, then she said suddenly, "Amabel. Will you lend me some money?"

"Yes, of course I will, Mother. I hope you haven't been lying here worrying unnecessarily about money," said Amabel. "'How much would you like? I'm rather well off just now, because they gave me an increase in salary at Christmas, and of course I get that flat free."

"I think not more than twenty pounds," said Millie. "Yes, that ought to be enough."

Very much surprised, but hiding it, Amabel said calmly, "Do you want me to draw a cheque and give you the money in cash, or what?"

"I think if you could pay it into my account at the bank, that would be best," said her mother, and added to Amabel's bewilderment by saying, "I want to buy Sam from Martin Heriot."

"What?" exclaimed Amabel loudly. "Sorry, Mother. I didn't mean to shout. But—I mean—why?"

"Because I want to be certain of keeping him. I can't let him go now."

She sounded a little excited, Amabel thought, and bit back all the questions she was longing to ask.

"Very well, Mother. That will be all right. I'll pay in twenty pounds, and you can arrange it with Martin Heriot," she said, "Doctor Wingate said you could see a few people now if you want to, so if Martin comes to—"

"I don't want to see him. I won't see him, Amabel!" Millie sat bolt upright, and a flush crept burningly over her cheeks. "You are not to let him come, please! I really mean this."

"All right, all right," Amabel said hastily. "Don't get in a state about it. You shan't see anyone you don't want to. You don't have to see people at all unless you like!"

Mrs. Maitland looked at her daughter rather piteously. The flush had gone, leaving her very pale. "I'm sorry if I'm being silly," she said.

"You're not being silly at all," Amabel reassured her. "I'll see about Sam, and all you will have to do is sign the cheque."

"Oh, thank you, Amabel dear. You're very kind and patient," said her mother.

"I won't be kind at all if you've upset yourself and don't eat your lunch," Amabel said threateningly.

"That's another thing," said Mrs. Maitland. "I'm afraid you will find cooking a great trouble. It takes so long if you aren't used to it—"

"Don't bother about that. I have a friend in the kitchen who knows *everything* about cooking," Amabel said. "If I have time I'm going to learn fancy ways of folding table-napkins from her as well!"

"Who on earth—?" began Mrs. Maitland, and Amabel laughed.

"You know her too," she said. "Her name is Mrs. Beeton! Now I'm going to give you your lunch, and then I'll ring up Martin Heriot about Sam. I can go to the bank to-morrow morning."

Leaving Mrs. Maitland smiling and once more calm, she went off to the kitchen again.

It was a severe shock, when she had got Martin on the telephone and told him why she was ringing up, to hear him say very firmly, "I'm sorry, but Sam is not for sale."

Amabel felt as if she had been slapped in the face. It had never occurred to her that he might refuse, especially as she had explained that Mrs. Maitland was worrying about Sam.

"Oh!" she exclaimed.

Then, as there was no sound from the other end, she went on rather sharply, "Look here, Martin, what *is* the matter? Have you and Mother quarrelled?"

"Not exactly," he said.

"Then what's wrong? She doesn't want to see you—won't see you, in fact, or so she says—and you refuse to let her have Sam—"

"I didn't say that I wouldn't let her have Sam," came Martin's voice. "What I said, and meant, was that he is not for sale."

"Well, it seems to come to the same thing," said Amabel in exasperation. "I can't imagine that she will accept him as a present, judging from both your behaviours."

"I don't suppose she will."

"I'm tired of all this mystery," said Amabel. "I'm sure it isn't good for Mother to worry when she really has been quite ill. If it is anything that I can put right, I wish you would tell me."

"I don't see how you can put it right," he answered. "If you must know, I asked her to marry me, and she refused in no uncertain terms. That's all."

Chapter 21

Amabel took the receiver away from her ear and stared at it in silent stupefaction. "Well I am blowed!" she remarked inelegantly. Then, feeling that this was not quite the right thing to say, she added into the telephone, "Martin, I'm sorry. I didn't know—"

"I didn't suppose you did," he answered gloomily. "Though I should have thought you might have guessed I was—fond of Millie by this time."

"But *everyone* is fond of Mother."

"I know. There's that old lawyer chap—what's-his-name?"

"Mr. Ramsay is *not* old," said Amabel indignantly. "And I'm sure Mother has never thought of him except as a friend. And as far as he's concerned—" She broke off, and a smile curved her lips, softening the normal severity of her face.

"Well, no use going on about it. We're only giving the exchange a treat," said Martin Heriot's voice. "I'll ring off now."

"Martin, wait a minute!"

But there was no reply. He had hung up.

More confused and at a loss than ever before in her life, Amabel went up to her mother's room again. She had no clue to Millie's feelings about Martin Heriot; she had never considered the possibility of his wanting to marry. Any preference he had shown had been for the society of little Mrs. Noble.

"I wonder if Mother refused him because of that?" thought Amabel, pausing on the top step. "Or whether she doesn't like to marry him while I'm unmarried? That would be silly but rather sweet, and quite typical! Or perhaps she just doesn't want to marry again at all?"

Then Millie called, and Amabel came to with a jerk and went into her room.

"Did you ring him up?" Mrs. Maitland asked at once.

"I did, but he says that Sam is not for sale," Amabel answered baldly. There was no use in trying to break it gently, it would only keep Millie in suspense.

"How horrible of him! Selfish, dog-in-the-manger creature!" cried Mrs. Maitland, her hand going out to he on Sam's head, which was not far off, because Sam, as usual, was on the bed. "He pretends to be f-fond of me, and yet he won't do the only thing I've asked of him! I suppose because he saved Sam's life he wants to have him back!"

"He doesn't want him. He said you could have him as a gift, but not to buy," said Amabel.

"He *knows* I can't accept a present from him!"

"Mother, I really think you ought to tell me a little more about this," said Amabel, noticing that Millie had eaten quite a good lunch. "It would be far better for you than working yourself up so that you have a temperature again. How did Martin save Sam's life, and when?"

"The day I caught this wretched chill, of course," began Millie; and with a little coaxing, told the whole tale to Amabel, who listened in silence until she had finished.

"Mother, I had no idea that all this was at the back of your chill. You might have been drowned yourself," she said at last. "It seems to me that Martin saved your life as well as Sam's, by rushing you home and then having the sense to ring me up."

"It was very interfering of him," said Mrs. Maitland ungratefully. "And I *will* buy Sam, if I have to see Martin Heriot myself to tell him so."

"I think it's your only chance of getting Sam," said Amabel.

"Very well. Then will you please ring up again and say I'd like to see him to-morrow afternoon?" said Mrs. Maitland defiantly.

Amabel raised her eyebrows. "I'm glad you feel well enough for visitors. What if anyone calls to see you to-day?"

"I'll see them," said Mrs. Maitland, reckless as well as defiant.

"Then you'd better lie down and have a sleep now while you've got the chance," Amabel recommended. She settled her mother comfortably, took up the luncheon-tray and left the room, restraining her smiles until she was safely on the landing. "No doubt about it, Mother's feeling better," she thought. "She's showing all the peevishness that worse-tempered convalescents show! I wonder how Martin will get on—*if* he has the nerve to come!"

"Come?" shouted Martin down the telephone when she rang him up again. "Of course I'll come. I'm not afraid of her!"

"Splendid. But please don't bellow like that. You nearly blew me away from my end of the thing," said Amabel. She was laughing, but sobered to say, "Don't forget that she has been pretty bad, Martin. I mean, don't send her temperature up."

"What I'd *like* to do is to shake her until she comes to her senses and says she'll marry me!"

"Well, why don't you? Not shake her, I don't mean that, but ask her again to m—oh, heavens, the exchange!" said Amabel. "I'll expect you to-morrow afternoon, then, about three-thirty."

This time she hung up first, and hoped that she had cut off his final remarks, for she felt he deserved it.

After she had washed up, tidied the kitchen, and gone softly into her mother's room to find her peacefully sleeping, Amabel decided to sit down beside the drawing-room fire with Mrs. Beeton for company.

She was deep in this entrancing work when the door opened and Mrs. Gray walked into the room.

"I didn't ring," she explained, "in case your mother might be asleep."

"She *is* asleep," said Amabel, laying Mrs. Beeton aside regretfully, and getting to her feet. "Won't you come and sit down for a little? She will wake quite soon, I expect, and I know she would like to see you."

"I'd have been here days ago," said Mrs. Gray, untying scarves and unbuttoning her heavy coat and flinging it wide as she took the offered chair, "but Doctor Wingate wouldn't let me leave the house.

He's a regular old wife, that doctor of ours! Singing *your* praises loudly just now, Amabel, by the way."

A short time before, Amabel would have bristled with indignation at this back-handed compliment; but now a tolerance born of contented happiness made her smile and think "How like Mrs. Gray!" She made a mental note to include the remark in her next letter to Edinburgh, and answered sedately.

"Doctor Wingate has been most kind while Mother was ill, and she and I think him an excellent doctor—"

"Oh, so do I, so do I!" Mrs. Gray hastened to agree. "Nothing wrong with his *skill*, but the man fusses so!"

"Ought you to have come here to-day?" asked Amabel. "There's a very cold wind."

"Snow on the way," said Mrs. Gray. "I can smell it." She sniffed the air like a questing bloodhound. "But I'm well wrapped up, and I have Wingate's permission. Now, tell me, how *is* Millie?"

After Amabel had given a full account of her mother's illness and her present satisfactory progress towards recovery, Mrs. Gray said: "*Well.* I'm thankful to hear it. She must have had a pretty bad time—worse than anyone suspected." She darted a sharp glance at Amabel. "You're looking a bit peaky. It's been a strain on you, with all the house on your hands as well."

"I'm afraid the house has been rather neglected," said Amabel, suddenly aware of dust on table-legs and a bowl of rather wilted anemones near the window. Mrs. Gray would notice every speck, every hint of tarnish on brass and silver! "But I just didn't seem to have time for anything but looking after Mother. I'm not good at housework."

"First things first," said Mrs. Gray. "Not much good polishing the silver and letting your mother get pneumonia or pleurisy because of it, is there?"

"That's rather what I thought, but—"

"You should have seen Netherton when I first got up," said Mrs. Gray grimly. "I don't know how they spent their time while I was in bed, but it certainly wasn't on dusting and sweeping! Two of them, too, mark you!"

Though Amabel felt sure that by her own standards Netherton had probably not fallen very far short of its usual polished and slightly bleak perfection, she agreed that it must have been very annoying for Mrs. Gray to find the house not just as she liked it.

"Oh, I soon got it to rights again," said Mrs. Gray. "I will say for those girls, they work very well when I'm there to supervise them. They aren't too bad. And Jean is quite a good cook. How are you managing about cooking?"

"I take a very long time over it," said Amabel a little ruefully. "But I haven't spoiled anything yet. I do exactly what Mrs. Beeton tells me—"

"Mrs. Beeton? But she's so extravagant!"

"No, she isn't really," said Amabel. "Of course if you look at things called Pound Cake or Baked Almond Pudding (very rich), you find they need a lot of butter and eggs. But for practical purposes I couldn't do without her. Besides, she's such fun! Imagine coming on a footnote headed Water Supply in Rome at the bottom of a page on pastry recipes!"

"My mother used to swear by Mrs. Beeton, of course," observed Mrs. Gray. "I daresay you couldn't do better than follow her instructions. You won't be attempting to bake, are you?"

Amabel shook her head. "No. That I know is beyond me," she said.

"Then you won't mind my having brought a little sponge for your mother's tea?"

"Mind? I'm delighted! I do think it was kind of you," said Amabel. "I was wondering what to do about Mother's tea."

It was a very great pity that none of the many persons who had so often seen these two eyeing each other with thinly-veiled hostility was not in the Fernieknowe drawing-room just then. Nothing short of the evidence of their own eyes and ears would ever convince them that Mrs. Gray and Amabel Maitland had been talking together like old friends for almost twenty minutes.

"I won't stay too long and tire her," Mrs. Gray promised, as Amabel took her upstairs after seeing that her mother was awake and ready for a visitor.

"I know you won't," said Amabel. "But she is much more easily tired than she realizes."

Mrs. Gray nodded. "And you go down and put your feet up on the sofa for a bit," she advised. "And read that book you were so engrossed in when I arrived. What is it, by the way?"

"*Mrs. Beeton's Household Management*," said Amabel with a twinkle.

True to her word, Mrs. Gray stayed for exactly a quarter of an hour with Millie, and then left, refusing Amabel's offer of tea because she wanted to get home before it became any colder and darker.

"I suppose Mrs. Gray put you up-to-date with all the news?" said Amabel when she carried in her mother's tea-tray. "It's amazing how she gathers it even when she has been in the house for a fortnight! It's like a magnet attracting bits of steel."

"Yes, she told me everything," said Millie, but she sounded subdued, and when Amabel put her tea on the bed-table her bedside light showed her pale and with suspiciously damp eyes.

"I liked Mrs. Gray better this afternoon than ever before in my life," said Amabel. "But if she has been depressing you or worrying you in any way, I shall kill her."

"That would be most unfair, for she has been saying such nice things about you," said Mrs. Maitland, trying to sound cheerful.

"What did she say to make you cry?" asked Amabel sternly, as she drew the curtains and poked the fire to a lively blaze.

"Nothing, dear, really. I expect it's just because I'm a little bit tired. She was telling me that Susan is expecting a baby in the summer. Isn't that lovely? Davina is quite excited about it."

"As she has—how many grandchildren? Six or seven—already, I can't see that another would be so very exciting," said Amabel, who was feeling tired herself.

"Oh, Amabel, don't be unkind!" begged her mother with a catch in her voice. "You know, being a grandmother *must* be exciting!"

"Poor Mother, do you want to be a grannie so much?" asked Amabel gently. She stood, tall and straight, beside the bed, looking down at her parent with an odd expression in her eyes.

"Well—I suppose every woman who has a daughter looks forward to being a grandmother one day," said Mrs. Maitland.

"It's a pity, Mother, that you didn't have nice satisfactory daughters like Susan or Pat Ross. They would really have suited you much better," said Amabel without a trace of hurt or offence.

Mrs. Maitland blew her nose hard. "I won't have you saying such things," she said firmly. "I'm perfectly satisfied with the daughter I've got—"

"Well, that's very sweet of you, Mother, though I don't deserve it." Amabel sounded unusually gruff. She cleared her throat and went on: "I can't make any promises about your being a grandmother just yet, it really is hardly decent! But how would you like to look forward to becoming a mother-in-law?"

"Amabel!" cried Mrs. Maitland, starting so violently that she upset her teacup and Amabel flew to mop up the stream of tea flowing across the tray. "Oh, never mind that just now! You aren't *joking*, are you?"

"Perfectly serious," said Amabel, scrubbing at the tray-cloth with a towel. "I didn't mean to tell you until you were better, but—well—you've got it out of me, and you had to know sooner or later—"

"But, Amabel! Can't you see that you're driving me mad? *Who* is it?" cried her mother.

Amabel turned away and began poking at the fire quite unnecessarily. "Can't you guess?" she asked.

"No, how can I? I *did* wonder if Martin Heriot, but—is it?"

"Martin Heriot?" said Amabel, turning back again to face her mother, her face pink with embarrassment, but scorn in every feature. "No, of course it isn't! It's Mr. Ramsay—and if you say he's *old*, Mother, I—I don't know *what* I'll do!"

There was a stunned silence for a moment. Then Mrs. Maitland said: "You—you are *quite* sure, Amabel?"

"Yes, I am quite sure, Mother. I have been for—oh, for a long time now. But I always thought it was you he cared about."

"Mr. *Ramsay*? Me?" gasped Mrs. Maitland, heedless of grammar. "How on earth did you get such an idea into your head, child?"

"Once, when I was quite little," began Amabel slowly, "—you remember, I hated him then? It seems funny now! I listened outside the door—he'd come here to see you about business!—and I heard him ask you to marry him—"

"How naughty of you, Amabel dear," said her mother, speaking as if the tall young woman were indeed that child of twenty-five years ago. "But if you listened, you must have heard me refuse him?"

"I didn't! I ran away! I was so afraid you were going to marry him, and I thought he was a beast!" said Amabel.

"He only asked me because he thought I was incapable of looking after you and myself," Millie said calmly. "It was very, very kind of him. I thought so then, and I still think so. But about you, Amabel. I *must* say this, whether you like it or not. He is a great deal older than you—"

"He's the same age as Martin Heriot!" flashed Amabel.

"Is he really? He seems older—"

"If he was as old as Methuselah I'd still want to marry him!"

"Ah, well. If you feel like that I'm satisfied," said her mother, and sank back among her pillows.

"You *are* pleased, Mother, aren't you?" asked Amabel rather wistfully.

"My darling child, I am delighted! And," added Mrs. Maitland with a chuckle, "won't Davina be surprised?"

"Won't she just!" said Amabel. "Mother, I'll take away this horrible mess and get you some more tea, and I'll have it up here with you."

"That will be very nice," said Mrs. Maitland. When Amabel came back with fresh tea, Mrs. Gray's sponge-cake and two cups and saucers on a clean tray-cloth, her mother said suddenly, "You know, Amabel, what I have been thinking?"

"No. What?" asked her daughter, pouring out scalding tea with brisk efficiency.

"At *last* I shall know Mr. Ramsay's Christian name. All these years he has been practically anonymous—'P. Ramsay'. What does it stand for?"

As Amabel said nothing, her mother went on anxiously: "You *do* know it, don't you? It is really too early Victorian to go on talking of him as Mr. Ramsay!"

"Mother, it's such a terrible name," confessed Amabel. "It's—it's—Pinkerton!"

"Madam Butterfly," murmured Mrs. Maitland.

"What do you mean?" said Amabel almost peevishly, for she had been through considerable emotional strain and was not accustomed to it.

"Well, that *was* the man's name in 'Madam Butterfly'," said Mrs. Maitland reasonably. "It is a bit fancy, but it isn't ugly, after all."

"It's so ridiculous to call anyone P-Pinkerton," said Amabel.

"Oh, you'll soon get used to it. Pinkerton. My son-in-law, Pinkerton Ramsay," murmured Mrs. Maitland. "Yes, I think I rather like it. It's dignified and unusual. It suits him. Can you imagine him as Peter or Percy?"

"His friends call him Spider and so do I," said Amabel.

"Horrid, and not at all suitable. I suppose it is a relic of school. Boys always give each other quite ridiculous names. *I* intend to call him Pinkerton," said Mrs. Maitland. "Please give me some more tea and a little piece of Davina's sponge, Amabel dear. I feel quite hungry after all this excitement."

Chapter 22

"Dearest Spider, I have told Mother. She needed to be comforted after hearing that Mrs. Gray is once again due to become a grandmother," wrote Amabel.

She was sitting in the kitchen as usual, scribbling away at the big table.

Martin Heriot's chicken was in the oven, a rather strange-looking mess purporting to be bread sauce simmered on top of an asbestos mat over a low gas, and Amabel's letter to her beloved was subject to frequent interruptions when she basted the chicken with anxious care, or stirred the sauce. One or two grease-spots and several crumbs added interest and local colour to the pages, and caused Mr. Ramsay to laugh a great deal when he read them. Mrs. Beeton, with the appropriate place kept open by a large spoon, was at Amabel's elbow to be consulted whenever necessary.

Upstairs Mrs. Maitland lay contentedly planning her daughter's wedding. The plans included the use of her own wedding veil and wreath, and a selection of small bridesmaids from among Mrs. Gray's convenient grandchildren, and though she was quite alive to the extreme improbability of Amabel's agreeing with any of them, Mrs. Maitland found it a very pleasant way of passing the morning.

After lunch (which was the chicken, beautifully brown outside, tender and white within, brussels sprouts and mashed potatoes, all very well cooked, and rather solid bread sauce—"but with an excellent flavour," Mrs. Maitland said—followed by a baked custard, and cream sent by Mrs. Gray), Amabel said, "Don't forget Martin Heriot will be here at three-thirty. You'd better try to sleep a little or you will be too tired to see him."

"Amabel, I'd forgotten all about him! I *can't* see him!" said her mother. "I won't see him. You must ring him up and tell him so."

"Mother, I really cannot ring Wardlaw up again," protested Amabel. "What the exchange must be thinking about it already I can guess! Especially as Martin is far from discreet on the telephone—"

"Then you must send him away when he comes."

"Ought you to behave like this to a man who saved your life?" asked Amabel.

"I wish you wouldn't talk nonsense, when you know quite well he did nothing of the kind," said Mrs. Maitland angrily.

Amabel sighed. "It's very hard to be the buffer state between two such difficult people as you and Martin, Mother," she said.

This had the effect she hoped for.

"I'm *sure* I'm not a difficult person!" said Mrs. Maitland indignantly, "And I don't see how you can call Martin Heriot difficult either—"

"He's not being exactly easy over Sam, is he?"

"Amabel!" Mrs. Maitland's voice was tragic "I'd forgotten all about Sam! I've been thinking so much about you, and what you will wear at your wedding—how dreadful of me!"

"It's nice to know that you do sometimes forget Sam and think about your daughter!" said Amabel with a laugh. "No, don't get into a frenzy of remorse, Mother. I'm only joking. But you will have to see Martin Heriot."

"Yes—all right—" Mrs. Maitland's mind had taken one of its kangaroo hops, and she was now picturing Amabel going up the aisle, all in white, with her mother's veil over her dark head. "Amabel—I think very heavy white satin, absolutely plain, you know—"

"What *are* you talking about, Mother? Oh!" and Amabel flushed scarlet. "Oh, I haven't begun to think about that—and anyhow, I should feel such a fool in a real wedding dress. I look so much better in a suit and a good hat—"

"I've still got my wreath of orange-blossom and my veil in a box on the top shelf of my cupboard," Mrs. Maitland went on dreamily. "I kept them for you—just think it over, dear. And now, if I've got to see this wretched man, I'd better rest a little." She closed her eyes, but opened them as Amabel reached the door and said, "If it weren't that I don't want to bother you, I wouldn't see him, you know. I could write about Sam."

Amabel said nothing.

"You know," murmured her mother, shutting her eyes once more, "white satin could be just as severely tailored as a suit, and it falls so beautifully."

"Camilla Maitland," said Amabel. "You ought to be ashamed of yourself. This is either blackmail or bribery—if it isn't both."

Mrs. Maitland's only reply was to turn on her side with her back to the door and pull the sheets up round her head.

"I would never have believed it of you," Amabel told the unresponsive white cocoon which was all that was visible of her parent. "The duplicity of it! I hope Martin is really tough with you!"

Mr. Heriot arrived as the grandfather clock half-way up the stair was striking its single note with a great deal of whirring and wheezing, for half-past three. And he looked so grim that

Amabel, quite forgetting her expressed wish for him to be "tough", exclaimed, "Now, Martin, you are *not* to bully Mother."

"I like that from *you*," said he, with a small unwilling smile.

"Well, no one is going to bully her but me," retorted Amabel. "Sit down and try to look a little more good-tempered while I see if Mother is ready to see you."

Mrs. Maitland had heard his voice in the hall—he had made no attempt to lower it on this occasion—and was sitting up in bed gazing anxiously at her reflection in her hand-mirror.

"What a fright I look!" she said. "Not that it matters in the least, of course! But I should feel more equal to arguing with him if I were looking a little more human!"

"A little powder," said Amabel consolingly, bringing it over from the dressing-table. "Not lipstick, I think. You look much more frail and helpless without it. Here's your comb—"

"I think I'll wear that silly little lace cap, my hair won't stay tidy," announced Mrs. Maitland.

"You mean that it's extremely becoming, really, I suppose," said Amabel indulgently, and took out the ridiculous trifle of old lace fine as cobwebs from a drawer.

The effect, when placed over Mrs. Maitland's silver curls, was enchanting.

"The marquise in negligée," said Amabel. "And that pale blue bed-jacket is just right. Take heart, Mother, you are panoplied against a much sterner foe than Martin is likely to be."

"Remember!" she said in her most threatening tone to Martin Heriot as she put out her hand to open her mother's door for him.

"All right. Charles the First to you!" said he, and walked in.

Amabel shut the door, leaving them together, and retired downstairs wishing that her upbringing and her principles did not forbid her to listen at the key-hole.

"As far as I can see, everything depends on Sam," she thought. "What a fuss about a dog. I can't understand it myself."

She never had known, and never would know, that her mother, imagining her heart to be set on Martin Heriot, had refused his offer of marriage with horror for that reason. Martin, equally in the dark, was as bewildered as Amabel to find that possession of

Sam was apparently the point at issue. While Mrs. Maitland had hastily shifted her ground and with a magnificent disregard for logic, a gift which she had more than once claimed for her sex, had succeeded in making herself believe that she had always known he did not really care for her because he would not let her buy Sam, and that she had been right to refuse him.

The atmosphere in her room was so electric with conflicting thoughts and feelings that Sam himself, after one hasty glance at Martin, crept to cover below the bed, while the two foolish humans to whom he had given his dog's heart stared at one another warily, wondering how best to open fire.

Each of them, however, had forgotten to allow for the effect of seeing the other for the first time since that afternoon by the flooded river. To Martin Heriot, Millie looked so small, so pale, and so frail among her pillows, with her pretty hair half-hidden by lace, that he knew he could not deny her anything she wanted. Mrs. Maitland, seeing him standing there tall and broad and strong, remembered how he had helped her, how gentle he had been, how kind, and she knew in her turn that she could not use her weakness as a weapon, even to gain Sam for herself.

And they spoke simultaneously. "If you really feel you must buy Sam, you shall have him," said Martin gruffly, while Millie was murmuring, "Martin, I didn't mean—of course you must keep Sam, he's your dog."

They looked at each other again, but in a different way, no longer as foes waiting for a lowering of the opponent's guard.

Martin Heriot spoke first. "Poor old Sam. It looks as if neither of us wants him," he said.

"We both do," said Millie. "It would need the Judgment of Solomon to settle this."

"Not at all. We can settle it quite easily ourselves," said Martin. "All you have to do is to marry me."

"To marry again at my age would be quite absurd," said Millie. "It's so long since I was married. I don't think I like the idea."

"I've never been married at all, but I'm willing to try it."

"And to marry because of a dog is so—so silly—"

"Now there I agree with you," he said heartily. "It's damn' silly. But that's the difference between us. You see, *I* wouldn't be marrying for the sake of Sam."

Mrs. Maitland gazed pensively down at her thin hands, folded on the sheet, as if she found them of absorbing interest.

"Then there isn't any difference between us at all, Martin," she said at last. "I'm very fond of dear Sam, but I wouldn't marry anyone because of him."

Amabel, standing in the hall listening for the sound of voices uplifted in angry argument, heard not a sound.

"What on earth can be happening?" she wondered uneasily.

"I hope that great idiot hasn't frightened Mother into a fainting fit! She really isn't well enough to quarrel—" The clock ticked slowly and loudly, until the second hand had jerked its way round its dial once.

"I'm going to see!" said Amabel, and walked firmly upstairs and into her mother's room.

Mrs. Maitland had not fainted. She looked rather pink, which was most becoming. One hand was lying on Sam's head—he had climbed up on the bed again, then! And the other was hidden in Martin Heriot's, who was sitting close beside her.

"H'm. 'Bridegroom to bride, pedigree black Labrador'," thought Amabel. Her sharp eyes did not fail to note that the little lace cap was more than a trifle askew.

Mrs. Maitland, turning even pinker, tried to pull her hand away from Martin's, but he held it fast, and looked at Amabel with a smile partly of triumph and delight, partly of defiance.

"I wondered if you were ready for tea," said Amabel mildly, ignoring the linked hands as if it were an everyday occurrence. "And have you settled about Sam?"

"Yes," said Martin Heriot.

"No, not exactly," said Mrs. Maitland.

Amabel hid her amusement by a look of polite surprise. "You don't seem to be in agreement over it, anyhow," she said.

"We are, really, only Millie won't admit it," said Mr. Heriot firmly. "We have decided to share Sam."

"That's more or less what you have been doing since last spring, isn't it?" said Amabel, rather despising them for being, as she put it to herself, exactly where they started.

"Not in the least," said Martin calmly. "When Millie and I are married Sam becomes our joint property. Up to now she has been looking after him for me."

"Oh! I—I see. And when are you thinking of getting married?" asked Amabel.

Martin gave her a quick look and the corners of his mouth twitched. "What about a double wedding?" he suggested innocently. "The Sunday papers will love to feature it. 'Mother and daughter wed.' You know the kind of thing."

"Martin, you are the limit!" said Amabel, and now it was her turn to blush.

"Only an idea," he said. "But quite practical, don't you think? One wedding, one reception—"

"Perhaps you will allow me to speak." This was Millie, with deceptive mildness. "In the first place, I think the idea of a double wedding of a mother and daughter is perfectly revolting. In the second place, I haven't said yet that I am going to marry Martin at all."

"You may not have said it in so many words, but your actions implied it, my love," said Martin, undisturbed. "Try to back out now and I'll sue you for breach of promise."

"I'm not joking, Martin," said Mrs. Maitland.

Amabel began to say something, thought better of it, and instead remarked that if they were still arguing they obviously were not ready for tea, and she would leave them to have it out.

"No, you had better stay," said her mother. "Because I know you are thinking me silly and unreasonable. But the truth is that I don't really know if I *want* to marry again."

"Widows so often do," murmured Amabel.

"Yes, I know, but usually not very long after their husbands die. I can understand that," said Mrs. Maitland with unusual eloquence and clarity. "They do it partly because they miss their husbands and are lonely. But I have been lonely for so many years that I'm accustomed to it. I—I almost like it! And Fernieknowe is my own home. It is very difficult to give up a house that has been home for thirty years." She turned her head to look at Martin. "This sounds horribly selfish, and as if I didn't care for you at all, Martin, but it isn't really. It's just that at my age I can't suddenly change my whole life without having time to think about it."

She spoke with a curious gentle dignity, and her daughter, with a most unexpected prickling sensation at the back of her eyes, realized that she had never fully understood or appreciated Millie Maitland as a person before.

Martin said quietly, still holding her hand in his, "Very well, my dear. I'm not trying to rush you. Think about it as much as you like—"

"Have *you* thought about it? You have a very agreeable life now, and you can amuse yourself by squiring people like Mrs. Noble whenever it suits you," said Millie. "I should not like it if you did that when we are married."

"I shouldn't want to, then," he said. It was evident that they had both forgotten Amabel's presence. "Loneliness affects me in a different way, that's all. I need company, and my wife's company would content me, I promise you. Besides, my dear, we're neither of us young. Don't you think old age is a frightening thing to face alone? But the two of us, together—wouldn't it be worth giving up something for that companionship?"

"Oh, yes! It would, it would!" whispered Mrs. Maitland, and now two tears trickled down her cheeks. "Only I *must* be sure—"

"I've no business to be listening to this," thought Amabel and managed to creep out of the room without attracting any notice. To her great surprise she found that there were tears in her own eyes. "I don't see how Mother *can* hold out against that. It's like— it's like John Anderson, my jo—"

She went down to the kitchen and took a long time over making tea, and when she carried the tray upstairs, she allowed the china to rattle very noisily, with a view to warning them of her approach.

Martin opened the door, took the heavy tray from her, and set it on a table.

"I haven't wished you joy yet, Amabel," he said. "I do, with all my heart, and I will give you even more good wishes if you and Ramsay intend to get married soon, because your mother says she won't begin to consider her own marriage until you are safely off her hands."

"So I'm to be the sacrifice, am I?" said Amabel. "White satin and Mother's veil and all, I suppose? Well, Spider and I have nothing to wait for, and he's been asking me if we can't fix a date, so—"

"A spring wedding is always pretty," murmured Mrs. Maitland dreamily. "Such lovely flowers, you know, and the little bridesmaids can carry posies of mixed—"

"Oh, *Mother*!" cried Amabel, but she laughed. "I can see you've got it all arranged for me already."

"Of course, dear," said her mother.

Chapter 23

"And that's all the news, Millie," said Mrs. Gray at the end of a long tale of real gossip. "Except—good gracious, I almost forgot the most amusing bit of the lot! Mrs. Noble's husband has turned that young cousin of his out of the house and issued an ultimatum to the fair Roxana: either she agrees to sell Logan's or Cherry Trees, as I believe she calls it, and go back with him when his leave's over, or she must live with his mother! You can guess which she has chosen, so Mennan will be rid of the horrid little creature quite soon. It can't be soon enough for *me*, I can tell you!"

"She sent me some lovely flowers when I was ill," murmured Mrs. Maitland, who had been promoted that day to the drawing-room sofa, on which she was lying with a Paisley shawl over her.

"Oh, Millie! I must say I thought that even *you* couldn't find anything good to say about that would-be home-wrecker! You'll tell me next that you are sorry she's leaving, I suppose!" said Mrs. Gray vigorously.

"No, I'm not sorry. I think she will be far better with her husband. . . . Davina, I have a piece of news for you," said Mrs. Maitland a little nervously.

"Really? Something I haven't heard?" Mrs. Gray sounded incredulous. "I thought I was pretty well up-to-date with everything."

"You won't have heard this, and I wanted to tell you before it is put in the *Scotsman*," said Mrs. Maitland. "Amabel is going to be married—"

"*What?* Has Martin Heriot—?"

"No. It isn't Martin Heriot," said Millie, hoping that the colour which she felt rising to her cheeks would be put down to maternal pride, for that it would escape Mrs. Gray's eagle gaze was too much to expect. "She is engaged to our lawyer, Mr. Ramsay. You met him when he stayed with us for Christmas. I am delighted about it," she ended to forestall criticism.

"Well, I must say this is a great surprise, Millie. I quite thought, after he took her to the Hunt Ball, that it was Martin Heriot? It is all very confusing," Mrs. Gray complained. "Of course I am *pleased*, my dear Millie, both for your sake and Amabel's! I only hope you won't miss her too much. I mean, somehow one never expected Amabel to marry."

"I can't think why, Davina." Millie could afford to be amused by this truly Davina-like remark which had lost any power to hurt her now. "Amabel is not quite thirty, and every girl doesn't marry in her first youth, after all."

"No, no, of course not! I didn't mean anything against Amabel!" cried Mrs. Gray hurriedly. "Handsome creature, and so very capable and clever! Mr. Ramsay is an exceedingly lucky man! I must be thinking of a present for Amabel. When is the wedding?"

"Early in April, we think," said Mrs. Maitland.

"She won't be wearing white, I suppose?"

"Certainly she will, and my wedding veil, only not the wreath, because Mr. Ramsay has a very beautiful diamond hair ornament which belonged to his mother, and it will suit Amabel better than flowers on her head."

"*Well!*" was all that Mrs. Gray could find to say.

"I am hoping that perhaps your Betty's twins and Margaret's girl would be bridesmaids," Mrs. Maitland continued tranquilly. "They will look charming—"

Mrs. Gray bridled with grandmotherly satisfaction. "I'm sure Betty and Margaret will be delighted," she said.

There was a pause, during which both ladies visualized the wedding.

Then Mrs. Gray said rather hesitatingly: "And—Martin Heriot? How has he taken the news—if he has heard it yet? I hope he isn't disappointed, Millie. He really seemed to have quite a fancy for Amabel."

"Oh, he has heard, and is very pleased about it. I can assure you, Davina, that he never had any wish to marry Amabel himself," said Mrs. Maitland.

"Well, that's a good thing! But what a great surprise this has been, Millie! It has helped you to recover from your nasty chill, at all events. You look quite blooming, my dear!"

"I feel very well now," said Mrs. Maitland. "I shall be out and about in a day or two."

Mrs. Gray got up to go, buttoning her coat and strapping its belt about her in her usual brisk manner.

"Give Amabel my love," she said. "And my best wishes. Really, an *immense* surprise. I don't know when I have been so surprised, and delighted, of course!"

Mrs. Maitland looked at her friend, and a dimple which had not been visible for almost thirty years suddenly appeared at the corner of her mouth.

"It is always a good thing to be prepared for surprises, Davina," she said. "Life is full of them. Who knows? You may have a greater one yet!"

Mrs. Gray swung round and stared at her.

"Millie, you are keeping something from me," she said sternly.

"Yes, I know I am, Davina. It's—it's not very easy to tell you—"

But now Mrs. Gray was on the alert, and she pounced like a hawk.

"Millie Maitland! *Another* surprise, did you say? Are you—you *are*! You're going to marry Martin Heriot yourself!"

Mrs. Maitland nodded.

"D—do you think it's very foolish, at my age?" she asked a little nervously.

"Foolish? I think it's the most sensible thing I've heard of for years," declared Mrs. Gray. "But what about Fernieknowe? And what about the dogs?"

"Amabel and her husband are going to have Fernieknowe for week-ends. It's my wedding present to them both," said Mrs. Maitland. "In fact, when Pinkerton retires, I shouldn't wonder if they settled down here. And as for the dogs—well, Davina, I shall always be willing to look after a dog for my friends. I couldn't do without them now."

"I don't suppose you could," said Mrs. Gray. Her eye fell on Sam, who lay beside the sofa within reach of Millie's hand. She gave her loud cheerful laugh. "*Now* I know why Martin was always coming here," she announced. "'To see Sam,' he said. He's a deep one, is Martin. And not a soul ever guessed that Sam was just an excuse!"

"No, Davina, not just an excuse," Mrs. Maitland told her gently. "Ridiculous though it may seem, I don't suppose Martin and I would be marrying each other if it weren't because of Sam!"

THE END

FURROWED MIDDLEBROW

FM1. *A Footman for the Peacock* (1940) . . . . RACHEL FERGUSON
FM2. *Evenfield* (1942) . . . . RACHEL FERGUSON
FM3. *A Harp in Lowndes Square* (1936) . . . . RACHEL FERGUSON
FM4. *A Chelsea Concerto* (1959) . . . . FRANCES FAVIELL
FM5. *The Dancing Bear* (1954) . . . . FRANCES FAVIELL
FM6. *A House on the Rhine* (1955) . . . . FRANCES FAVIELL
FM7. *Thalia* (1957) . . . . FRANCES FAVIELL
FM8. *The Fledgeling* (1958) . . . . FRANCES FAVIELL
FM9. *Bewildering Cares* (1940) . . . . WINIFRED PECK
FM10. *Tom Tiddler's Ground* (1941) . . . . URSULA ORANGE
FM11. *Begin Again* (1936) . . . . URSULA ORANGE
FM12. *Company in the Evening* (1944) . . . . URSULA ORANGE
FM13. *The Late Mrs. Prioleau* (1946) . . . . MONICA TINDALL
FM14. *Bramton Wick* (1952) . . . . ELIZABETH FAIR
FM15. *Landscape in Sunlight* (1953) . . . . ELIZABETH FAIR
FM16. *The Native Heath* (1954) . . . . ELIZABETH FAIR
FM17. *Seaview House* (1955) . . . . ELIZABETH FAIR
FM18. *A Winter Away* (1957) . . . . ELIZABETH FAIR
FM19. *The Mingham Air* (1960) . . . . ELIZABETH FAIR
FM20. *The Lark* (1922) . . . . E. NESBIT
FM21. *Smouldering Fire* (1935) . . . . D.E. STEVENSON
FM22. *Spring Magic* (1942) . . . . D.E. STEVENSON
FM23. *Mrs. Tim Carries On* (1941) . . . . D.E. STEVENSON
FM24. *Mrs. Tim Gets a Job* (1947) . . . . D.E. STEVENSON
FM25. *Mrs. Tim Flies Home* (1952) . . . . D.E. STEVENSON
FM26. *Alice* (1949) . . . . ELIZABETH ELIOT
FM27. *Henry* (1950) . . . . ELIZABETH ELIOT
FM28. *Mrs. Martell* (1953) . . . . ELIZABETH ELIOT
FM29. *Cecil* (1962) . . . . ELIZABETH ELIOT
FM30. *Nothing to Report* (1940) . . . . CAROLA OMAN
FM31. *Somewhere in England* (1943) . . . . CAROLA OMAN

FM32. *Spam Tomorrow* (1956) . . . . Verily Anderson
FM33. *Peace, Perfect Peace* (1947) . . . . Josephine Kamm
FM34. *Beneath the Visiting Moon* (1940) . . . . Romilly Cavan
FM35. *Table Two* (1942) . . . . Marjorie Wilenski
FM36. *The House Opposite* (1943) . . . . Barbara Noble
FM37. *Miss Carter and the Ifrit* (1945) . . . . Susan Alice Kerby
FM38. *Wine of Honour* (1945) . . . . Barbara Beauchamp
FM39. *A Game of Snakes and Ladders* (1938, 1955) . . . .
. . . . Doris Langley Moore
FM40. *Not at Home* (1948) . . . . Doris Langley Moore
FM41. *All Done by Kindness* (1951) . . . . Doris Langley Moore
FM42. *My Caravaggio Style* (1959) . . . . Doris Langley Moore
FM43. *Vittoria Cottage* (1949) . . . . D.E. Stevenson
FM44. *Music in the Hills* (1950) . . . . D.E. Stevenson
FM45. *Winter and Rough Weather* (1951) . . . . . . D.E. Stevenson
FM46. *Fresh from the Country* (1960) . . . . Miss Read
FM47. *Miss Mole* (1930) . . . . E.H. Young
FM48. *A House in the Country* (1957) . . . . Ruth Adam
FM49. *Much Dithering* (1937) . . . . Dorothy Lambert
FM50. *Miss Plum and Miss Penny* (1959) . Dorothy Evelyn Smith
FM51. *Village Story* (1951) . . . . Celia Buckmaster
FM52. *Family Ties* (1952) . . . . Celia Buckmaster
FM53. *Rhododendron Pie* (1930) . . . . Margery Sharp
FM54. *Fanfare for Tin Trumpets* (1932) . . . . Margery Sharp
FM55. *Four Gardens* (1935) . . . . Margery Sharp
FM56. *Harlequin House* (1939) . . . . Margery Sharp
FM57. *The Stone of Chastity* (1940) . . . . Margery Sharp
FM58. *The Foolish Gentlewoman* (1948) . . . . Margery Sharp
FM59. *The Swiss Summer* (1951) . . . . Stella Gibbons
FM60. *A Pink Front Door* (1959) . . . . Stella Gibbons
FM61. *The Weather at Tregulla* (1962) . . . . Stella Gibbons
FM62. *The Snow-Woman* (1969) . . . . Stella Gibbons
FM63. *The Woods in Winter* (1970) . . . . Stella Gibbons
FM64. *Apricot Sky* (1952) . . . . Ruby Ferguson
FM65. *Susan Settles Down* (1936) . . . . Molly Clavering
FM66. *Yoked with a Lamb* (1938) . . . . Molly Clavering
FM67. *Loves Comes Home* (1938) . . . . Molly Clavering

FM68. *Touch not the Nettle* (1939) . . . . MOLLY CLAVERING
FM69. *Mrs. Lorimer's Quiet Summer* (1953) . . . MOLLY CLAVERING
FM70. *Because of Sam* (1953) . . . . MOLLY CLAVERING
FM71. *Dear Hugo* (1955) . . . . MOLLY CLAVERING
FM72. *Near Neighbours* (1956) . . . . MOLLY CLAVERING

www.ingramcontent.com/pod-product-compliance
Ingram Content Group UK Ltd.
Pitfield, Milton Keynes, MK11 3LW, UK
UKHW040037220126
10239UKWH00048B/79